Lucy Beresford

INVISIBLE THREADS

First published in 2015 by Quartet Books Limited
A member of the Namara Group
27 Goodge Street, London W1T 2LD
Copyright © Lucy Beresford 2015
The right of Lucy Beresford to be identified
as the author of this work has been asserted
by her in accordance with the
Copyright Designs and Patents Act, 1988
All rights reserved
No part of this book may be reproduced in
any form or by any means without prior
written permission from the publisher
A catalogue record for this book
is available from the British Library
ISBN 978 0 7043 7385 3
Typeset by Josh Bryson
Printed and bound in Great Britain by
T J International Ltd, Padstow, Cornwall

For Laurel Remington

'The best times are the talking times…'
Love is a Learning Thing, Stuart Shaw

PROLOGUE

The evening after her world fell apart a second time, Sara finally has the beginnings of a plan. She steadies her hand, and knocks.

'I need to talk to you.'

Without waiting to be properly invited, Sara steps past Trevor Islam into his consulting room, crosses the plush carpet and occupies the chair next to his desk. It is gone seven o'clock, but she knew he would still be here. He is doing some last minute prep before appearing tomorrow as an expert psychiatric witness in a trial.

Sara isn't focusing on the trial. Instead she is staring at her knees and trying in this gap of time, this cushioned silence, to control her breathing. Given yesterday's news, she is desperate to stop her mind unravelling by keeping active, by focusing on something ordinary, reliable. And knees are extremely ordinary, extremely reliable. Everyone has them. Unless they are blown away.

Her palms scrape the armrests of the chair. 'I was thinking of taking a holiday.'

'Well done.' Trevor flips the end of his tie. Trevor's ties are so excitable they should be on Ritalin. 'Where to?'

'India.'

'Ah, my home,' he smiles. Rocking in his ergonomic chair, Sara's clinical supervisor embarks on a description of India as the land of reinvention. Very subtle.

'Yes. I thought it was time I discovered what makes you so warm, so empathic.' She manages a smile. 'So I was wondering, where should I stay in Delhi?'

1

'My home *town*,' he muses. 'And why Delhi?' he adds, tipping back alarmingly in his chair. 'Most people go to Goa, for the beaches. Or to Agra, for the Taj Mahal. Or to Rajasthan, for the camel fair. Delhi's just the political and military capital.'

She widens her eyes as if, really, she didn't know. As if she hasn't already been scoping out India's Ministry of Defence and the British High Commission in Delhi on Google Earth, hasn't already found the website for a company which—for an eye-watering fee—can facilitate an Indian visa in three days flat. She stares back at her knees, avoiding eye contact like a patient who has forgotten to bring their weekly cheque.

Trevor springs forward in his chair. 'More to the point, how long are you going for?'

There is something beady in his question. It makes her look back up, makes her sense that he knows she isn't intending to stay for just a week or ten days, riding an elephant or being photographed sitting wistfully in front of the Taj Mahal. Her planned response to just this kind of question was going to be 'two weeks tops'. But it is as though he can read her mind.

'A friend came to my house last night. An old colleague of Mike's. Told me Mike didn't die in Afghanistan, but in India.'

Trevor steeples his long fingers. 'Ah. Do you want to talk about it?'

Hearing the phrase she has so often used with her own patients jolts her. She certainly doesn't want to talk about it. Or to even think about it, or for any of it to be true. For eighteen months she has found it impossible to shut out the memory of that first knock at the door, when she first heard the news that Mike had been killed in Afghanistan, destroyed by one of the bombs he was so skilled at diffusing. A skill for which he'd won numerous medals. Sara hasn't wanted to dwell on the details, but in her more tortured moments has presumed at the very least knees blown away, limbs scattered over a wide area, torn flesh clinging to leaves, fragments never to be reunited.

And now there has been a second knock at the door, from Mike's corporal Tom. She closes her eyes, as the conversation from last night replays itself in her mind.

'I just thought you should know the truth,' Tom had said.

Sara paces the room, hugging herself. 'Just tell me again.'

Tom sighs. 'Sara, we've been over this a dozen times—'

'Just—' Sara rakes her fingers through her unwashed hair. 'Just *tell* me.'

'I was discharged at the weekend and I thought you should—'"

'Yes, I get why you feel you can tell me this now—' she pauses, trying to rein in spikes of fury and frustration. Yet by suppressing those, she now finds herself swamped by guilt, wondering whether there was, in fact, a body to be claimed. Whether Mike did, God forbid, die in agony after all.

Tom holds out his hands. 'I just thought it might help you to start to move on,' he says, clutching at a well-known straw. 'I mean, it's what you people do, isn't it? Make sense of the past? Move on?'

'You people?' How can she disillusion him, reveal that therapists are the most screwed up of all? Tom—Mike's ammunition technician in the disruptions of the IEDs, the one colleague of Mike's she has always had a soft spot for— how is he to know she isn't ready to move on? How day after day, week after week, her grief has mutated until what is left isn't so much bereavement as a holding pattern. And now Tom has appeared, with his shiny new information, and dragged her back to that dreadful place she stood in eighteen months ago, dumbstruck, to when *the family has been informed.*

Only, this time, she has to fight the urge to rush to the bearer of this surreal news and shake him violently, as though Mike will come spilling out of Tom's pocket. Her eyes rest on the Afghan oil painting Mike brought back from one of his tours: a bowl of blushing apricots, a crop which thrives in the harsh winters of the region. A delicious symbol, Mike used to say, of never giving up hope—in a place or its people. A symbol of Afghanistan, not India.

'But, why India? What the hell was he doing there?' A flash of terror burns her heart. 'Mike never mentioned India in any of his letters, not once. Nor in any of his phone calls. Not even on leave. So why was he there?' And she has a sudden image of him, kissing someone in the shadows. A secret life. A loud ringing starts up in her ears.

Tom's lips are moving but she isn't listening. She is deaf from dread, at the information to come, like patients receiving a second diagnosis which turns out to be as deadly as the first. There must be implications stemming from this revelation, although her mind can't quite grasp what they might be.

She tries not to start pacing the room again, and yet she finds she has to. 'Why was he there?' She knows she has said this already, but she can't help repeating herself. 'Look. Tell me again, what you know. Don't leave anything out.'

A spasm of pain spoils Tom's features. A micro-gesture, that subtle psychological incongruence between body language and speech. He obviously feels conflicted. He clears his throat. 'If a death occurs on operations overseas, the Royal Military Police here and the Coroner's Court where the body is to be repatriated are informed.'

'But with Mike, it didn't happen like that?'

'Exactly. I was back in Brize Norton at the time and all we got was a death certificate from AFG with instructions not to contact the other authorities.'

'But I still don't get it. Why all the secrecy? Why did no one tell me? I was his wife.' Tears prick at her eyes. A wife in name, at least. The ghost of him kissing someone floats once more in her mind and she shakes her head to get rid of it.

'No idea. The only thing I can think of is that he was working undercover.'

Sara flings her hands to her face. 'Oh for God's sake, that's ridiculous. You'll be telling me next all this secrecy *from me* was vital for "national security". As if I'd tell a soul. You forget, my day job is about keeping secrets.'

Tom concedes the point. 'Like I say, I don't know.'

A wave of heat flashes over her scalp. 'Maybe he'd met someone,' she says quietly.

Tom looks genuinely shocked. 'Mike? Now that *is* ridiculous. He adored you. You know that.'

Sara is unable to meet his eye. 'But why India? And why did no one tell me?' I am babbling, she thinks.

Tom sighs. 'In the army, you learn not to ask questions.'

She recalls the grand ceremony with which friends and family bid Mike a war hero's farewell, with the gold brocade, the gleaming trumpets playing 'I Was Glad', and the speeches celebrating male camaraderie. Had anyone else that day known that Mike's death—'killed instantly'—was not as it seemed? Had anyone else asked awkward questions?

And then the penny drops. She spins round. 'But *I* could ask questions.' She glimpses another micro-gesture ripple lightly across Tom's features. A faint hint of a smile playing on his lips. And she sees immediately how it is, why Tom really paid her this visit today, five days after his own discharge from the army. An idea planted. Non-attributable.

Her skin tingles, her mind wild and curious for the first time in months. India. She imagines the heat on her English skin, the way it might cause her to unfurl.

5

Trevor takes her glittering eyes in his professional stride. He stretches his tall frame across the tooled leather of his desk and spins a Rolodex until he reaches a particular name. 'Here. This might help.' He unhooks a business card and hands it over. 'Dr Mathur. He's an old mukka of mine from St Stephen's. At med school we were known as Laurel and Hardy. Me the tall, thin Muslim, he the short, fat Hindu.' He laughs, fondly.

Sara scans the florid font. 'I don't understand. Does he run a hotel?'

Trevor flips the end of his psychedelic tie. 'Other side. He runs a clinic. I'm sure he would love to have you work there for a while.'

Trevor's empathic ability to read people and situations is a talent she has long admired, envied even. That and his reputation for being a Catherine wheel, shooting off clinical sparks. It's why she applied straight from King's to work at this clinic, to learn from the eminent Professor Islam, foppish hair going grey at the temples, just old enough to be her father.

Sara turns the card over, reads the meaningless address of the Mathur Clinic for Mental Disorders. 'I don't see how this will help. I don't speak Hindi or Urdu or whatever it is they speak over there. And there will be cross-cultural issues. I could get things wrong, make things *worse*.' What she really means is, how can I possibly find out what happened to Mike when I'm busy seeing patients I can't understand?

As though reading her mind, Trevor continues. 'If you want to find out about how Mike died, you'll need a structure once you're there. Colleagues to give you support, and something to take your mind off things when you meet an obstacle,' he chuckles, as if to say, after all—this is India we're talking about. 'As for the work itself, you underestimate yourself.

You're the best therapist I have. You combine empathy with insight. And you don't give up on people.'

Mike, she thinks. I can't give up on Mike.

'And believe me, there will be plenty of work for you to do.' His eyes dart to the papers on his desk and Sara remembers guiltily about Trevor's important witness appearance tomorrow in the trial of five men from Hounslow, who—allegedly—trafficked girls from India to—allegedly—fund a cell planning to blow up one of London's landmark hotels. She had almost forgotten Trevor was working on it. India. Always India.

'After all, India is a country in transition. It won't be what you expect.'

She smiles. This is the Trevor way. Challenging your blind spots, your prejudices, and dismantling them towards the path of Trenlightenment. 'And what will I be expecting?'

'The Happy Poor! Waiting to be Rescued!'

'I think the movie *Slumdog Millionaire* ruined any romanticised notion we in the West might have about that.'

Trevor nods. 'Westerners have been drawn to India for centuries. They usually go to find themselves,' he adds, with a hint of contempt. 'They imagine India will be pure, unsullied, exotic. A country where old values and traditions have been preserved.' Now he stops rocking and leans forward. 'But there is something called India Psychosis. Travellers lose their bearings. They become so consumed by their quest—for spirituality, for answers, for meaning—that they develop a mental illness, a full-blown psychosis. They lose touch with reality.'

She bridles, to think that Saint Trevor could cast her in such an unflattering light, but says, 'Thanks for the heads up. I'll take extra care that doesn't happen to me.'

'Good. And remember, India is what it is. It's just an ordinary place, operating in extraordinary circumstances.'

7

Then out of force of habit, he stands up to indicate to the person in the chair opposite—who, unlike Sara, usually has their face buried in multiple tissues—that the session is now at an end. 'Contact Mathur,' he adds, reaching her chair. 'Don't worry. I'll write a glowing reference for you.'

Sara stands. 'Anyone would think you're happy to get rid of me,' she jokes.

Trevor places a hand on her shoulder, a large one with buffed, healthy nails. 'Sara,' he says, 'you haven't been yourself for eighteen months. I'm doing this to get you back.'

1

As the plane begins its descent towards Delhi, the man in the next seat leans towards her. So close, their foreheads almost touch; she catches whiffs of breakfast coffee. Beyond them, the dawn sky spreads out like a bolt of silk.

'You be lucky to be being by the window,' he murmurs. 'I be desperate to see my home town from the air, before we land. May I?' he adds.

Before Sara can answer, the man releases his seat belt and twists—making an unfortunate noise on the faux-leather—to lunge across.

'I don't mind swapping,' she says, unlocking her seat buckle. But a flight attendant who witnesses this minor rebellion points a Damson Crush talon at the lit-up Fasten Seat Belt sign.

The passenger acknowledges Sara's attempt to be kind. 'I be running import-export business,' he says proudly, pressing his business card into her hand. 'So can I be asking you, why you be coming to India?'

What to say? That she was lied to about her husband's death and wants to find out the truth. That her boss thinks she is falling apart. Or that her life is on hold. 'I've come for answers,' she says, hoping to sound more confident than she feels. And as the plane lands, she experiences the full force of all she hopes to achieve here bursting in her inner ear.

Stepping outside at Arrivals—waved through by yawning men in khaki—Delhi explodes into bedlam around her. Men yell taxi prices, horns blast incessantly and boisterous passengers shriek their joy at being met. The clamour hits her like a rugby tackle. Everywhere she turns, eyes seem to glare at her. A solid heat clamps her jeans to her legs and every time she breathes in, she smells animal dung, fried food, paraffin.

Hobbling along, dragging her loaded suitcases behind her, she smiles at everyone, in an effort to look fearless. Yet inside she has a chronic urge to escape the crush, to turn straight round and fly back home. Without warning, a man without legs scoots past her on a skateboard, knocking her off balance. She yelps, both at his sudden appearance in filthy rags and at his blatant deformities, the distended skull, the twisted limbs. She stops dead, in semi-shock. Is this where Mike landed, when he arrived in India? Was he as overwhelmed as she is, by this chronic assault on the senses?

Her heart pounding, she takes a moment to gather her thoughts. The Arrivals concourse carries an air of urgency and panic. Sara knows the feeling. Physician, heal thyself.

Just then, a young man emerges unruffled from the crowd and stands before her, clean-shaven, his serene face bathed in sunlight. Stitched onto his crisp polo shirt is the name of Mathur's clinic. She is about to put out her hand to shake his when he places his palms together to greet her. 'Namaste Miss Sara,' he says. 'My name is Hemant. It is my pleasure to welcome you to India.'

The directness of his gaze startles her, the way it seems to own the space between them and, by implication, her day. Her future, even. She looks at him closely, with his kind face, his slender frame, his capable hands.

Sara lets go of her cases and repeats his gesture, enchanted. 'Thank you, Hemant. Thank you very much.'

He reaches for the suitcase handles.

'Don't worry,' she grabs for them too. 'I've got them.'

But those agile hands get there first. Turning on his heels, he leads her through the shrill crowds, pulling her cases effortlessly behind him.

Something expands inside her. As she follows him, her neck muscles relax and she can sense herself walking a little taller, as though pulled skyward by an unseen thread. And as the air brushes her bare limbs, heavy and warm—almost amniotic—she is conscious that she is touching the same soil, *the very same soil* that Mike trod.

⚜

On the drive into town, Sara tries to get her bearings using the maps in her guidebook, but for now Delhi is simply a blur of traffic hysteria and heartbreaking scenes of the elderly sprawled on pavements and snot-encrusted beggar children. Their scabrous hands smack against her window. Hemant the driver is good—careful—and Sara thought she was prepared for the sights, familiar from documentaries, of human misery. Yet to see it up close is a different matter. She is so tense, sitting so rigidly in the back of the clinic's minibus, that her left leg has started to jiggle. She was mad to come to India.

Two drawn out hours later, and she and Hemant have dropped her luggage off at her hotel and she is now standing in the peeling courtyard of the clinic. The tops of her feet are frying. A lizard darts around a waterless bird bath. A dozen people stand before her, the sun beating down, clutching garlands of marigolds. She is so relieved to have made it here in once piece, that she has a fierce longing to open her arms and hug them. Unsure as to whether this is the moment to perform the driver's enchanting palms-together thing, she smiles but they do not catch her eye.

A stocky man in his sixties trots forward. His expression suggests he has just rammed an empty chocolate wrapper into his pocket.

'Dr Mathur?' she says.

11

'Absolutely. Welcome, Sara.' Dr Mathur presses his palms together, saying namaste as he does so.

She repeats the gesture, and the word. 'Thank you so much for letting me spend some time at your clinic. Dr Islam has told me all about you.'

He waves away the implied flattery. 'Sorry to put you up in an hotel. The flat I have for you, she is not ready.'

'Please don't apologise, the hotel is stunning.' She is not lying. The Majestic is quite magnificent, with a stratospheric staff-to-guest ratio. The flower display in the lobby is the size of a family car.

Dr Mathur poses with her for photos for the clinic's website, and then briskly excuses himself. She watches him disappear into the cool of the main building with something close to envy.

The people holding the marigolds are introduced by a nurse as patients. In silence they place the heavy loops around her neck, and are then led away, shuffling across the courtyard. The sun is so high in the sky that their shadows appear grotesquely foreshortened, as though what bobs at their feet is a small yet solid ball and chain.

⚜

After a selection of greasy vegetable pakoras in the clinic's small canteen, Sara is shown to her office by a nurse who then excuses herself. Sara jiggles a key into an unfamiliar lock. A bead of sweat dribbles down the side of her waist, and it occurs to Sara that Mike would open this in a flash. Mike, who was trained to think twenty moves ahead, to clear surrounding areas, to save lives. Taking a pause, she tightens her grip on the key, turns it more deliberately, feels it ease into place.

Inside, her office proves to be small and airless, with telltale bulges of damp at the skirting boards and a dead insect lying on its back. A metal desk stands in the middle. She sinks down on a metal chair and pulls open one of the drawers. A paperclip glares back at her, reproachfully. She sticks her tongue out at it and, using her iPad, plots a route for this evening from this clinic to the British High Commission. In the past week, in a sort of manic delirium, she has Googled, India and Anglo-Indian cooperation, India's army regiments, counterterrorism and, in a flight of fancy, kidnappings. She has scoured the websites of the *Times of India* and *Hindustan Times*, and has even fired off emails to the British Ministry of Defence demanding full and open information about how Mike really died. These emails have bounced back, address unknown. She twists her wedding ring.

Now she is in India she realises she isn't entirely sure how to proceed. She is by nature an observer, watching for nonverbal clues. If she appears to hold back, it is because she trusts in treading carefully until you know what you're dealing with. It is all Sara knows how to do, since she lives in her head, whereas Mike was always out in the world, a man of action.

'But you hold people's hands,' Mike would say, when she felt as though her job had no value. 'Metaphorically, anyway. You're on that journey with your patients, never knowing if it will end. I snip a few wires and it's all done.'

Modest to a fault, that was Mike.

Later that afternoon, her first patient arrives to sit opposite her—Dr Mathur is certainly getting his pound of flesh in quick. The woman is young, small, compact. Sara explains who she is and what her role will be at the clinic, giving one-to-one therapy. The tidy woman takes it all in and nods, but volunteers nothing of her own.

'So what brought you to the clinic…' she glances at the file, 'Kanan?'

Kanan looks down. Around the two of them hangs silence. And the heat, that thick, sliceable heat which the decrepit ceiling fan cannot hope to eliminate.

'Can you remember what happened before you came here? Did someone in your family bring you?'

Kanan tilts her head. 'Uncle.'

Sara nods. 'And what did your uncle think was wrong with you?'

'Nothing.'

Classic case of denial, thinks Sara. She smiles kindly at Kanan. 'Sometimes we don't know we need help.'

Kanan balls her sari into her fists. 'I refused…'

'You refused to come here?' In denial *and* admitted against her will, she decides.

'I refused to die.'

Sara blinks. 'Someone wanted you dead?'

Kanan tilts her head. 'My family wanted to burn me, when my husband died.'

Her hand shaking, Sara reaches into her bag and passes the woman a pack of tissues. Sara has read in her guidebook about sati, the old practice of burning widows on the funeral pyre of their husbands—although the guidebook also maintains that the practice has died out, having been made illegal across India.

A thought forms. 'So how long were you married? You're only just eighteen?'

'We were betrothed when I was eleven. I saw seven Diwalis as a wife.'

'So your husband died young.'

'Not so young. He was sixty-four.'

Sara wants to be outraged but in this moment is reminded of Mr Finn, her Maths teacher. Drove a yellow TR7. Finn

14

had seen her when she was fourteen, walking in the rain to the bus stop. Drew up by the kerb and invited her in. And that was that. Home and dry.

It is now Sara catches sight of the scarring all the way up Kanan's arm. The skin is raw and shiny and knobbly. And she has an image of the woman being dragged towards the flames, screaming, before pulling away, maybe her clothes on fire.

Kanan catches Sara studying her scars. 'Do not be worrying, these are not from the fire.'

Sara looks up and sees a fierce pride in the woman's eyes. 'Not the fire?'

'I burn myself with acid. I think to myself, they will say I am mad. No man will want to touch me if I am mad. For years in secret I teach myself English. I learn from the newspapers about places like this, this clinic. I think to myself, they will bring me to a place like this. And then I will be safe.'

Sara feels a smile forming, at the girl's presence of mind, yet she is also appalled at such a dreadful situation. To feel the need to pretend to be mad, to escape the pressures of family or tradition.

'I will be safe here, won't I?' Kanan adds, and it is only now that her eyes become filmy with moisture.

Dr Mathur drops by. 'Settling in, my dear?'

'Yes. But what a dreadful story Kanan has to tell.'

'Yes, my dear. The perils of a nation that subsidises kerosene. But Trevor tells me, you have your own sadness too, about your husband. How you wish to find out what happened to him. How is your search going?'

She doesn't know whether to be irked at Trevor's indiscretion or relieved that she doesn't have to explain herself. 'I phoned the British High Commission on the way

15

here from the airport, but no one on the twenty-four hour switchboard even knows where to direct my call. My plan is that if I go in person, they'll find it harder to get rid of me!'

Dr Mathur tilts his head in understanding. 'I hope you find out something, my dear. But even if not, the pain, it does subside. Not all at once, but gradually. When my wife died, I couldn't imagine having a life again. But I had my patients. They kept me going. And my son of course,' he adds, almost as an afterthought. 'So go. Go. Today, we are done.'

Ten minutes later, she is sprinting to the six-lane highway where she hails a battered green and yellow motorised rickshaw. Once again the traffic carnage means the driver cannot drive fast, so she has the perfect opportunity to see more of the city and start to make sense of it. The sunlight dazzles in rainbow colours off the battered bonnets of cars, and cows meander contentedly down the middle of the road. The elderly she saw before lying on pavements are evidently part of extended families, playing with babies, and when she glimpses into one-room homes she sees they are spotless and tidy, the cooking utensils stacked and brightly polished. She smiles at these incremental happy discoveries.

What is more, Trevor was right, Delhi has confounded her expectations. The clinic is located in a dusty lane on the edge of Delhi. It has grey walls and the slight air of abandonment. The High Commission turns out to be a bougainvillea-draped bungalow standing in wide lawns. She'd expected the people living in plastic tents on the pavement, the stink of rubbish rotting at the kerb, the occasional dead dog lying rigid in the street. What she hadn't expected were the avenues, the creamy Lutyens architecture, the swanking opulence.

In her hand she clutches a letter addressed to the Ambassador. She treads the gravel path towards the High Commission building—the unusual smell of damp earth speaks of intensive irrigation—and once there, hands the

16

letter to a gentleman in military uniform and white gloves who has watched her arrival. His salt-and-pepper moustache is wider than his face.

'Ambassador,' she says, handing it over.

The tone in which the man glances at her tuk-tuk and repeats the word doesn't inspire her with confidence. She is suddenly wary of letting this letter go.

She repeats the name on the envelope, triple-checked online.

The man takes the envelope. 'No,' he smiles.

'What do you mean, no?'

The man doesn't reply.

'Not today? No, not here? Or no, you won't make sure he gets it?' She holds out her hand to take the letter back.

'Consulate.' His grin broadens.

'The Ambassador is at the Consulate?'

He waves her envelope energetically. 'Ambassador.'

Sara takes a deep breath. Pointing at her feet, she says, 'Commission.'

'Commission,' the man agrees, with a grin.

Sara points behind her, in the vague direction of the centre of town. 'Consulate.'

Much energetic head tilting.

Sara holds up her hands in a questioning posture. 'Ambassador?'

The man waves her envelope again, as if the double-barrelled man in question, CBE, KCMG, is actually to be found within the sealed folds of paper.

'Where is your husband?' the man suddenly says. She can almost see his moustache twitch in contempt, as if to say, I prefer to deal with the man of the house.

Something burns within Sara, an urge to shove this wall of a man out of the way. But being a rebel, a troublemaker, doesn't come easily to her. Dogged persistence in the face

17

of the void—to sit for example with the same patient for five years, inching towards change—*that's* what gives her the ripple of a high. So for now, in front of this obstacle, the epitome of the infamous bureaucracy of India, she feels deflated.

⧜

That evening, dodging the eager concierge's attempts—'I am clocking off in half an hour'—to entice her to one of the hotel's many VIP social events, Sara chisels lengths in the hotel's outdoor pool decorated with plaster fish. She is trying to derive, in the Zen-like rhythm of her swim, inspiration about where next to look for information about Mike. Sometimes, in that quasi-meditative zone, she can almost hear Mike's voice, soft in her ear, sense his breath warm on her skin, humming the odd Afghan ballad. Or she can hear him telling her animatedly about his passion for apricots, how they could become the miracle crop in Afghanistan, trumping opium.

And she remembers Tom just before he left last week, clearing his throat again. 'My father died last year.'

'I'm sorry to hear that,' she said.

'A stroke. Unable to communicate. But I knew he was in there somewhere. So I just used to hold his hand and talk, you know? Let him know we hadn't given up on him.'

She wishes she had asked, How did you start to get over it? Please tell me, as I am currently stuck, how to get over to the other side of grief.

And as she swims, she allows herself to remember the last time she watched Mike leave for Afghanistan, the military heft of him bulking out his clothes, the Blakeys on his shoes ticking the pavement, his blonde hair enamelled in London's splinters of sun.

18

2

One morning, Sara emerges from the metro through the crowds of commuters in shirts and ties, and the men in turbans armed with cotton buds—the ear cleaning wallahs. The heat is stifling so she tries to keep to the shadier side, and imagines Mike seeking out its coolness as well.

As she strolls up the lane to the clinic she thinks back to the world of the metro. To her great surprise, the carriages on her train were segregated. Male passengers, at either end, leered and whistled at the forbidden fruit; Eve Teasing is the trivialising euphemism she has seen the media here use, for all forms of sexual harassment. And as she sat there, between stations, Sara had felt a sense of what it might be like to be an Indian woman. An object in a tunnel, with no easy escape.

As she approaches her clinic she passes her favourite sign of the trip so far. *Pants-U-Like: made to fit.* The shop's plump owner, wearing a grubby lungi, sits outside the yellow windows, picking at matching jaundiced toenails. Sara and he are already on nodding terms.

In front of the clinic stands a large crow, its jet feathers metallic in the sunshine. Sara's now well-thumbed guidebook has warned her about crows, who have filthy beaks from pecking at cow-dung. Two small boys taunt it, an act of bravado, since this creature is almost their size. Sara smiles.

Suddenly a slim young woman in a sari appears, her ruby lips parted in a high-pitched holler, a glossy, sensuous 'o'. She claps her hands to shoo the crow away, bangles tinkling and glittering in the sunlight as they slide down her wrists. It is beautiful to watch this woman's taut body as she raises her limbs, the swell of her firm breasts against the cotton of her blouse, her hair honey in the sun, unravelling from its bun with every wild gesture. Insolently, the bird flaps barely out of reach, staring her out.

Sara could watch this woman all day. The liquid flow of her body in the sari. And the building. She hasn't really noticed it before. Some sort of temple, perhaps. Pale and crumbling and huge. She resolves one day to go in and properly explore.

That is, of course, if she stays here in Delhi. This morning back at her hotel, she opened on her laptop a fobbing-off email from India's Ministry of Defence, saying that owing to the sensitive nature of ongoing military operations, they are unable to confirm or deny Tom's information and do not consider a meeting worthwhile. Distraught at the casual snipping of this lifeline, she grabbed Mike's T-shirt from under her pillow where she keeps it, and crushed it to her face, inhaling his familiar, comforting, yet increasingly faint, scent.

Turning her back on the crow, the woman readjusts the wispy fabric over her head, clips the boys round the ears and ushers them round the stone gateway. Sara hopes with all her heart that the woman has a husband.

⚜

Sara skirts the dried-up bird bath in the courtyard and heads for her office. There she fires up her iPad, Googles the Delhi Police Force and works out the nearest station to the clinic.

Deepak, a male patient, arrives, stinking of booze, his eyes bloodshot. Deepak used to work with his father as a pimp, but he was caught having sex with his father's favourite prostitute and beaten up and thrown out of the family home. He turned to whisky as a crutch. His detox has been going slowly. When the session ends, Sara can smell alcohol on her skin.

At lunchtime she grabs a chicken wrap from a kiosk on the highway and takes a tuk-tuk to the police headquarters for the central Chandni district. For good measure, she got her concierge this morning to write out directions in Hindi script and, at her request, has practised with him some key words—left, right, thank you—for added consideration.

The station waiting room is framed on all sides by chairs, only one or two of which are occupied by docile locals. Perhaps crime is extremely low in this district.

'Passport number?' asks a junior officer at the front desk. 'Previous countries visited? Father's occupation?'

'In what way is my father's occupation relevant?'

'Station very busy,' he replies, incongruously, gesturing at all the empty chairs.

Just then a door opens and a man strides out. Like the junior officer, this man wears a short-sleeved biscuit uniform, but only this man sports epaulettes thickly decorated with stars, only he has a jet black comb-over gleaming with brilliantine, only he wears tinted sunglasses.

Instinctively Sara knows this man to be important.

She blocks his path. 'Good afternoon,' she says, before the junior office, can intervene. 'My name is Sara Young. I'm over from England and I'm trying to find out what happened to my husband, Michael Young, who apparently died in India.'

Passang Kasturirangan introduces himself, offers his condolences for her loss and invites Sara into his office.

His desk is submerged beneath an in tray that would take at least a decade to clear. A small flag of India flutters in the breeze of an equally small fan. And the pleasantries are endless, as Passang seems obsessed with Sara's constitution. All women, he announces, have delicate constitutions and need looking after, to be kept pure.

Sara catches an undertone of infantalisation and straightens her spine. 'Thank you for your concern. And I won't keep you

21

long, but I need help tracking down information about how my husband died. Do you, for example, have any national databases which might link deaths both in Delhi and in other cities? Deaths which were unresolved maybe.'

Passang sits back in his chair and steeples his fingers. 'So what we be talking about in essence is Missing Person, yes?'

'Well, sort of. Yes.'

Passang puffs out his chest. 'We have new national web-based application for the Missing Persons.' The senior policeman switches on his bulky computer and the two of them wait in silence as it noisily warms up. Sara is about to ask why he doesn't have it on all the time, when he interrupts her thoughts with a sheepish grin. 'Power cut.'

He spins the screen to face her. 'We log the relevant info into the Daily Diary and this is flashed electronically to Police Control Room, State Crime Bureau, National Crime Bureau and Anti-kidnapping Bureau. We can also give publicity in the area where the person was last seen, using loudhailers.'

Loudhailers. 'Heavens.'

'And we use these modern techniques both for Missing Persons and for dead bodies found without identification card. And already I am pleased to say we be having twenty-seven per cent success rate of discovery. The first fifteen days are crucial for finding said Missing Person. Speed is of the very essence. When did you say your husband died?'

Sara's mind has already snagged on the phrases twenty-seven per cent and fifteen days. 'Eighteen months ago.'

Passang looks appalled. 'And only now you be coming to register him as Missing Person?'

Sara juts out her chin and explains about Tom's revelation.

'But this means Backlog. Do you not know, nearly five hundred people go missing in India every day, including nearly two hundred and fifty children.'

'Five hundred people *a day*?'

22

'Exactly so. Eighteen months is a long time.'

Although not long enough to complete the grieving process. Sara slumps under the strain, which seems to galvanise Passang. 'Tell you what. Give me all his details. I can also get my men to scrutinise the National Register of Unidentified Dead Bodies. Do you have a photo?' he adds.

'Here, I brought a few.' Sara hands one over. It is of Mike and her at a regimental dinner, Mike in military blue, apparently happy to be home. Passang promises to be in touch but somehow, as the glossy paper leaves her fingers, Sara has a hunch that if the British military has hushed things up, it is unlikely that the Indian police will find anything at all.

Sara takes a tuk-tuk back to the clinic. Nearly five hundred people *a day*. She plays with her necklace, Mike's last birthday present to her, sliding the opal from side to side on its silver chain.

At a set of count-down traffic lights, Sara's eye is caught by a beggar woman strolling between cars, carrying a mobile phone. She isn't using it—she might have just found it, it might not be hers—but she is carefully carrying one. As though on some level she is aware that to possess such an object is crucial, as though it renders her immune. The woman's hair is matted, her turquoise sari filthy, but she is carrying a mobile phone. She belongs to the modern India. But she doesn't have any shoes.

3

Two steamy weeks after her arrival, Sara is writing up notes on a patient when a sharp rap on her office door makes her jump. The door bursts open and a man enters wearing mirrored sunglasses.

'You must be Sara?'

He slides the sunglasses into his hair and approaches with one hand extended. The man's nose is as sharp as the creases in his jeans. 'I'm Rafi,' he says. His speech is dynamic, a burst of automatic gunfire, but his handshake is limp. 'I see Dad has put you in the broom cupboard!'

'Dad?'

'Owns the clinic? Your boss?'

'Ah yes. You've been on holiday in England. Whereabouts?'

Rafi frowns. 'He said that?'

'Word for word.' It's the professional hazard of being a therapist, photographic hearing. 'You weren't in England?'

'I was *working*.' He checks his watch. 'Listen, do you fancy a drink? A lime soda?'

She has no idea what a lime soda is, but she can't imagine it could be amazing enough to justify delaying her return to the hotel to research the names of other diplomats at the British High Commission. And yet she can almost see the condensation-dappled glass in her hand, feel the iced liquid sliding soothingly down her throat, the burst of energy such refreshment would provide. 'Actually I need to clear up a few things here first,' she says. 'Some notes.' The excuse sounds as lifeless as her hair.

'Absolutely. Anyway, I'm in the room above if you need me. And—' he executes a mock solemn bow, 'welcome to India.' She nods in return.

After he leaves, Sara perches on the edge of the desk and breathes out deeply. Staring at the floor, she sees herself running up the stairs and knocking on Rafi's door, sees in an inspired pause a life in India filled with sociability and *moving on* from Mike.

She picks up a blue Manila folder, which bends in the humidity. She needs to be out there in the world. She won't find out the truth about Mike in her head. And maybe Rafi knows someone who knows someone. Abruptly she pushes off from the desk.

Rafi beams at the sight of her at his door.

'I'd love to, thank you. But just a quick one,' she adds.

'Absolutely!' Eagerly locking up, he leads the way out of the clinic, scrolling all the while through messages on his BlackBerry.

They walk down the lane, in the opposite direction of the highway, dodging steaming pancakes of cow-dung. To the left of the clinic is a plot of land, with what look like foundations for a building, now overgrown with weeds.

'My father's next project, the next phase of the clinic,' says Rafi, striding ahead. 'When he can stand still long enough to plan it properly.'

They are, it seems, on the very edge of Delhi. The few shops opposite the clinic quickly give way to fields on one side and a long dun wall on the other. Dusty children and the odd masticating goat gaze at the two of them curiously. The churning heat presses in on her skin, so intense it is hard to draw breath.

And then she sees it, an enormous tree in the next field, with its soft grey bark, its perfect leaves and tiny white flowers. Its canopy opens out against the luminous sky and seems to welcome her towards it. Beneath it stands a wooden cart, with maybe a dozen people gathered round. More relax in the shade of a faded block-print sheet slung between some branches. She sees jugs and glasses, and piles of limes still with their leaves sweetly attached. Saliva stings in her mouth.

They watch a man slicing up limes, before squeezing them deftly with one hand into various glasses. Next he pours in a measure of viscous liquid which shimmers in the sunlight. Rafi explains that proper lime sodas contain a mixture of salty and sweet. 'The perfect rehydration tonic!' Rafi adds, as though intoning for an advert. Adding soda, the man whisks until the liquid is the palest pistachio.

Rafi holds up his fingers, places an order.

'I love the way this chap is able to rustle up several orders at once,' she says. 'Like experienced bartenders all over the world.'

'Rustle up?' chuckles Rafi. 'You're speaking like an Indian already.'

She grins. 'I love reading the newspapers over breakfast at the hotel. All that antiquated language. *Scarpered, preponing…*'

'*Doing the needful!*'

'My favourite is, *Change is on the anvil.*'

Rafi's eyebrows knit together. 'Apart from the fact that India is too stubborn to change. As you will quickly discover.' He hands her a glass.

'What do you mean?'

'India's stuck.'

'Rubbish,' she laughs, gesturing towards the highway, with its shopping malls and HIV clinics and 4x4s. 'Two hundred yards away from here, it's like another world.'

The bartenders calls out that their order is ready.

The soda bubbles tickle her nose.

'Again, welcome to Delhi,' says Rafi, raising his drink to her.

She downs hers so quickly it dribbles down her chin. The sugary liquid is not especially cool, but it sets off thrilling little taste explosions in her mouth.

Before she has finished, Rafi says, 'Another?'

Sara nods. She watches as Rafi hands over a small denomination note. Mike always called her a cheap date. And from nowhere, a sudden flash of anger surges over her. Why India? And why keep it a secret *from me*? And there it is again, that vision of Mike walking away from her. She chokes on the last of her lime soda.

Rafi turns. 'You OK?' His forehead is dappled with perspiration. 'Shade?'

She nods again. 'So what do you do, Rafi? Are you a psychiatrist, like your dad?'

'Am I like my dad?' he says, slowly. He sips his second drink, as though the more he drinks, the more his thoughts, or some association with them, will be diluted. 'And what brings you to India?' he says, finally.

Sara registers the sidestepping of personal questions and determines to be more open. 'I thought my husband died in Afghanistan but it turns out he died here, in India.'

'How awful. And how bizarre. Why was he here? How come you never knew?'

Sara hesitates, a spasm of guilt twisting in her stomach. The first question she would agree, is a mystery. The second question, if she is really honest, maybe not so much.

'Hard to say. I imagine he found something here of great value.' Something which gave him more than our marriage could, she almost adds.

'So where have you tried?'

She tells him about the farcical experience at the High Commission and the marginally more depressing one with Passang Kasturirangan at the sleepy police station.

Rafi rolls his eyes. 'This just proves my point about change. India will always be bogged down by the three Cs: caste, chaos and corruption. I mean, look at this place—' he gestures contemptuously at the fields, the stall. 'We could overtake China, if we really put our minds to it. There is so

27

much potential. But India is stagnating. India suffocates. It's like being in a relationship with the wrong person. To stay sane, you must leave.'

'Hang on, I've only just got here,' she laughs.

Rafi's eyes twinkle.

'And you've come back,' says Sara.

'Who said I've come back?'

She frowns. He isn't seeing her in front of him. Other audiences have heard this outburst before. This is an old, old conversation. No, not a conversation. A monologue.

She leaps in to stop Rafi descending into a self-pitying spiral. 'So how can I get to meet a British diplomat, if no one will direct my calls, answer my letters or even give me an appointment?'

'I guess you need to hang out where they hang out.'

Sara glances back at the beautiful tree and the pop-up stall. She can't imagine a British diplomat trotting down this semi-rural lane anytime soon. 'So tell me, where in Delhi do British diplomats socialise?'

'You mean, where else can Delhi's hungry high rollers go to be served champagne and foie gras by a waiter who grew up in a slum? At the smart hotels, of course.'

Back at her hotel, Sara makes a beeline for the excitable concierge. 'You know those special VIP events you've often told me about, that take place in this hotel? I was just wondering, is anything happening here this evening?'

Nearly fainting with pleasure, the concierge offers her a choice of the launch party for a perfume, a lecture on the Last Mughal by a famous British writer and an exhibition stroke Mexican buffet in the hotel's ballroom. She agrees to go to all three.

After all, it's not like she has socialised much these past eighteen months. When Mike died, everyone spoke of how strong she was being, how resolute. That was the word they used: resolute. As though she had resolved something, come to conclusions, when in fact some days she could barely do much more than stare blankly for hours on end at the contents of her sock drawer. Numerous friends would ring, but she took to unplugging the phone. An understandable tactic—given the tragic circumstances—but strangely not one that has since made it into the NICE-recommended medical guidelines as a treatment for grief.

Up in her room, Sara showers and towels herself dry. Bits of pink fluff stick to her skin. Barefoot, she looks in the mirror. The woman gazing back has a sunburnt nose, a dimple denting a small chin, straggly chlorinated hair—less blonde when wet—and dark circles under the eyes. Average height, protruding ribs, and a current BMI of eighteen, which—in clinical terms—is a cause for mild concern.

She thinks back to the women she sees every day, loitering opposite the clinic outside the building Sara reckons might be a temple. They stare at her with their unsmiling eyes, some of them fingering loops of red and white beads around their necks. She hasn't seen again the beautiful woman who shooed the crow away, the lithe woman with unbiddable hair. Sara plucks tissues from a box and drapes them over her head. Studying her own reflection, she tries to work out how that temple woman manages to look so deeply alluring from behind the gossamer of her veil.

She slips into a cotton dress—her body gives off a mild pong of chlorine—but struggles with the top bit of the zip at the back. And this makes her think again of Mike. Mike, who in the early days used to finish zipping her up by kissing the nape of her neck.

Her hands shaking, she turns up the volume on the television. Channel V is on, and Simon and Garfunkel are passionately advocating protection against heartache by being a rock or an island. It could be her theme tune. She sprays herself in a cloud of insect repellent and makes sure she has got her room key. It's all very well, she thinks as she slams shut the bedroom door, urging patients to rake up the past, but sometimes the past is surely best left dead and buried.

She looks in on the lecture about Mughals but the audience is respectfully hushed, so she decides to return later in the evening when guests are mingling. The perfume launch is running desperately late, with premature guests nursing cocktails while an events team tests the strobe lighting. Which leaves the photographic exhibition stroke Mexican buffet in the hotel's ballroom.

In the corridor, Sara braces herself at the sound of manic chatter. Who would care, if she slipped away now? She could easily spend tonight, as she has every night, planning trips to Delhi's military cemeteries or writing to the Ministry of Defence. And she has become rather partial to the room service murgh korma. She promises herself a five minute sidle round the room, and then back for supper in front of her laptop.

'Miss Sara,' cries the concierge, his evening now made. And he steers her tenderly round the room, introducing her to senior members of staff, who then introduce her to other guests.

She meets Steve from Slough, who makes her laugh with his tales of running multiple call centres, and Nigel from Clapham, who works for the Delhi arm of a British investment bank. She even meets the Mexican cultural attaché. As she says to Steve from Slough, 'When in London would I ever get to meet a Mexican cultural attaché?'

A white woman in a shiny sari glides by, saying goodbye to people. The Mexican cultural attaché clasps her arm.

'Everyone. This is Kate. From the British High Commission.'
Kate namastes them all.

Sara steels herself. 'Hello,' she says, without waiting to
be introduced. 'Sara Young. I'm British too.' Then she gets
into a muddle about whether to shake the woman's hand, or
namaste her, which makes Kate laugh. It is a laugh with an
earthy throatiness, which makes Sara like her immediately,
which she suspects is the supreme attribute of a diplomat.
Late forties, with cropped blonde hair, good teeth and
blue, Lady Di eyeliner to match the sari. For some reason
it makes Sara think equestrian. She also clocks the lack of
a wedding ring. Someone married to her job. Like being in
the military. Like Mike.

'Do you have a card?' says Sara quickly, fumbling in
her bag for one of her London ones with her mobile on it.
Someone behind Kate reminds her that they were meant to
be leaving. Kate namastes her goodbyes to the group.

Before she knows what she is doing Sara is suggesting to
Kate that maybe, you know, if you're not busy, a coffee or
something…

That boisterous laugh again. 'A coffee? When it's a hundred
and four in the shade? But an iced tea. I'd love to meet you
for an iced tea. Let's text. But it must be early in the morning.
That's my favourite time to see Delhi. This weekend? Are you
staying in Delhi that long?'

Sara smiles. Just as long as it takes.

4

Five forty-five on Saturday morning, and Sara waits outside the hotel. Brimming with nervous energy, she performs step-ups on the hotel's stone steps. While the rest of Delhi sleeps, the vultures circle high in the sky. To Sara they look like the dregs of tea-leaves. She hopes it's a good omen.

Two minutes later and Kate trundles through the hotel compound gates in a cycle-rickshaw. Today the woman wears an orange sari, which clashes magnificently with the blue eye-liner. Sara returns her namaste eagerly, but wonders if Kate isn't taking the whole 'going native' thing a bit too far.

Janpath is refreshingly light on traffic, the only sound the bicycle chain catching with each revolution. The calves of the cyclist bulge with the effort, standing on the pedals with his broken sandals to get better purchase. At first Sara is uncomfortable at this immense physical effort on her—on their—behalf, but something in the easy way Kate speaks to him in Hindi, makes her want to enter India more deeply.

'You're very brave,' she says, 'to wear a sari. Aren't you afraid it will unravel?'

'Oh, it's all in the pleating. We can go shopping after we've had tea if you like?' Kate leans in as she says this, and Sara can smell her perfume. It is a reliable, old-fashioned scent, like lily of the valley, which Sara finds oddly comforting.

The taxi-wallah takes them to the Old City, and they wind their way into ever-narrower lanes festooned with wires and cables. Although it is early morning, Indians are out enjoying the coolest part of the day, trying on sandals, drinking chai, fingering fabric.

Soon the two women are taking iced tea at low tables of beaten silver and eating sugary jalebis fresh from the fryer.

'If there is one thing which would make me leave India, it would be these things,' says Kate, licking her fingers. 'They are annoyingly irresistible.'

Sara swoons. 'Well, I'm overdosing on pappads and biryanis.'

'And dahl makhani. Have you tried dahl makhani? It's a North India speciality.'

'Dahl makhani is the food of the gods. I'm addicted to dahl makhani. In fact,' Sara adds, 'I think I've hit on my perfect job. Curry taster for a major supermarket chain!' They both laugh, and each pinch another jalebi.

As Sara sits chewing, various versions of a request for help for information about Mike ricochet around her head. But by the time she is sure she won't sound selfish, as though she only ever had an ulterior motive for suggesting tea, the moment to speak has passed.

'Right,' says Kate, dropping some tatty rupees on the silver, 'let's get you Desi'd.'

'What's Dezzid?'

'Desi. Let's dress you as a local. Like me!'

Speaking Hindi, Kate instructs the rickshaw-wallah through tighter lanes until soon they are clearly in a garment district.

The shops they visit are quickly transformed into theatre, where iridescent streams of fabric are unfurled with a flourish and held against skin and wrapped and folded and draped around waists and try this one and that's definitely your colour. Sara can't resist touching and stroking the fabric, the chiffons and brushed cotton, and silk so soufflé-soft it can pass through a wedding ring, or sprinkled with sequins or beads or tiny mirrors or stiff with embroidery. In one shop, Sara holds a swatch of crimson brocade and marvels aloud at the weight of it, while not quite being able to stop thinking about all those underage fingers no doubt involved in its manufacture.

Between them, Kate and the shopkeepers explain about a sari's five metres of petticoats and the drape of the pallu over the shoulder and about the need to test the stitching of the choli under-blouse, and to get a snug fit. They show Sara how the wispy ghoonghat veil can be tugged over the face, should a woman suddenly find herself talking unexpectedly to a man. And using pattern books they show her how a sari can be worn in over fifty different subtle ways.

'The shopkeeper says that the important thing is the flow,' says Kate. 'Any cutting or stitching detracts from the movement of the silk. So buy as much fabric as you can afford.'

Sara had meant to go along with Kate's shopping idea just to be friendly, and to buy herself time to pluck up the courage and ask for help, but when the billowing sari folds are draped around her and she sees in the mirror the vibrant tones against the incipient tan on her skin, it takes her breath away. Colour in her cheeks, after all this time. Or maybe she is blushing, with a thought to the way the slippery skein could be peeled off by a lover in a matter of seconds. But that silhouette! She feels taller somehow, more elegant, more empowered. 'If only Mike could see me now,' she murmurs.

In the end she buys two salwar kameez for work, one lavender, one mint-and-cream; two saris, one pink shot through with gold, and one embroidered ivory for special occasions—as yet unidentified—and, from a dizzying range of colours, four toning pashminas. She also buys some tooled leather flip-flops. The thong of them is stiff, but she figures it will get more supple over time.

'You look fabulous,' says Kate, as they walk to where their driver waits in the shade of a jasmine tree. 'Your husband or boyfriend will be most impressed when you go back home,' she adds.

Sara slides awkwardly into the rickshaw, trying not to drop her many parcels wrapped in brown paper. 'Actually, my husband died. I'm a widow.'

Kate grasps Sara's hand. And perhaps because the diplomat is also diplomatic enough not to rush to fill the silence with crass offers of regret, or perhaps because Sara now has an old memory of coming home from a different shopping trip with a scarlet fitted sheath of a dress which Mike had made her put on again just so he could unpeel it and make love to her, Sara finds herself, as they squeak and bounce back through the lanes, telling Kate how she and Mike met, at a wedding in a hotel beside Tower Bridge.

How Sara had been serving champagne when she should have been revising Winnicott, for Child Psychology. Mike was a friend of the groom, majors all in Number One Dress; all dark blue high-necked coats and gold trim. She hadn't been attracted to the uniform, has never been one for uniforms. Which might explain why she never dated boys from school—unless you count Mr Finn...

She remembers the soldiers at the tables, their faces comically sunburnt in November. Boisterous, they were. To her 'Prawns or goat cheese, sir?' she had endured variations of 'I'd rather have you' from most.

At the lamb, she had accidentally-on-purpose poured redcurrant jus into one obnoxious lap. His mate with a blonde cow-lick had leaned across an aunt of the bride and made a great show of dabbing at Sir's groin, looking up at Sara as he did so, his broad smile firing off little rounds of ammunition in her heart.

'Later, he rescued me from the DJ,' Sara says to Kate, her eyes glistening at the memory. 'During the speeches I was tidying up the room where the drinks reception had been

35

held and where the disco would be. The DJ was meant to be setting up but he kept pinching crisps and pinching my bum, and asking me what songs I wanted to hear. I kept saying it wasn't my wedding, at which point he'd winked and said it could be. At midnight, when I left to get my coat, he delegated the disco to his junior and stalked me. Tried to kiss me.' She grimaces. Even now she can smell his cheese and onion breath.

'You OK?' called a voice.

She turned her head, and there was the soldier with the untamed cow-lick.

'What's it to you?' The DJ peeled his crisp-greasy hand away.

'That depends.'

The men were now facing each other, like stags about to rut.

'Depends on what, army boy?'

From the far end of the corridor came the screech of feedback. The DJ cocked his head, swore, and sprinted for the disco. At the door he nearly collided with a guest, the bride's aunt who was beckoning Mike in for more of a boogie.

Sara turns to Kate. 'That's when I fell in love with him. For the whole evening he'd been dancing with aunts and grannies. Five months cooped up in barracks and yet his priority was to give them a great evening. His manners were impeccable.'

She had forgotten that. She had forgotten the precise moment of falling in love, because of Mike's generosity of spirit. Arguably the most important moment of her life and it has been buried beneath the sickening freight of all that came later.

And yet India has brought it back. Or Kate has. Or this journey.

'It's good you have warm memories. No one is truly gone if you have those.' Kate's grip on Sara's hand tightens for a moment.

36

In a rush she says, 'The army told me Mike died in Afghanistan, but recently I learned he died here, in India. But no death was ever logged with the coroner. And when I contacted the MOD, they fobbed me off.'

Kate sits silently for a moment. 'I'd say someone wanted to tidy things up.'

Sara tries to picture Mike and untidiness, but she can't do it. Fastidious. That was a word used about him at the funeral. Not a soldier to leave loose ends. 'Why, though?'

Kate shrugs. 'There *is* intelligence sharing between India and the UK. But we'd only get involved if there was a strategic imperative.'

'Meaning?'

'Meaning something threatening Britain's security. Which also means, that it would have to be denied. Which is maybe why you've drawn blanks. Where else have you tried?'

Sara describes her multiple internet searches and the sorry time with Passang Kasturirangan. 'And I wrote to the British Ambassador here. Went in person, to the High Commission.' There, she has finally done it, made the link explicit. Maybe Kate will feel offended—used—but she holds on to the hope that if Kate has ever loved and lost she will understand her desperation.

Kate has a serious look on her face. 'Was Mike a Special Forces operative?'

'Not that I know of. I thought he was in bomb-disposal. Should I have known?'

'Not every partner is told. Sometimes it's safer that way—' Kate clears her throat. 'Send me what you know. Regiment, dates, anything at all. The Ambassador's away, so I'll dig around—oh no, what's this?'

Sara jerks her head and looks beyond the rickshaw. They have turned left at a roundabout and have ploughed straight into a demonstration. Hundreds of people, a thousand? Sara cannot tell, but the road is utterly blocked. People chant and wave placards. A line of police thump batons into their palms, their expressions suggesting they are looking forward to using them.

Before the driver has had a chance to reverse back to the roundabout, the rickshaw is engulfed by the crowd. It rocks alarmingly, and Sara flinches as random hands graze her shoulder and thighs. Leaning forward, Kate barks in Hindi at the driver, who peers over his shoulder and tries to reverse. Sara grips the side of the rickshaw with one hand, slaps away wandering hands with the other and braces herself for the crunch of bones beneath tyres.

'What is it?' she cries, gripping her seat.

'It's a demo against compulsory school for girls.'

'What? *Against?*'

Using hand gestures, Kate urges the driver to try a different route. She looks back at Sara. 'If your daughter's at school, she can't be out earning you money.'

Each road they try seems similarly impassable, and for about twenty minutes Kate and the driver chunter at each other in Hindi as they try out alternative routes. But eventually, directed by the traffic police, they find themselves stuck in ordinary, unthreatening, noisy gridlock.

'What you were saying earlier, surely if a daughter had a better education, she could earn more money for her family. Especially in the long term.' As if to prove her point, two children try to scramble on board the rickshaw, their hands cupped for begging.

Kate shoos them off. 'A bird in the hand. If you're planning to marry your daughter off by the age of twelve, you want to tap into that earning potential as soon as you can, to stash that dowry.'

Sara is recalling her guidebook. 'I thought dowries were illegal now, aren't they?'

'Yes, although nearly eight thousand women died in dowry disputes last year.'

'That's medieval.'

Kate nods. 'I don't know how much you've seen, but women in general have a very bad time of it here.'

'But I thought the head of the country was a woman?'

'She is. Sonia Gandhi. Daughter-in-law of the great Indira. But even so, millions of female foetuses are still aborted and millions more girls than boys die in childhood, either from violence or, one suspects, from deliberate neglect.'

'So how can things change?'

'Delaying marriage and motherhood would help, as would better salaried jobs. But it's more cultural than economic. It's still completely acceptable here for a man to grope and attack and harass women.'

Sara toys with the opal at her neck, trying to take in Kate's words. And she thinks about her patient Kanan, married off at eleven. And how all the men in one carriage on the metro leered at all the women in the next door compartment, including her.

They are now grinding along a road Sara doesn't recognise. Despite the early hour, this strip is humming in the dawn light. Yet it isn't the usual commerce Sara has come to expect from Delhi, no tiers of pirated DVDs, no rows of copper pots, no gaudy piles of mobile phone covers. Instead, outside every shack, above every dilapidated shop, behind every iron-grilled balcony, girls sit on low plastic stools, plastered in make-up. As though on display.

From her vantage point in the stationary rickshaw, Sara watches other women stick their heads out from doorways whenever a man walks by. Like a hen with chicks, these older women adjust a veil on a young girl here, smooth the hair there, nudge the girls into sitting straighter on their stools. Sara stares with horror. None of the girls looks older than about fourteen.

The gazes of the girls slide over Sara's body. Their mouths smile, but not their eyes. Some of the girls display the 'pinprick' pupils associated with morphine addiction. One girl in a pink polyester sari meets Sara's eye and can't help moving seductively, writhing almost. Sara shudders, and diagnoses hypersexual personality. A possible sign of abuse.

'Is this what I think it is?'

'G.B. Road. Delhi's largest red light district. Can't imagine why the traffic police diverted us here, unless they're drumming up extra trade for their pimps on the sly,' Kate adds wryly. 'Not quite the sights I was planning to show you this morning. Sorry.'

Sara's gaze is caught on the girl in pink polyester. She looks to be about eight or nine, draped in cheap jewellery, her legs bruised. She is sucking her thumb. 'No, don't apologise,' she says softly, craning her neck to continue watching a middle-aged man approach the girl and start a conversation, 'I had no idea.' She sits back in her seat, thinking. 'So where are the girls from? They're just kids. Are they born into it?' She can't quite bring herself to say the word: prostitution.

'Some are. A trade handed down from mother to daughter, you might say. But some are kidnapped, or openly lured to the cities with the promise of clean jobs. In other words, trafficked.'

'Trafficked? What, like women taken to the bright lights of London?'

'Exactly. Smuggled from one end of the country to another.'

Sara is thinking of the trial Trevor was an expert witness in, and about Passang's Missing Persons database. And about his claim, that two hundred and fifty children *a day* go missing. 'And no one goes in search of them?'

Kate shrugs. 'Most poor families have neither the money nor the time.' Kate holds up her hand. 'And before you say it, no, it's not the West's place to mend what is broken in India.'

Sara can feel herself simmering, although whether it is because of the sights she is witnessing or Kate's well-meaning rebuke, she can't say. And Trevor did warn her, about being seduced into thinking she could rescue the Happy Poor. Not that anyone on G.B. Road this morning looks remotely happy.

Gradually she is aware that the rickshaw driver has become agitated. He and Kate are in frantic discussions about something and he is now trying to mount the pavement.

'What is it?'

'Some of the pimps have recognised our driver.'

Sara glances back again and notices a group of men, staring at their rickshaw, muttering to each other. 'Why is that a problem?'

Kate barks further instructions. 'Many of the rickshaw-wallahs are in the pay of the pimps, providing customers.'

'So with us in the back, the pimps are getting suspicious?'

'Quite so. And our driver's panicking. I've heard him trying to tell them about the demonstration and how we're only on a detour, but they are having none of it. We need to get out of here. If I were you, I'd hold on tight. This next bit could get bumpy.'

Back in her room, Sara spreads her purchases out on the counterpane, and then sinks onto the bed herself, profoundly weary. And she wonders what the girls in G.B. Road get to sleep on, if anything at all. The guilt at not leaping off the rickshaw and rescuing them lingers.

She rolls on to her side and strokes the soft pashminas and shimmering saris. And it occurs to her that saris like these probably cost more than a trafficked girl could earn in several lifetimes.

And yet she wishes now more than ever that Mike were here to see her, the new her, a woman trying to engage more with the world, maybe more like a wife should. He would be stunned. In the old days, he could barely get her to leave London.

'It's Miami, not the moon,' he said.

'It's not the distance, it's just that I'm happy honeymooning in England.'

'You'll be having us honeymoon in your consulting room, next.'

It was a jest tinged with concern, at Sara's difficulty in leaving her comfort zone.

G.B. Road is definitely out of her comfort zone. She has glimpsed India's shadow side. She slides the tiny opal on her necklace from side to side.

She rummages in the brown wrapping paper. Her favourite is the pink fabric shot through with filaments of gold. Yet when she takes it to the window and holds it up to the light to hunt for the precise weave of gilt thread, it has somehow disappeared.

5

On Sunday Sara sits at the desk in her bedroom and types a long email to Kate. From time to time she looks up to stare out the window and watches guests padding across the lawn to the pool. The routine of a swim would be delicious, but she is determined to get all the information about Mike over to Kate.

The facts are plain: age, regiment, and the evidently fake details she was given at the time of death, together with the lack of personal items sent back, not so much as a military dog tag or wedding ring. She touches the opal at her neck. She doesn't want to get Tom into trouble, even though he is no longer in the army, so she avoids mentioning him by name, but she types their conversation word for word. She pauses, scanning her marriage, wracking her brains for any piece of information, any mention of India, any Freudian slips, any inconsistencies during any of their conversations.

The sleeping memories yawn and stretch, and she is back in Mike's hotel room, the one for his friend's wedding, a frenzied blur of sex, reports from Iraq on the TV, and the bartering of trivial intimacies. She is twenty-five, and one month shy of her viva in psychotherapy; Mike is twenty-nine, going on fourteen and forty-five at the same time, on leave for the wedding from Baghdad. He bends her gently over the desk, with CNN turned on low in the background.

'So, do you have a girlfriend?' Sara says later, over room service breakfast.

Mike is enjoying a dream mouthful of bacon, white bread and brown sauce. He shakes his head. He chews and swallows. 'Is this your way of telling me you've got a boyfriend?'

Sara smiles. Now it's her turn to shake a head.

'That's good,' he grins, 'me neither.' And he turns back to the TV.

And that's it. No prying. No competitive tally games. No, 'How many lovers have you had?' No, 'How many lovers have you had *in your own age group?*' She thinks back to inappropriate Mr Finn. And once again, folds herself neatly into the life of a man who is ever so slightly out of reach.

'But I warn you, we're bad news, us army boys,' Mike adds, buttering more toast. She duly laughs. 'I'm serious. We're always on manoeuvres, we might get killed, and the widow's pension's lousy.'

'But by then I'll have our children keeping me company,' she dares to say.

He looks at her, serious for a moment. 'Not children. Sons!' And he grins.

She throws a triangle of toast at him but deep down her muscles unknot with relief. She thinks about telling him he is her youngest lover. Or that she lost her virginity to her Maths teacher. She could say, I want to love you, but then I won't be able to trust you. But she doesn't. Because that would mean stepping into no-man's-land.

❧

Tucked into an alleyway full of minuscule shops off Connaught Place she finds a printer who—*for special price, memsahib, one hundred rupees*—runs off five hundred copies of a simple poster she created on her laptop. Passang Kasturirangan's mentioning of Missing Persons gave her the idea, as did the current constant squirming in her heart for

44

the families of bruised, missing girls like the ones on G.B. Road, lured into the sex trade.

She has also indulged in some artistic licence. Influenced by seeing how those who live on the street happily ignore dead dogs and comatose neighbours, she has put above a head-and-shoulders photo of Mike in a T-shirt the word MISSING, in large caps, and then underneath details of who he was, the date he died and an appeal—in English and Hindi, thank you Mr Concierge—for any information, no matter how small. At the bottom run columns of sideways numbers, her mobile, and for an hour over a mango lassi, she snips each side of these columns, like a fringed skirt, for easy retrieval.

Later she climbs into a motorised rickshaw. She shows the driver a list of all the main shopping malls and parades in central Delhi, again written down by her friendly concierge, in English and Hindi. For a laughable flat rate of one hundred and fifty rupees, the driver and she then spend the afternoon puttering back and forth across the city, so she can find places to put up posters.

In the shiny shopping malls, the escalators are crammed with India's middle classes lapping up the air conditioning and foreign brands, out and about, being seen. She targets the kind of shops she imagines Mike would have frequented—sports clothing, mainly, plus ice cream parlours and a Ferrari store—and asks, 'Would you mind putting up a poster of my husband?'

Everyone is happy to do so, which makes her feel properly excited.

Normally the driver sits in his tuk-tuk. At Khan Market, out of the corner of her eye she is aware of him getting out of his cab and going to one of the mom-and-pop stores. After talking to many of the dark men loitering around the front, he brings one of them over to Sara, who is by now standing in the shade of a tree.

45

'What are you doing with the posters?' asks the dark man from the shop. He has a cleft lip.

'This man is my husband and I'm trying to find out information about him. Why, is there a problem?' And it occurs to her that this being bureaucratic India, maybe you have to seek permission in triplicate to pin a poster on a tree.

The driver and the dark man confer.

'This man is my uncle,' says the dark man.

Yeah right, thinks Sara.

'He asks me to translate for him. He says you have been visiting all the malls, yes?'

'Yes.'

'And have you been putting the posters up in the malls?'

'Yes.' And for an awful moment she has a vision of being locked up, for fly-tipping.

'My uncle thinks you should be putting the posters up in the smaller markets too. Where ordinary people will see them, not just Delhi's Big People. People like other drivers and maids and waiters. People who see things, who might have information. Who like to gossip.'

'That sounds like a brilliant idea,' she says, and starts to search in her bag for more rupees. The driver waves away the idea of extra payment. Instead, beckoning her to follow, he hops back enthusiastically into his tuk-tuk and revs up the moped. She namastes her gratitude.

By the time night falls, they have visited four other markets, with their smoky alleyways divided into distinct bazaars. And as she lies back on her hotel bed, sniffing Mike's T-shirt, she thinks back fondly to the epidemic of Mike's face—augmented by a fresh batch of photocopying—which has now broken out across the city's lamp posts and telegraph poles.

6

On Monday, staff arrive at the clinic early for a breakfast puja, or worship. Everyone crowds into the ECT Suite, where the innocuous metal box of the Electro Convulsive Therapy equipment has been placed for today on a table at the far end of the room. Sara has apparently arrived just in time, because a doctor with startling maroon hair is calling for hush with a few nervous claps. Sara sidles up to Rafi.

'This is all very intriguing. What's going on?'

Rafi gives her a sideways look, as if to say: you are not going to believe this.

And indeed she doesn't. As Sara understands it—and the doctor's hair *is* rather distracting—they are all gathered in this room to pay homage to the ECT equipment.

'As though the equipment were a god?' she whispers.

Rafi waggles his head. 'Our clinic is honouring this branch of modern science which has been so helpful, so meaningful to its patients.'

A nurse holds garlands of marigolds at the ready, and Sara recalls the surprising weight of them from her welcome ceremony, how the petals pressed on her skin because of their droop. One by one, members of staff take a garland and shuffle forward to offer prayers to the ECT machine. Sara has a lump in her throat, watching their devotion, and sees in a nutshell the essence of India, with its new technology and old traditions.

Over coffee, Rafi introduces her to Shakeel, the doctor with maroon hair, hair which hints at an impulsive side to this otherwise formal man.

47

'—and then it turns out my husband died here in India,' she says, in answer to one of Shakeel's questions.

'Oh, I am terribly sorry,' says Shakeel and then, ever the clinician, 'How?'

'I don't know.'

'But, the body?'

'No word.'

'Maybe he was working not for the British but for the *Indian* army?' says Shakeel.

'I think you mean the *Russian* army.' Rafi stirs in three sugars.

Shakeel waves a biscuit, dismissively. 'We may buy all our kit from the Russians, but our true allies are the US. And the UK, of course,' he adds, to Sara.

'But how do you find a body when you don't know where it died? It's driving me slightly mad. It's like doing brain surgery blindfolded.'

'But do you need to find out?' says Rafi.

She twiddles with the opal on her necklace. Maybe she is searching for information about how Mike died for the wrong reasons, to prove to the outside world that it was a stronger love than she feared it to be.

'After all,' adds Rafi, draining his cup. 'All this talking things through. The infamous talking cure. Does it ever cure anything? Does it do any good?'

'If all our patients thought that, we'd be out of a job!' laughs Sara.

But Rafi looks from one to the other. 'I'm serious. Tolerating the unknown. Isn't that the best we can hope for?'

'That reminds me of my mother,' she says. 'She once told me she used to leave me in the pram at the bottom of the garden so that she couldn't hear all the crying.'

Rafi chuckles. 'There you go. We all have an urge in life to smooth out the lumps.'

Sara is standing at her office window, playing with her necklace, looking out over the lane towards the temple. She is watching people, or rather women, wander in and out. There is something odd about the temple, which she can't quite put her finger on. And it occurs to her that of course, in this land of many faiths and none—where even ECT machines are venerated—she could always go to the temple today and pray. Pray for answers about Mike. Pray for a lead. Pray to be unlocked.

As she gazes out she catches sight of the woman with her sensual mouth and pliable torso, looking back at her. Well, maybe not at *Sara,* but at the clinic, through the gauze of her veil. She watches as this woman slips a mobile phone out of a pocket and studies the screen.

There is a light tap at the door. On opening it, Sara finds a new patient, an inpatient, hovering in the corridor, escorted by a nurse.

'Hello Pritti. Welcome. Come in.' She opens the door wider.

The new patient is a young woman, tall yet with a self-effacing stoop, and a narrow face framed by two dark plaits hanging over her shoulders. They remind Sara of exclamation marks. 'Come in,' Sara says again. But for nearly ten minutes this young girl refuses even to cross the threshold, instead standing motionless in the corridor. Her stillness is extraordinary. Sara has the sense that the girl is absorbing everything. Either that, or trying to make herself invisible.

Her pulse quickening, Sara tries to recall Pritti's referral form lying on the desk behind them, scrawled by Dr Mathur with the girl's diagnosis and history. Pritti's father died when she was six and she and her mother went to live with the mother's brother. Soon after, her mother fled India, apparently to be with her Muslim lover in Lahore and her maternal uncle has raised Pritti in his family ever since. Sara gazes at Pritti, who is staring at Sara's sandals on the lino, like a wasp alert for the swat.

Sara hasn't moved. If later she were called to justify her behaviour, she would say her immobility was designed to show she was giving Pritti her full attention, but she knows this to be disingenuous. For reasons she can't explain, she finds herself drawn to—identifying with, almost—the suppressed energy of this still woman. And it comes to her, what to say. 'You're safe here.'

She touches the door, as though to pull it back further and Pritti tiptoes into Sara's space, only to slide slowly to the floor against the wall. Once settled, she fiddles purposefully with the borders of her olive green sari. Sara nods at the nurse to leave, but wedges the door half open with a folded piece of paper. In a steady monotone, Pritti relates the story. It sounds as much like a rehearsed script as Rafi's outburst about India. While she speaks, Pritti gently rocks herself.

In a random flash of inspiration, Sara asks, 'How old are you?' The person on the floor in front of her is—Sara discreetly rechecks the notes—nearly seventeen, but she has the air of someone much more innocent.

'Six,' says a child's voice. 'Six and a bit.' Her bottom lip juts out truculently.

The rocking continues, accompanied by a sort of mantra, as Pritti whispers about being plagued by *illusions, delusions, and confusions*. Whenever Sara asks a question, Pritti hesitates, and then reverts to her mantra.

Sara tries to find a way in, to break the logjam, but soon her thoughts float away to the rhythm of Pritti's voice. And she has an image of Pritti trapped in Delhi, pacing her room, up and down, while her mother lives an unknowable life in far-off Lahore, longing for the one thing you cannot have.

50

7

Notes for the day written up and safely stored, now Sara is standing between the crumbling stone pillars of the temple opposite the clinic, her skin prickling with sweat. She isn't sure what prayer she will actually say for Mike, but trusts something will come. She finds comfort in the familiar sight of Mr Pants-U-Like in his grubby lungi, attending to his toenails. She nods, and he nods back, as though giving her permission to enter.

She finds herself in a large courtyard, dominated by a massive stone building, tapered like a pyramid. Squares of patchy grass surround it. A man in a cotton dhoti crosses the courtyard and disappears through a door.

Just then, she sees a familiar form, a small boy in a torn T-shirt, pottering along, out between the pillars and off down the lane in the direction of the busy highway. Her heart thumping, Sara scans the courtyard for his mother. And in an instant, Sara can visualise it, this boy darting into the traffic. Or being kidnapped and forced to work on some male version of G.B. Road.

She rushes after him down the lane, amazed at his speed. Grabbing for his shoulder, her hand snatches at air. Lunging for the boy again, this time she lands a touch on a pudgy forearm. The boy turns as she crouches down. 'Hello,' she says, hoping her smile and soothing tone will convey her good intentions. 'Where's your mummy, eh? Shall we try and find her?'

She holds out her hand—a white hand, smelling of recently applied suncream—and the child studies this

51

unfamiliar object as though it has landed from Mars. Luckily, to her immense relief, the little chap takes it. 'There we are.' And hand in hand, they toddle back up the bucolic lane with its nutmeg trees and bitter gourds drying on doorsteps in the sun.

Suddenly a woman darts in front of them, screaming in Sara's face. Sara recognises the supple body, the honey of her hair, the sensuous mouth contorted in agony. Yanking the boy roughly by the arm, it is clear, even though Sara can't understand a word the woman shrieks, that she blames Sara for the child's disappearance.

'I didn't take him,' pleads Sara. 'I would never have taken him.' And frantically she looks up and down the empty lane, in the vain hope that someone, anyone can corroborate her story. 'Please, I was only trying to help—'

The pain and fury in the woman's eyes tug at Sara's heart but it is the stray tendrils of hair—a bun unravelling with every flaying gesture of the arms, every smack to the head— which speak most eloquently of a mother's turmoil, a woman ever so slightly teetering on the edge. Helplessly Sara can only stand and watch, as the woman shoves her son between the stone pillars and into the temple.

Legs shaking, Sara steps towards the stone posts, hoping to see the woman again, to explain.

'Sara!' calls a voice.

She spins round.

'Are you all right?' It's Rafi, wiping sweat from his neck.

'No!' Instantly she regrets snapping. 'Sorry. Some woman thought I'd tried to kidnap her child.'

'Ah,' says Rafi. 'A boy, no doubt?'

'Yes,' her voice a little sharp. 'Why?'

'This is India. Boys are more valuable than girls. Obviously!'

'What?' But then she remembers what Kate said about aborted foetuses and infant neglect.

52

'There is an old Indian saying: "Why water your neighbour's tree?" Girls will eventually be handed over to their husband's family. Of course *I* don't subscribe to that nonsense. But many people—'

Sara feels a stab of irritation, yet sees how hard it must be for Rafi. Just because he dresses in Western clothes doesn't mean he isn't deeply influenced by centuries of India's traditions. And once again she is reminded of the young girls on G.B. Road, as it occurs to her that some families might even be glad to be shot of an extra mouth to feed.

She tries to shake off a sense of despair but it is resilient. 'Well, this wasn't about gender as such,' she says at last. 'It was an awful misunderstanding. I just wanted to explain.'

'Well, I am glad I caught you out here. Do you fancy meeting up tomorrow tonight? Some friends and I are going to a restaurant,' he adds, in case she fears it's a date. Or maybe it's an Indian thing, this constant nod to the need for a chaperone.

She accepts his kind offer—her first social engagement since Mike died—and watches as he heads off home down the lane.

Her first social engagement since Mike died. She doesn't know whether to laugh or cry. And it occurs to her that part of her longs to give in to Rafi's kindness and yet the other part of her is weirdly superstitious that a night off searching for information about how Mike died will cause her to miss something vital.

Still, maybe the gods of the temple will explain, in all their infinite wisdom. She isn't sure why, but something about this temple is drawing her in. Perhaps it's the stillness, like her new patient Pritti with the plaits. She turns to face its entrance and reaches out for one of the pillars. The plaster is old and cracked and Sara senses centuries of supplicants' hands gripping its coping: pleading, longing, grateful hands.

Out of the corner of her eye she senses movement. It is Mr Pants-U-Like, holding something out to her, flapping it, a length of fabric. He mimes putting it round his waist—he'd need a circus tent for that waist!—and then shakes the fabric out. Clearly he wants her to wear it, to cover her legs.

'Thank you,' she breathes, as he hands it over.

He smiles, his teeth tawny from chewing paan. The heavy cotton rubs against the backs of her legs. And as she steps between the stone pillars, it is as though she has become absorbed into something protective.

She peers round for some kind of chapel or small room in which to pray. Her eye is caught by a skinny monkey, on its haunches, biting its nails and studying her. Then it sprints up to the first tier of the structure, like a magician's assistant at the moment of the big reveal. The tiers are formed by rows of sculptures in bold relief. This close, she sees they are the coquettish bodies of men and women, all fulsome breasts, tweaked nipples, and robust lingams. The building seems alive with athletic coupling. Women impaled on glorious erections, women sandwiched between lusty males, or sucking virile members, their peach perfect hemispheres unaffected by gravity.

A wave of hotness wells up inside her. She blinks away a tear, feeling hundreds of stone carved eyes boring into her, judging her and her years of marital celibacy.

And then she realises that some of the eyes are real, women moving seductively, writhing almost, watching her like the girls did on G.B. Road, with those same eyes, dark and mistrustful. And just like before, it unsettles her, these girls moving in such a provocative way in front of her, as though they simply can't help themselves.

Sara hurries deeper into the temple's courtyard, where whispers of incense reel her in. Through a carved archway she can see flickers of candlelight. As she is about to pass through, she glances up again at the erotic carvings. She can do this.

Inside the dimness, the air is thick with the sweet notes of jasmine and butter. Flames from ghee lamps cast shadow butterflies on the walls. Barefoot women walk around the large main room, tending, sweeping. Sara removes her flip-flops and walks too, feeling herself slow down to their rhythm. The black stone statues gleam with oil.

As Sara's eyes adjust, she works out that each chamber houses a different version of the same statue, of a penis. With the women's devotional humming, the beguiling lighting and the fabric clinging to her legs, Sara is suddenly much more conscious of her own body, its curves, its hidden folds, its intimate spaces. The abnormal rhythm of her heart disturbs the thin cotton of her top.

She bows her head and prays for Mike. Prays fiercely that he died without pain. Prays too—if God doesn't regard this extra request as too selfish—for information to come to light soon, so that she might have what her profession calls closure. And prays above all that, if there is nothing to be found, she will have the strength to tolerate the unknown.

As she turns to walk out, she notices the column beside the entrance. It is a stone carving of a man sucking his own penis, the shaft of it as long as his body. With its proud domed top and inviting slit, it makes her tremble in its simple, familiar beauty. It begs to be stroked. She glances sideways to check if anyone is watching. The stone is cool under her hand, and deliciously smooth where her lips kiss it.

8

The following evening, she stares at herself in the bathroom mirror, flicking on mascara, a sweep of eyeliner. She almost doesn't recognise herself, what with her skin nicely plumped out with Delhi's humidity. Magazines would normally be starting to call her skin crêpey. Well, not now. It positively glows. And she is reminded of Mike in the early days, his capacity to make her glow inside. His eyes on her, her body enflamed, all its synapses firing off breathy, urgent signals.

Rafi rings up from the lobby. She checks she has her phone with her, in case somebody finally decides to call her number from one of the 'Missing' posters, takes one last look at herself in the mirror and blows herself a Rouge Caresse kiss. *Her first social invitation since Mike died.* She is surprised at how jittery she feels.

Rafi squires her out of the hotel. The evening air is humid and stodgy with pollution, making her eyes itch. After a string of people carriers, a midnight blue Mercedes saloon glides up. The throb of its engine vibrates through her as it idles in the drive. Rafi gestures that she should get in.

It is deliciously cool inside the car, with mellow lighting, like the bewitching interior of a mysterious cave. Its seats are yielding, their leather the colour of clotted cream. The heavy sculpted door clunks securely shut with impeccable Teutonic engineering before the Mercedes pulls smoothly away. Night curls itself around the car, deadening any sense of speed and distance.

Rafi murmurs quietly into his BlackBerry, so Sara gazes over the driver's shoulder at Delhi in the dark. Gradually she is aware that the driver is studying her in the rear-view mirror. The directness of his gaze takes her back to when he collected her from the airport. She looks away, a tiny pulse fluttering at her throat.

She tries to concentrate on the roads crammed with shops selling jewellery, cooking utensils, Halal meat. Another street sells tyres and car parts, its workshops open to the road. Half-naked men stand welding, their bronzed skin glistening in the flare of kerosene lamps. As the Mercedes slides past, one man stops to wipe the sweat from his brow with the back of his hand. At first he watches the car admiringly—cars are his life—and then his eyes discover Sara's and lock on to them. The whites gleam from the smut on his face. As she looks away, an incipient blush rising from her neck, she is aware of Rafi's driver's eyes also still on her.

She forces herself to breathe. Lowering her gaze she notices the driver's hands resting on the steering wheel, their smooth caramel skin, their grip firm yet relaxed. An utterly unexpected and slightly ridiculous thought strikes her: she wants to be held by those hands.

Rafi finishes his call. 'Ah,' he says, twisting in his seat. 'On your side, you will see one of the stadiums we are building for the Commonwealth Games. And that,' he adds, as they cross a six lane carriage way, 'is a bridge that collapsed. Did you hear about that?'

Sara wrinkles her nose. 'Not India's finest hour. Remind me what happened.'

Rafi rolls his eyes. 'The usual. Corruption, politics. India will never change.'

The driver's shining eyes catch hers again in the rear-view mirror. She fights the impulse to engage him in conversation, where he comes from, whether he likes his job, what his name is, whether he has a girlfriend. She must be out of her tiny mind.

The driver turns into a hotel driveway, where there is a security check with sniffer dogs, and then they purr along to the hotel entrance. She swings her legs out into the evening heat. Maybe she will never see this driver again.

Yet just as she and Rafi reach the hotel's revolving doors, they hear a shout. Turning, they find the driver jogging up to them, her evening bag in his hand. In her daft stupor she must have left it on the back seat.

She reaches out to take the beaded purse he holds out, their fingers not quite touching. For the first time she is able to look properly at his face. With his strong forehead and brows he looks rather determined. Deep grooves either side of his mouth draw attention—like elegant punctuation marks—to something significant. But it is his full mouth, the lower lip fractionally plumper than the upper, which is confusing.

'Thank you,' she gabbles, in Hindi, then in English, then in Hindi again.

He tilts his head. 'Once is enough,' he says, smiling.

The melody of his voice makes her tremble. Despite the humidity, she pulls her pashmina around her, the soft wool brushing her nipples.

The hotel's top floor restaurant is clearly the place to be, all candles, throbbing bass and granite. Amitabh Bachchan, apparently, ate here only last Thursday. As they are shown to their table, they pass a wall of celebrity photographs and an open Visitors' Book, and Sara feels compelled to flick through its pages in case, in case... But for the weeks leading up to Mike's death she can find no sign of his name, handwriting or signature.

They are six in total, and soon Sara is sipping a cocktail and scanning an international menu where the speciality pizza costs—bloody hell—a hundred and forty pounds sterling. The bread arrives. She picks up her butter knife, its brushed metal weighing heavy in her hand.

Rafi catches her. 'Who would have thought it, eh? Delhi, city of collapsed bridges and seven star temples to gastronomy!'

'A city possibly turning itself around?' she counters.

Rafi concedes the point. 'Reinventing itself.'

She grins. 'A city tailor-made for psychotherapists, then.'

'So, welcome back from the UK, yaar!' says a lawyer called Pradeep. He raises his Johnnie Walker to chink glasses.

Rafi grins. 'Missed me?' he says. He has tucked his first drink away already.

'Some more than others,' says another chap called Alok, with a wink.

'Well, I am here now,' says Rafi, slapping Alok on the back.

The first platters of food arrive; Barkha has already ordered for the table. Barkha is an actress—*just a silly part in a daytime soap*—which perhaps accounts for the hypnotic layers of kohl weighing down her eyelids.

In the fashionably uncooperative light, Sara finds a king prawn, giving off the most heavenly scorched sea smell. Her jaw stings, to think of the juicy charred flesh. Just how far away is Delhi from any natural source of shellfish? Just how bad could a bout of food poisoning be? And could it ever be as bad as missing out on sinking her teeth into something so heavenly, so forbidden?

She yanks off a head and sucks the brains from the shell, her tongue seeking out the sweet pulp. She swallows greedily, then twists off the tail and pops the whole prawn into her mouth. It is tender and sweet. She glances up—Rafi is in the middle of a funny story about falling off a London Boris

Bike—and sneaks another prawn. A third she uses to scoop up black dahl served in bowls of beaten copper, topped with fried onions and slivers of garlic. Then she sits back and licks each finger thoroughly in turn.

Looking up she finds Barkha staring at her. 'Do have some,' mumbles Sara, reluctantly pushing the dahl towards her fellow guest.

'In India we say it is a sin to eat onions and garlic,' Barkha murmurs.

'Psychotherapists are very familiar with sin,' laughs Sara. 'Guilt keeps us in business.' As she says this, her chest clamps tight. This is madness, but the image of Rafi's driver is now in her head. Or at least those hands. Hemant's elegant, capable hands. She fiddles with her necklace. 'Isn't that right, Rafi,' she adds quickly.

'Absolutely,' Rafi says. 'Onions and garlic are aphrodisiacs. They arouse people. People might even,' he pauses dramatically, 'have sex! And then where would we be? The great Mother India will unravel.'

Sara has a sudden image of the bruised girl sucking her thumb on G.B. Road and of the penis temple and of the voluptuous images of female goddesses she sees on temples, in adverts, on T-shirts. Is there nowhere in India you can go to escape sex?

'So, Sara. How are you liking India, and all?' says Rupa.

'She will hate it as much as we do, soon enough,' says Rafi.

'Speak for yourself,' joshes Sara. 'I love it. The clothes, the colours—' The drivers.

Rafi drums the table. 'She has hardly seen the real Delhi. She is staying at the Majestic! My dad was supposed to fix her up with a flat. Told me it was sorted.'

'Well, you know your dad,' says Alok, with another one of his facial twitches.

Rafi rams his cigarette into the nearest ashtray.

60

'I hear the Majestic's lovely, and all,' says Rupa, her voice as soothing as one of her massages.

'Stunning pool, I gather!' says Pradeep, lighting up a fat cigar.

Sara laughs. 'If you like plaster fish!'

'Right. I am sorting this out now,' barks Rafi, reaching for his trusty BlackBerry. His thumbs scurry across its keys.

'Don't worry, I'm thinking of renting a flat.' Now where on earth did that idea come from? Sara feels the tips of her ears go hot.

Rafi gives her a look as though she has just stripped naked. 'Did you not hear what Delhi's Police Commissioner said today? About women's safety?'

'*Only go out at night with your brother or driver,*' quotes Pradeep. 'Ridiculous.'

'And what if you don't have either?' asks Sara, surprising herself by accepting one of Pradeep's fat cigars. It is lighter than she expects. Papery. Very phallic.

'Abso*lute*ly!' says Rafi, flinging his BlackBerry onto the table. 'He has basically admitted that the Delhi police are incapable of keeping women safe.'

'Then the girl must get a boyfriend—and fast!' laughs Alok.

'But there was that girl with her boyfriend, on the bus,' says Rupa, carefully.

The group is silent for a moment. Everyone on the planet knows about the murdered girl on the bus. A medical student, the victim of multiple rapes by slum dwellers, plus assault with a crow-bar. India's shadow side, laid bare for all to see on the front of the world's newspapers.

'Your dad?' says Alok, with a nod towards Rafi's BlackBerry. A tiny red light is pulsing, like a distress flare.

Rafi sets his cigar down. He pauses, to read what his father has deigned to type. '*Flat not ready. Major issues. Please send*

61

Sara warmest apologies.' Rafi looks up at Sara. She takes in the shame clouding his eyes.

'Honestly, it's OK,' she says. And then she remembers the nights alone sniffing Mike's T-shirt. 'Unless, of course, any of you know of a flat I might rent?'

'Well, there's always the athletes' village,' smirks Barkha. 'For our national triumph, the Commonwealth Games. Very cheap. Very empty.'

Pradeep looks appalled. 'It's not even finished yet. She'll be all alone.'

Sara fiddles with her necklace. How attractive that statement sounds. She could sing along to Simon and Garfunkel to her heart's content. Keep Mike neatly dead and buried.

There is a silence, broken only by the rhythmic sound of Rafi flipping his BlackBerry over and over. 'Come live with me,' says Rafi, suddenly. 'I've got space.'

'Oh listen, I couldn't...'

'It is a really nice place, and all—'

'Two cleaners,' chips in Barkha, unable—oddly, for an actress—to hide her envy. Which suggests she might not be a very busy one. 'A cook, a flower arranger, driver—'

'She won't need a driver,' snaps Rafi, in the manner of someone with a driver who has never really had to think much about how to get from A to B. 'She can have a whole floor to herself.'

'No, but honestly, the Majestic is—'

'—is a colonial theme park aimed at tourists,' says Rafi. 'And you are not a tourist, right? Anyway, it is the least I can do. It is my dad messing you around.'

'Just watch Rafi yaah doesn't make you clean up after him,' says Alok.

'Yeah, you don't need a wife, Rafi. You need a *mother*,' says Barkha.

At which point the platinum pizzas arrive.

62

Around midnight, they all decide to show Sara the flat, and race there in a convoy of spluttering tuk-tuks. To one side of the front door squats a carved elephant god statue, sitting cross-legged in all his pot-bellied glory.

The 'flat' is actually a town house, on five floors, with a roof terrace. Sara can have a floor to herself. Already, she can tell that this building is well-finished, with vast rooms, a waterfall feature, enormous unused landings, a TV room with ornate swinging daybeds, a room with a couch for private consultations, and a central stairwell flooding the entire flat with crepuscular light. Clearly India's mental health industry pays well.

But it is the roof terrace which seduces her. Stepping through the floor-to-ceiling windows, her head brushes some wind chimes which tinkle happily. She leans against the warm bricks of the balcony and gazes out, captivated by Rafi's residential enclave. All of ordinary India is here, the lads playing night-time cricket, girls standing around pretending not to watch, two Sikhs taking a late-night stroll, sharing a giant bag of potato chips, overtaken at one point by a woman in shorts, jogging to her iPod. A man in the lane below polishes a luxurious blue saloon. And in the distance soar cranes and blocks of flats topped with enormous billboards, for brands of rice or Citibank money transfers.

She could watch this clash of cultures all day. She chooses this view, hugs it close.

Back downstairs, the party is breaking up.

'I'll take it!' she laughs, and they are all—Rupa, Alok, Barkha, Pradeep—thrilled, although whether for her or for Rafi, she isn't quite sure. And then they are gone.

A stillness settles on the house.

'Tea?' Rafi asks.

Sara accepts and Rafi shouts in the direction of the kitchen. A young lad with thick glasses steps out to receive instruction.

Sara asks Rafi whether he lives here on his own, which leads him to explain that his father lives opposite, 'So he can keep an eye on me!'

'Are you that disobedient?'

'Hardly! But I suppose, in my father's eyes, yes.'

Before Rafi has a chance to elaborate, the tea arrives, with saucers of aniseed, and the conversation turns to other things, such as Sara and Rafi both losing their mothers to cancer in the last five years, and both being only children. And for a beat, each privately glimpses in the other the sibling they never had but always wanted.

Rafi yawns. 'Forgive me.'

'You've been most kind. I should get a cab.'

Rafi tosses his head. 'Hemant will take you.'

God, no. The kitchen boy looks too myopic to slice a carrot without chopping off his finger, let alone drive a car in twilight. 'That's very kind, but no—'

'My driver. He's outside. He is ready when you are.'

With a jolt Sara remembers the driver, whose hands held the steering wheel like a father cradling a baby. And something very English and middle class kicks in, that to borrow a driver is ridiculous. The height of indolence. 'Oh, I couldn't possibly,' she hears herself say. And yet here she is, brushing imaginary crumbs from her clothes, reaching down for her bag, popping her head round the kitchen door to say thank you—in carefully enunciated Hindi—for the tea, running her free hand through her hair.

Rafi follows her down the path to the front gate. At the road, Rafi stares diagonally ahead at the residential block opposite. 'That is my father's house.' He plucks a leaf on a hedge and shreds it as he strides towards the parked Mercedes.

64

Hemant walks round the front of the car, his eyes on hers, brown orbs with flecks of topaz. Reluctantly she climbs in the back. And though it stings that she is nothing more to him than a passenger, their present differences goad her, excitedly, to close the gaps.

She beams at Rafi. 'I'm looking forward to living here. And thank you for this—' she gestures at the car, at Hemant. 'You really didn't have to.'

'No, I insist. Hemant's reliable. Hemant will keep you safe.'

Rafi pushes the door closed. The interior light dims efficiently and she is alone with Hemant. He pulls away. Neem twigs crackle under the tyres until the car leaves the enclave, and soon the only noise is the lullaby hum of the engine.

She feels restless; what she wants is to see Hemant's eyes. Lust does terrible things to one's dignity.

'So you are moving in,' Hemant suddenly says, beaming.

She is glad he seems happy. All the same, he probably shouldn't be eavesdropping.

They cruise on. The street lamps light up the interior intermittently and gradually, below the sleek buttons for temperature control and entertainment options, she becomes aware of a miniature brass version of the elephant god, tucked into the moulded compartment near Hemant's knee. 'Oh, how lovely. You've got a statue like Rafi's.'

He glances down. 'That is Ganesh,' he says, looking back at her in the mirror. 'We say he is the remover of obstacles.' He holds her gaze for an extra beat.

At the hotel, a tall Sikh opens the car door and salutes. The evening heat gropes Sara's bare legs and she longs to tuck them back in and slam shut the door, to stay in Hemant's air-conditioned cocoon forever.

Instead, she gets out, thanks the Sikh, and half turns, unsure. She has been in Delhi about a month but already she

65

knows—and has to rapidly remind herself—that an embrace in India, between memsahib and driver, is not appropriate, is almost a taboo. But still, does Rafi ever thank his driver?

'I thank you and Ganesh for driving me carefully,' she says, in hesitant Hindi.

Hemant executes a mock pout. 'I am disappointed,' he teases, in English. 'You have only said it the once, this time.'

Ah yes, she thinks. It has begun. And silently the car pulls expensively away, taking something of her with it.

9

Lying in twisted bed sheets, she wonders what Mike would have made of them all tonight, the golden youth of Delhi. Mike adored impromptu parties—was happy to dance with maiden aunts, no less—so he would definitely have had a ball. He would even have bantered about cars with Hemant... She stops herself going down this path and turns over, her fingers reaching for the cotton of Mike's T-shirt under her pillow. It was in bed where she and Mike got on the best, so it is in bed that she finds she misses him the most. But he is never coming back. Not ever, ever.

And even after the buzz of the evening, the jokes, the new friendships, even after her absurd—embarrassing—minor infatuation with Rafi's driver, the loneliness aches. She blinks back the tears, tightens her grip on the crumpled T-shirt, and forces herself to admit that for the last year or so of marriage she had felt lonely even when Mike was home on leave. He had become withdrawn. Even their vigorous sex life had withered. And it occurs to her: that she had been searching for him even before he died. That somehow she was to blame for the increasing distance between then, and therefore his secret life.

She turns over onto her other side, her stomach gnawing away. When she eventually drops off to sleep, she dreams of Mike and Hemant meeting, swapping marigold garlands and then walking off hand in hand.

In the morning, she wakes with a start, her heart as well as her head thumping. She switches on her phone and waits with increasing resignation for a little beep to tell her that the 'Missing' posters have prompted a text, or an email, or a voicemail. But there is no sound.

The call from Kate comes as Sara is emerging in a crush from the metro. They agree to meet after work and by the time Sara has had Kate repeat herself because of the noise in the street and has jotted down directions of where to meet, Sara is late.

On her office door is Sellotaped a piece of paper: *Come and find me. Rafi.* When she reaches his room, staff are perched on every available flat surface. An emergency meeting is clearly in progress.

'And you are saying she was violent?' Rafi asks a nurse in a salwar kameez.

'Threw chairs. Ripped up her bedding.'

'And scratched me,' chips in another nurse, absently rubbing his own forearm.

'Patient PB,' says Rafi, looking at Sara. 'One of yours.' He turns to Dana, the nurse in the salwar kameez.

Dana speaks without notes. Her voice is light but clear, a trickle of water in a desert. 'No longer oriented in time or place. Thought disordered, no eye-contact—'

'Is she still taking her medication?' asks Sara.

'Diazepam,' says Rafi. 'Ten milligrams,' he adds, turning to Dana.

Dana tilts her head in assent. 'She took it,' Dana checks her fob, 'at nine-oh-ten.'

'One-to-one obs in place?' asks Rafi.

'Absolutely.'

'Any idea what might have triggered this violent outburst?' Rafi asks Sara.

Sara clears her throat, playing for time, thinking back to how still Pritti had been in their first session, how contained. 'It could be a number of things. Possible distress from our

68

first session, stirring up buried emotions. Or today could be an anniversary of some kind. Or it could simply be a classic case of transference, that I'm an echo of someone from her past, someone with whom she has unfinished business. Please let me see her,' she adds.

The guard unlocks the grille and Dana escorts Sara down an unfamiliar corridor to a room at the back of the clinic. Through a window in the door, Sara sees Pritti curled up in a foetal position on the floor, her long plaits like arms around her own shoulders.

'Dana,' she whispers, 'what do you think this is all about?'

'Miss Pritti kept saying she wanted to go home. We had to get Sanjiv to hold her down,' she gestures in the direction of the guard, before adding in a whisper, 'and he has no medical training.'

'I didn't think Pritti's family lived near here?' They are, she seems to recall, from a village on the outskirts of the state. Took them hours to get here.

'Not *that* home. To be with her mother. In Pakistan.'

'Her mother's been in touch?' Sara is rapidly trying to recall Pritti's notes.

'Not once. As Pritti knows. Her uncle is adamant she has been told this repeatedly over the years. It is just that I think she doesn't *want* to know it.' Dana glances around. 'To be honest, I don't even know if her mother is alive.'

'What makes you say that?'

Dana glances around again, and then leans closer to Sara. 'Even today, women who marry across caste or religious lines are often murdered,' she whispers. 'Sometimes by their own families, seeking to avenge the shame.'

'And the police do nothing?'

Dana's expression says, Well what can you expect from *them*?

Sara looks at Dana, her hair tied neatly with a ribbon, the neckline of her kurta beautifully embroidered. Sara has an

69

image of a tidy home, a handsome boyfriend, parents who love her. All of which could be false.

She gazes back through the window at Pritti, collapsed on the floor, rocking. Sara knocks. Inside, Pritti doesn't stir. But her lips are moving, endlessly. *Illusions, delusions, and confusions.*

Sara opens the door and steps into the room, unsure as to whether her presence will be an answer for Pritti, of sorts, or an additional complication.

'Hello Pritti,' she says.

Pritti's voice gets louder, the rocking intensifies, the mantra is muttered with more conviction. A wall of words, keeping people out. Sara turns to where Dana waits in the doorway—ready to call for Sanjiv again, perhaps—and nods at her to leave. Dana closes the door quietly.

Sara walks slowly towards her patient and crouches down. 'Hello Pritti.'

She is on a level with Pritti, her patient's face sheeny in the humidity. Pritti fingers the pallu of her sari, trying to hold herself together, soothing herself with repetition, like the repetition of a nursery rhyme. The pallu thread has been pulled so far it has completely unravelled. The woman is shaking.

And so Sara does the only thing she can think of, which is to lean in and wrap this girl in her arms so that for a while the world comprises just the two of them, rocking gently. She whispers—*It's OK, it's all right*—and lets her patient weep, all the while tracing a circle with the heel of her palm on the woman's shuddering back.

Instead of heading back to the Majestic—to pack and to take one last dip among the plaster fish before moving in with Rafi—Sara takes the metro to the Central Secretariat and walks according to Kate's meticulous directions. The heat is fierce. Despite the view out towards India Gate, this is not a tourist area, and for twenty minutes she is stared at for being white and looking sweaty and anxious before finding the correct low-built building made of rose-coloured stone.

A loud roar rises up in her ears. What on earth does Kate have to tell her? Because, to be honest, having come this far, she isn't sure she wants to know. She remembers the night she was told originally about Mike's death, how she had crumpled. She isn't sure she can go through that again.

'Hello lovely,' says Kate at the entrance.

By floridly waving a High Commission pass in a duty guard's face, both women are let through the turnstiles. As they sign in, Sara slyly flicks back the pages of the fat Visitors' Book, to take a look at the weeks leading up to Mike's death, but no familiar name or signature leaps out at her.

After endless corridors, Kate shows her into a musty little room lined with glass cabinets. Even once the lights are switched on, the room is depressingly dim.

Kate closes the door. 'I have to confess that my initial search and conversations have drawn a blank, which suggests to me Mike must have been involved in an operation unknown to the High Commission. So we must explore other avenues. Now,' she adds, gesturing at the cabinets, 'some of what you may read here is highly confidential. In fact, you and I haven't been here at all. Do you understand?'

Sara nods. She feels an enormous debt of gratitude for the risks Kate is taking on her behalf.

'This room contains the files of Anglo-Indian military cooperation going back to 1848. We can get the files for the months around when Mike died. I'm hoping there might be some information, even if it's just a code word or nickname which might resonate for you.'

'Nickname?' And then she remembers.

'Who are "Pondy" and "Trigger"?' she asked, when he told a story, home on leave.

'We never use our own names, even to each other. We use nicknames, picked up in training. Fast on the guns, "Trigger," always wet, "Pondy."'

She threw her arms round his neck. 'And what's yours?'

But he wouldn't tell her.

'I always thought the whole nickname thing was a bit silly, very comic strip.'

Kate shakes her head. 'No it's deadly serious. It's why they never use a physically identifiable part of the body, like Ginger, or a shortening of a real name. Still, even if Mike went under an assumed name, you might notice it in a way that I can't. Take your time. I've got plenty to do here,' she adds, pulling a laptop out of her bag.

Sara scans the spines for dates and then opens wide a tall cabinet door. Standing on a chair she eases down three huge files. For over an hour Sara studies their pages, detailing unfamiliar events and locations, while Kate taps away on her laptop. Nothing leaps out as offering even the slightest hint that Mike is being written about here.

After an hour, she thanks Kate for giving her the opportunity to research something concrete, and gathers her things. Together they return the files to their slots. It is only when Sara hears the click of the cabinet being closed that she starts to cry.

'So you found something?' says Kate, heading towards the panel of light switches.

Sara shakes her head. She had thought there would be answers, clarity. Because without answers, the imagination runs riot. So why in the world is she crying?

She covers her eyes with her hands and tries to breathe, tears spilling from between her fingers. Kate will think she is thinking of Mike, but she is thinking more of their marriage,

72

and in particular of what Sara came to think of as Mike's vacant, Thousand Yard Stare.

And the pain comes back to her then, the increasing sense of distance between them, the way they stopped properly communicating, the way they stopped making love once they were told Mike couldn't have children. 'I've never told anyone this before, but I'd lost him well before he died. He had become so remote. And I tried to talk to him, I really did. My work is about getting people to talk. But he stopped telling me about his worries, and increasingly there seemed this part of him I couldn't reach—'

Eighteen months on, she cannot say who first stopped raising the subject of adoption, of surrogacy, of donor sperm, who first edged away in bed. How much was she to blame for the gaping hole at the heart of their marriage and, by extension, Mike's secret life?

'What are you most afraid of?' Kate asks, doing her best—diplomatically—to hurry Sara out of the room, the room where they are not meant to be.

Trevor once told her that people don't come to therapy because they want answers. They come because they have worked out the answer and are absolutely bloody terrified. When she looks up into Kate's face she sees that she doesn't need to spell it out.

10

'Ladies and Gentlemen, please be staying calm. Staying calm.'

In the lobby the next morning, the concierge is swamped, so Sara and her checking out suitcases must wait patiently. And all because of a Slutwalk.

If in Delhi the success of a demonstration is measured by civic disruption, then Delhi's Slutwalk is already, at eight in the morning, a resounding triumph. Roads are so jammed that even metro staff are unable to get into work. When Sara phones Rafi to warn him she will be late, he says he will send Hemant over. She tries to talk him out of it, but he is insistent. So she agrees. It is only a lift, after all. And yet when the call ends, she glares at her phone as if it is complicit. The shiny buttons stare back at her innocently.

Not surprisingly, Hemant takes an age to arrive. Meanwhile, the lobby throbs to rumours of civic scuffles. Fresh Twitter hashtags—#delhiwomen, #NoMeansNo— burst onto laptops. Sara admires the women's courage and her thoughts turn to Kanan and Pritti and Pritti's mother, fighting to be themselves in a country where a woman's behaviour is often misinterpreted as shaming the family. Above all, her chest aches for young Pritti, bravely crossing the threshold into Sara's consulting room. Something about this young woman—pining for years—has pressed a button in Sara.

What she knows is that both she and Pritti have an infinite capacity for longing. Growing up with a single mother, Sara used to play for hours constructing a father in her head. It was a composite of the scraps her mother provided—tall, handsome, can't remember—and certain classic childhood wishes that he be rich, powerful, and coming home soon. Facially, his appearance changed according to the fashions of the day. But one factor never changed: he always came back.

She fantasised about bumping into him in the street. Or hoped that the rare male standing at the school gate was him, come to take her home. She pictured herself running into his arms, him swinging her up into the air, promising never to leave her again. She once wrote to *Jim'll Fix It* to ask if he could Fix It for her to meet her dad. Five years ago, when she cleared out her mother's belongings at the hospice, she found a small wooden box. Among the dried flowers and polaroids of Sara as a child was the letter to Jim, never posted.

She has never known her father. She has only had relationships with men like Mr Finn and Mike, Alpha males she could romanticise, hero worship, love from a distance. She tugs the opal on her necklace from side to side.

'Madam, your car is here now.'

Sara gets up ready to follow the bell-hop, but there now unfurls a minor panic, in which it transpires that Sara never filled out the Visitors' Book at check-in. Those stiff, hallowed papers constituting a hotel's history. The Manager and Duty Manager and Marketing Director and Concierge all now descend, bearing The Book.

Eagerly they show her the names of previous eminent guests, decades of ambassadors and politicians she has never heard of, whose flamboyant signatures adorn its pages—although this does give her the opportunity to linger over the pages from eighteen months ago, just in case… They are buoyed by her apparent interest, want to wish her well, give her a good send-off, this esteemed client, this possible repeat guest. Yet above all, they want concrete proof she lodged under their roof. Eventually she squiggles her name and makes up something nice in the comments column about the pink towels. The staff beam, utterly beside themselves with promotional joy.

Conscious of keeping Hemant waiting, she dashes from the hotel; doesn't see in the bright sunlight the Mercedes right in front of her; can't see Hemant holding open the door. She walks slap into him, her right breast bumping into the ripe mango of his bicep. She jumps, as if from an electric shock. His sculpted mouth curves into a smile.

Sara takes an instant dislike to that smile. Angrily she climbs into the car and tugs the door shut. It crosses her mind to tell him that she is in Delhi simply to understand how Mike died, that she loved her husband very, very much and that as soon as she has found out all the necessary information, she will be returning to London. She folds her arms and stares out the window.

The main road is crammed with people and banners. She follows with her eyes a passing sign, *My dress is not a yes.*

'Makes me proud,' Hemant says. 'Delhi is one of the few cities left in the world which actually *needs* a Slutwalk.'

She feels this last word brush her skin, her senses annoyingly alert—despite Dana's warnings about cross-caste relationships—to the micro-movements of air between the two of them.

'My sister Varsha, is walking today,' he adds. 'She is passionate about women's rights. Women of all ages are taking to the streets and men are supporting them. It is a good thing for my country.'

'What does your sister do?'

'When she isn't watching Shah Rukh Khan movies?' he laughs. 'She is a university student. St Stephen's. She will do politics one day.'

She hates to have such a condescending thought, but his English is impeccable.

As if he can read her mind he adds, 'Both my sister and I were made to speak English at home by my father. Varsha was in the top four in her school this year. I keep telling her, she will be running the country one day.'

Sara shifts in her seat. Her shoes land on something hard and unexpected. It emits a plaintive wail. She laughs—'I thought it was a cat!'—and reaches down, to find a guitar. An electric one, scarlet and silver. 'May I?'

Hemant smiles. She picks it up by the neck, feeling the uneven weight of it in her hand. It's a magnificent beast. She strokes its plush enamel and plucks the fattest string with her thumb. The twang resonates deep inside her. 'Is this yours?'

'I am in a band,' he says simply, and a warm feeling blooms across her chest at this man's hidden accomplishments.

Reaching down to put the guitar back, she finds a pile of papers. Leaflets. A flyer for a gig. She folds one and tucks it into her handbag.

When they reach the clinic, she offers to help Hemant carry her cases, but he ignores her. No, not ignores her, just gets on with his job. He is Rafi's driver. Perhaps hers now too, she isn't sure.

Hemant turns to go.

'Do you ever teach the guitar?' she says, on impulse.

'Sure,' he says, taking his leave with a deep namaste and then closing the door behind him.

She is left with an excitement so intense it is almost pathological.

11

It is mid-morning and Rafi and Sara are grabbing a quick coffee at the clinic before heading off to one of Dr Mathur's mental health conferences for local office workers. The door opens and Shakeel pretends to stagger exhausted into the room.

Rafi looks at his watch and taps the face.

'What's your car gone and done now?' giggles Sara, happy to play the straight man. Shakeel's car is always *giving him gyp* and the saga of its daily ailments is an enjoyable soap opera.

'Minor matter. Oil leak. I know, I know, you both think I should get rid of it.'

'I just love that you're so attached to it,' says Sara.

'Because,' Shakeel nods at Rafi, 'it is an *Indian* car. Not one of your imported tanks, nah.'

'I like my Mercedes. It makes me feel safe and protected.'

'And who, or what do you need protection from, Rafi?' laughs Sara.

Rafi ignores her. 'Nor do I feel loyal to India. India is going to hell in a handcart.'

Shakeel chuckles. 'Well, I am proud to drive a Tata.'

'What's a Tata?' asks Sara.

'Mr Tata used India's problems as the spur for good design. Better suspension because of our potholes, one windscreen wiper instead of two to keep costs down, and a hollow steering shaft to reduce the amount of steel. It's the perfect Indian car, nah, because we are so poor.'

Rafi pretends to choke on his biscuit. 'You are not poor, Shak. You are idealistic. You can afford to drive a car like mine, it's just that you don't.' And he pulls a face. It is clearly an old sore, and both men love picking at it.

Sara's phone beeps. It is a text from Kate. *Call me.* Sara's stomach spins so violently she thinks she might be sick. She sprints into the clinic courtyard for better reception.

'Where are you?' barks Kate, picking up.

'At the clinic. Why? Have you found something about Mike?'

'Oh, thank God.'

'Why? What's happened? What have you found?'

'There's been another bomb at the High Court. Round the corner from where you and I were looking at files the other day—' Sara hears her new friend almost choke. 'I thought, you know, you might have gone back looking—'

'Oh my God, are people hurt?'

'No, thank God. We're getting reports of a few light injuries apparently, nothing more. Not as bad as the one there two months ago. But still—'

Sara has a sinking feeling in the pit of her stomach. She can guess what Kate is thinking. They were there. It could have been them.

Sara races back to the canteen and tells the others the news about the bomb.

Rafi throws his hands up. 'Two in two months. It is Mumbai all over again.'

Sara has a vague memory of watching something on the news back home. 'What happened in Mumbai?'

'Paks blew up hotels, a cafe, a synagogue—'

'—*allegedly* Paks,' warns Shakeel.

Rafi shrugs. 'Over one hundred and sixty killed. Over three hundred injured.'

A chill washes over her. This carnage smacks of Mike's world.

'We refer to Mumbai as India's Nine-eleven—' adds Shakeel.

'I'm not surprised,' she says, shaking her head. 'And now they're targeting Delhi?'

'Who knows,' says Shakeel. 'Could be outsiders. Could be home-grown…'

'Listen,' says Rafi, checking his watch and almost spilling his coffee, 'if there's been a bomb in central Delhi, it's going to be chaos out there. The police will be running round like headless chickens. And we've got to get to my dad's conference.' Rafi pushes his chair back.

Sara looks up at him, incredulous. 'You think your dad's conference will still be taking place? After everything that's happened today?'

Rafi puts a hand on her shoulder. 'India loves a crisis. We want the gods to admire our stoicism. Then our rewards will be plentiful, in the next life.'

A lopsided banner welcomes them to a seminar on *Women in India Today*. Dr Mathur is holding court outside surrounded by journalists and cameramen. As they approach, Sara overhears him say that India needs to *fly the flag for women*. 'Good for you,' she murmurs.

He beckons them over. 'And here are some of my staff. Flown from Yoo-kay.'

She smiles, as he pulls Rafi and Sara to him. Yet a moment later Dr Mathur's pudgy hand grasps her shoulder, squeezing her as though she is a piece of fruit to be bought. A ripple of revulsion courses through her.

Inside they take their places on a raised platform, for a panel discussion for human resources staff on mental health. But firstly Dr Mathur thanks them all for coming under the difficult circumstances, and holds a minute's silence for those injured in the bombing. Then he invites the women to *pile in* with their questions.

'How do I cool the ardour of two colleagues having an affair?'

'Help me, please, with nymphomania in the typing pool.'

'What can I do if I suspect a colleague is being beaten at home by her husband?'

Sara leans towards Rafi. 'I thought we were here to talk about mental health,' she says, out of the side of her mouth.

For over an hour the three of them take turns to offer insights, with Dr Mathur beaming at their side. Then a lady in a gorgeous lime salwar kameez half-stands and raises her hand. 'What do I do if I suspect some of the cleaners are secretly Devadasi?'

Sara has never heard the word before, but she definitely hears the sharp collective intake of breath in the room. The woman in green is now standing, but it is as though the other ladies have drawn back somehow, so that she stands as the one street lamp in a bad neighbourhood.

Dr Mathur, sitting beside Sara, reaches across and grabs the shared microphone. 'Ladies,' he says, clearing his throat, 'this is very controversial subject. Taboo we might be saying. As we know, this is an ancient Hindu tradition, made illegal some thirty years previous. So, unless your junior colleague is also ancient,' he pauses for the expected ripple of laughter, 'I doubt she is Devadasi.'

The lady frowns, as if to say *I don't need a history lesson, I need concrete advice.*

Sara is aware of how rigid Rafi has become, beside her. Meanwhile, the lime green lady is being heckled by the other delegates, who tug at her salwar kameez, at the very threads around her neck, as though intending to lynch her. The noise levels spiral, until the piercing shriek of microphone feedback bounces off the walls, with Dr Mathur rapidly *preponing* lunch. He clambers down off the podium and leads the way, pointing to a break-out room at the back.

'Tell my father I am not feeling well,' mutters Rafi, extracting a cigarette from its packet and striding out of the room.

Over lunch the audience are far more interested in the buffet and gossiping about this morning's High Court bomb than approaching Sara or Shakeel to ask questions. Dr Mathur fills his belly with conspicuous practice, and then takes his leave of the paying delegates. He hasn't noticed Rafi's absence.

Sara suggests to Shakeel that they too slip away.

Soon the two of them are walking back through gridlocked streets to the clinic.

'Probably didn't want to take any exercise,' jokes Shakeel. 'Prefers his limo, does Rafi!'

Sara grins. 'So, what is Devadasi?'

'Whereas I prefer to drive. As I always say, find a space on a road in India, and an Indian will put a car in it!'

'Shakeel?'

Shakeel's eyes remain glued to the street, as though he fears marauding potholes.

'Why was everyone so hostile to the woman in lime green?' She is aware of the same tight silence as existed in the seminar room. 'Shakeel?'

'When I was a student doctor,' he says in a rush, 'I trained at a clinic in a poor part of Mumbai, which had a temple for Dalits, the Untouchables in the area. The young girls in the district were still being married off to the temple. Do you see what I'm saying?'

Married off to the temple? 'No, not really.'

He breathes out heavily. 'Families dedicate their daughters to the temple before puberty. The girls earn money for their families, for schooling, for healthcare, for weddings. And they earn this money by performing tasks. You know, everything you would do if you were married?' He glances at her. Please, the frown on his forehead begs, follow what I'm saying.

Sara hasn't a clue what he is talking about, and yet is amazed Shakeel is finding this conversation so hard. She tries to understand by creating a context, by imagining the only temple she is familiar with, *her* temple opposite the clinic, where women sweep and light candles. And men wander in and out.

'Heavens,' she says, wondering why she hasn't thought of this before. So that's what was slightly odd about it. Her temple is actually a brothel. 'So Devadasi are prostitutes?'

Shakeel grabs her wrist 'Please. Keep your voice down. It is not that simple. In pre-colonial days, women who became Devadasi were of all castes, not just Untouchables. They had high status. They were seen as devoting their lives to the gods. They danced, played instruments, some were accomplished poets. Most importantly, they had financial independence. Even today, the Devadasi say that marriage to the deity gives them responsibility, power—'

'But not everyone agrees?'

Shakeel allows himself a wry smile. 'You British came over here. Taught us that sex outside marriage is wrong. Devadasi are now seen as working exclusively in the sex trade and are therefore seen as failed members of society. In psychiatry, they are evidence of India's shadow side.'

Sara thinks for a moment. 'I don't get it. Everyone was sniggering quite happily over nymphomania in the typing pool and then this one word gets mentioned and everyone goes berserk.'

'I know. We are very muddled about sex here in India. We are the home of the Kama Sutra and yet we are obsessed with women being either pure or defiled.'

'How come?'

'Attitudes are partly to blame. Sex education, for example is rarely taught in schools. So prostitution in general is a hard problem to talk about, let alone tackle. When I was training, most of our time was spent just dealing with the fallout.'

'The fallout?'

'For example, men who pay more for sex don't have to wear condoms.'

Sara shudders. 'The rates of HIV and AIDS must be sky-high.'

Shakeel tilts his head. 'Added to which, today the government denies that dedication of young girls to the temples even takes place. In villages Devadasi is easier to outlaw because the communities are smaller. But that just pushes families who have fewer choices to sell their daughters to prostitution gangs in the cities. Or they are kidnapped, with little effort being made at home to find them,' he adds, unable to look her in the eye.

Sara is remembering the young girls on G.B. Road, and Rafi's comment, about why would you water your neighbour's tree. 'Because daughters can be a financial burden?'

'Girls must have a dowry when they marry. Families get desperate. They sell their daughter into prostitution. Or if she is kidnapped they see it as one less dowry to find. Even some *wives* are sold into prostitution, especially by their husband if she has not given birth to sons.'

'And either way, the women end up in the rape trade.'

'I wish your phrase weren't so horribly accurate,' says Shakeel, his voice flat. 'Trafficking. It's one of the fastest growing industries in the world. And though it shames me to say it, India is right at the centre of it.'

By now they have reached the clinic and clearly Shakeel is unwilling to continue the conversation while they might stand a greater chance of being overheard. She resolves to go and seek him out again this evening, to find out more about the Devadasi and sex trafficking.

As they enter the clinic she glances back at the temple opposite. 'And our temple? Just so I know.'

Shakeel's grimace tells her what she needs to know.

84

In her mind, Sara sees the taut physique of the woman who fascinates her, with the sensuous mouth and unravelling hair and the dear little boy. She waits to feel some sort of revulsion, but it doesn't come.

❧

Later that afternoon, Sara hears noises—shuffling, murmurs—outside her office and opens the door. She finds Pritti and her one-to-one obs nurse lurking in the corridor.

'Hello Pritti. I wasn't expecting you this afternoon.'

'Miss Pritti wanted to be coming to see you,' says the nurse. 'Very insistent.'

'Sure. Come in.' She opens the door wider. But Pritti merely stands on the threshold and peers in, scrutinising the room.

Sara wants to laugh: there was a time when it was impossible to get Pritti to leave her own room, and yet here she is, making an unscheduled visit. It could be a cause for celebration. But Pritti's face is deadly serious. 'Did you leave something behind?' Sara asks, glancing at the obs nurse. 'Are you looking for something specific?'

'I am checking you are here,' says Pritti, boldly.

'Me?' Sara looks at Pritti, the angle of her lean into the room speaking of great urgency or desperation. 'I'm here,' she says tenderly. She turns to the nurse again, and murmurs, 'Is this about the bomb this morning? Has she become more clingy?' The nurse doesn't comment. Sara turns back to Pritti. 'I'm here, Pritti. I'm still here.'

And Pritti looks back at her, eye to eye, before shuffling back towards the inpatient block.

For once, Pritti has sought out Sara, not the other way around. Progress. Sara feels the hairs stand up on the back of her neck.

85

At the end of the day, Sara is just locking her files away before heading off to Shakeel's room when there is a respectful knock at her door. It is Shakeel, looking furtive.

'Am I interrupting?' In his hands he holds a bulging scrapbook.

'Not at all,' she smiles. 'What have you got there?'

'It's not much, but I thought you might be interested.'

She takes hold of the *not much*, and is surprised by its weight. She remembers her disappointment at the files in the Army Archive, and how much she had wanted to find something, *anything* there about Mike. A quick flick of Shakeel's file tells her it is crammed with scribbled notes and yellowed cuttings and photos. 'Wow. This goes back years.'

'I try and keep everything I find on the subject. I may write a research paper one day. Who knows? But it is tricky, nah. Even to investigate it, is to challenge the system.'

'The system?'

Shakeel double-checks that Sara's door is closed. 'Underage sex. It is a huge problem here in India. But the government, the authorities, the police, they all deny it. They say they have got it licked. The problem is, in some places, even the Hindi word for rape, *balatkar*, is still taboo. So we can hardly have a national conversation about our ill-treatment of women.'

Sara strokes the rough Manila of the cover and thinks again of the young girl in cheap jewellery, sucking her thumb on G.B. Road. 'Then I look forward to reading it. And thank you,' she adds, 'for trusting me with it.'

Already she can guess what it has cost him to show this murky information to someone else.

12

That evening, Sara has invited Kate to join her and Rafi and his gang of friends to knock back impromptu beers, and discuss survivor guilt. Everyone in the open-air café is drinking wildly, discussing this morning's bomb at the High Court. Rumours fly that the next terrorist target will be a shopping mall, or a busy cinema. Maybe even the swish new airport.

Pradeep, Rafi's lawyer friend, sucks rabidly on one of his cigars. 'It's outrageous. There was a similar blast near the High Court two months ago, and at the time the government promised to put in CCTV cameras there. But have they been installed?'

Everyone knows the government too well to be surprised they haven't.

'Do they know yet who was behind the bomb?' asks Sara.

'Yes,' says Rupa, 'what's the latest?'

Pradeep's chest expands. 'The latest theory is that the bomb was intended for one of the High Court judges, presiding over a case involving a sex-trafficking gang from Pune. Which is highly unusual.'

Sara frowns. 'In what way?'

'Normally the cases don't even come to court. The verdict is expected tomorrow, so if he was the intended target, this bomb was meant as a warning.'

'Of course,' says Rafi, or Rafi's whisky, 'if the Mumbai bombings are anything to go by, there'll be another spike in the birth rate in nine months time.'

'Is that true?' drawls Barkha. 'Are we still programmed to survive?' Barkha's kohl is particularly heavy this evening.

Rafi gestures to Sara, as if playing her in, the fount of all knowledge. After all, this is her territory, her Freudian patch, this whole survival instinct business.

She takes a long swig of beer. 'Before my husband Mike died, he was a bomb-disposal expert in the British army. Whenever he was asked if he was frightened doing his job, he'd say that we will walk on two legs, kill our siblings, do whatever it takes to ensure the survival of our own genes. Danger focuses the mind. Survival trumps fear.'

And in the respectful silence that follows her mention of him, Sara is struck by the thought that at the very end, maybe even Mike had been afraid. She drains her bottle of beer.

'Well, that's the one reliable thing about India,' jokes Alok. 'Human life will always survive here, against the odds. There are a billion plus plus of us already, as it is.'

Everyone laughs. Everyone is merry and noisy. Everyone is drinking and swapping seats. Sara grabs another bottle of beer and engineers a perch closer to Pradeep.

'Can I ask your professional opinion?'

Pradeep beams the smile of a man secretly happy to be permanently on call.

'My husband was in India doing something I didn't know about. He died here and the authorities back in England hushed it up. As a lawyer, where would you start?'

Pradeep considers the question and then grabs a paper napkin. Taking a pen from his jacket he draws two circles, overlapping. Sara watches as he labels one circle India and the other UK. Then he taps the intersection in the middle. 'I'd think about where the two worlds meet.'

'And where do they meet? What does that bit in the middle represent?'

Pradeep glances swiftly around the table and then leans in. 'Officially? Tourism, curry and Bollywood music.'

'And unofficially?'

Pradeep leans so close their foreheads are almost touching. 'Drugs and people.'

'How does that involve Britain?'

'Not only is Britain a market for both the drugs and the girls, but the money made in India through both those commodities is often laundered via the diaspora into legitimate British businesses, like restaurants, and then used to fund more nefarious activities.'

'So do you or your law firm ever get involved in trying to stop it?'

Pradeep sucks on his cigar. 'Officially? No. It's definitely not my area and very few law firms take on the work.'

'Because?'

'Because it is a dangerous business and it is impossible to bring convictions.'

'Because?'

'Because everyone, the police, the taxi-drivers, the nearby shopkeepers, they're all getting kickbacks from the pimps to provide customers. Pimps are very wealthy, very powerful.'

'And they'll cut up rough if anyone tries to interrupt their revenue stream?'

'Exactly. The head of my chambers was stabbed last year, for defending a man simply trying to get a brothel next to his investment bank closed down. So no one on that side of the transaction talks.'

'But what about the victims, the women? Surely they'd do anything to get the men who traffic them put away?'

'Even if we do get the victims to talk, it can take months to befriend them, arrange for translators. Or they retract their stories. Or they disappear, are moved on. With few prosecutions and even fewer precedent decisions, even the most determined victims can lose faith in the legal process.'

'So what about going after the clients, men who use prostitutes? After all, it's rape.'

'Have a guess how many rape cases are pending in India at the moment.'

Sara thinks big. 'A thousand. No, five thousand.' Pradeep stays silent. Sara bites her lip. 'Ten thousand? Twenty?'

'Twenty-four thousand. Pending. And that's before we add in all the ones yet to be committed tonight. And that's probably not including all the marital rapes, committed on women within the home where the woman can't see the point in reporting it to the dozy police. Or the crimes committed during trafficking. So, as you can imagine, the courts are at breaking point.'

Sara thinks for a moment. 'OK. That's officially. But unofficially?'

Pradeep pulls out a silver case from his jacket, extracts a business card and gives it to her. 'Unofficially my chambers sometimes works with charities and NGOs trying to get different things changed. We help on raids of brothels or in filing complaints to the police or to help charities and NGOs lobby for revised legislation. My chambers, for example, is pushing for the creation of fast-track courts across the country for any crime at all related to the abuse of women. But as I am sure you can imagine, it is a long haul.'

Just then, the café owner turns up the tape deck to full volume. It is strictly cheesy Bollywood here, and the beat is hungry, driven, sexy. Sara takes another long swig of beer.

Rafi sidles up and flings a drunken arm around her. 'Having fun?'

'Yeah.' She burps. 'But I feel bad—'

'Bad? Why? We're alive. We've survived.'

'I know. But staying out with you guys, getting drunk, when I should be out finding out about Mike—' Although, she hates to admit it, she has slept better here in Delhi than she has done since Mike died.

'It is OK to still miss him,' says Rafi.

Sara shakes her head, dizzy from thinking about the bomb and G.B. Road and losing Mike. 'I wanted to hate India, for taking him away from me…' She feels she might burst.

Abruptly she stands up and launches herself at a space on the floor, fists punching the air. Kate follows, in a delighted show of support, and then Rupa and Pradeep and Alok, and then Rafi dragging Barkha.

Before long, most of the café has caught the mood, a mood of defiance, eager to lose themselves in the music. Sara dances wildly, fearing—with her two left feet—for other people's shins, but no one seems to care. Mike insisted on at least one ballroom lesson for their first dance. Which suddenly strikes her as immensely funny. Mike in clod-hopping army boots and her draped in bridal organza. 'My first post-Mike joke!' she yells in delight above the music, to no one in particular.

Kate sees her laughing, and grabs her new friend's hand, lifting it up. Makes her do a little twirl.

❧

Later Sara helps Kate climb unsteadily into a waiting rickshaw. Perched high on the seat behind the cyclist, she wraps her scarf Bedouin-style around her head against the pre-monsoon dust.

Kate leans back out, her speech slurred. 'Darling, I nearly forgot. We're having a reception soon at the Ambassador's Residence for one of the Queen's thingies. Just a little do. Can you come? You might meet someone there who has better contacts than me, who might shed some light on Mike. I'll send you and Rafi invites.'

And without waiting for an answer—it is perhaps more of an instruction—Kate prattles to the driver in Hindi and is off.

Another possible route to Mike. Sara watches the cycle-rickshaw disappear down the street.

⚜

Back in her room at Rafi's house Sara downs half a litre of bottled water, lifts Shakeel's heavy scrapbook from her bedside table and places it on her bed. The cuttings are probably dry and dull, but she'll just read one or two. She grabs some cleanser and cotton wool from the bathroom and returns to sit on the bed. And, while she removes her make-up, she idly turns the first page. It is stiff and cracks with glue.

The early cuttings comprise Shakeel's notes on the prostitutes he came into contact with during his medical training in Mumbai. Some jottings are on scraps of paper, but some are photocopies of file notes made on clinical paper. Sara knows immediately how this compromises Shakeel: the information in these notes should never have left the clinic where he was training.

She reads about Akanksha, kidnapped from her village and brought by train to Mumbai, Deepti whose parents sold her to what they thought was a construction company, but who were then told she had run away, and Indu who was drugged and abducted from her slum cluster in rural Maharashtra.

In Shakeel's blue biro she reads: *All three girls are clearly under eighteen but they insist they are in their twenties. Having brought them to the clinic, their madams now won't let me speak further to them—'over twenty' and not allowed to speak for themselves!!!!!*

In another note he writes: *A D + I are forced to have sex multiple times every day to earn their keep. Some of the girls must take part in gang rapes. None are given the money they have been promised to send back to their families.* In red he writes, *Their bodies are covered in cigarette burns—presumably as punishment.*

Suddenly Sara feels terribly sober. She thinks back to the woman at the temple opposite the clinic—her temple—the woman with the sensuous mouth and lithe body and tinkly bangles. Sara doesn't want to think about her being forced to have sex with lots of different men.

She hunches further over the scrapbook and reads some of the historic information of Shakeel's essay—the Devadasi wear necklaces of red and white beads to identify their status—until her eye catches on a sentence Shakeel has also underlined in pen:

Even though the Devadasi system has begun to disappear, many of the temples still in existence claim to practise the Devadasi tradition but are in fact brothels in anything but name. They are run by the sex trafficking mafia, generating huge incomes for clans both in India and overseas.

A bolt of understanding forces her upright, thinking of her temple. This isn't just some academic issue. This is part of her community. She is blithely working opposite women who may have been abducted, abused, sex trafficked; sisters in spirit to the bruised women and girls on G.B. Road.

Her skin prickles with the realisation that life always throws up the unexpected. Or as Trevor used to say in supervision sessions, 'Remember, the only consistent thing about life is change.'

That right when you think you have a plan, something happens to throw you off course. Something that gives your life value.

13

Sara leans her skull against the cream leather headrest. A nail is being hammered into each socket, the size of a pylon. It flashes all the colours of titanium.

Keeping her head stable whenever Hemant navigates a roundabout, she sends a BBM to Kate: Hung-over?

Ha! Despite heat am having restorative coffee. But thanks for inviting me :)

Cautiously—no, more than cautiously—Sara turns her neck and gazes out at Delhi's morning routines, at Dilliwallahs shitting, shaving or sluicing toothpaste in the street. Her head reverberates again and all she can think of is how on some level all this pain must be a punishment. Punishment for frittering away an evening when Mike's body lies unclaimed. Punishment for not being a better wife. And punishment for knowing that even though her patients suffer, she is only in India temporarily and at some point will abandon them. That all her life, her attachments have been flimsy. That she is to blame.

The guilt is almost as unbearable as the agony it so recently replaced. Back in London, she had been so melancholy that she felt she had fallen into a yawning chasm. Whereas in India, she now feels conflicted. She loves her new friends, mourns her husband and wishes she knew how to rescue a prostitute young enough to suck her thumb. While her inner therapist is thrilled to see progress, to see that Sara is once again capable of reaching out to the world, as a grieving widow she still has obligations.

Quickly she scrolls through the contact list on her phone.

'Hello. I'd like to make an appointment to see Passang Kasturirangan today.'

Pritti is chatty this afternoon, co-operative. No sign of the stunned young woman of yesterday who seemed to fear Sara might have died. Instead, she is sitting on the chair not the floor, her plaits like plumb lines anchoring her to something like reality. Sara watches her patient's hands, folded neatly in her lap, delicate dark hairs on dark skin. Pritti's eye contact is good, and she seems oriented in time and place, keen to ask about the real world outside the clinic. *Has the monsoon started?* Sara is encouraged.

And then Sara notices the bruises. Dark welts on the upper arm, disappearing under the sleeve of Pritti's sari under-blouse. She tells herself to stay focused, stay with what is in the room. 'I see bruises,' Sara says, touching her own body in the same place.

Pritti's expression changes fleetingly—another one of those micro-gestures before speech, betraying difficult emotions—and then back to neutral. 'They say the monsoon is late, don't they? Will it be heavy? Will this year's rains be good, do you think?'

'Has someone hurt you?'

'Or maybe no rain. Poor farmers.' Then Pritti stops talking. And then the rocking starts, the agitated stare, the mantra. *Illusions, delusions, and confusions.*

'Did you hurt yourself?' Inpatients can start to self-harm, especially with little else to do. But are the bruises even self-inflicted? Were they instead made by another patient? Or a member of staff? It would be fatal to jump to conclusions. She asks again, more softly this time, 'Pritti, I want to help you. How did you get those bruises?'

But the mantra is now firmly in place, the defence shield up. The session is lost. Half an hour later, she closes the door having seen a mute Pritti safely into the hands of her one-to-one nurse. In her mind she has registered everything about her patient, the stoop, the clasping of her elbows, the slight rocking, as though being able to mentally describe her accurately might bring back the rapport so recently won. But the look on Pritti's face, as her eyes went to the nurse and then back to Sara, jolted her. On Pritti's face, she saw fear.

She joins Rafi for a ward round.

'I need to speak to you about Pritti,' Sara describes the session and the bruises.

'Do you think they're self-inflicted?'

'They look more like someone has grabbed her. You know, fingerprints.'

'That is a worrying development.'

'Have you noticed other patients with them?'

Rafi confesses that he hasn't.

'In which case we need to monitor who comes into contact with her.'

Rafi agrees, but seems distracted.

Sara adds a note to Pritti's file. 'Is everything OK?'

'Yes. Just a bit hungry, I reckon.'

'I couldn't help noticing you left the seminar yesterday before lunch.' She has never known Rafi not to be shoving something in his mouth. Classic oral fixation.

'All that spiritual mumbo-jumbo—' he tails off.

'You mean the Devadasi and their temples? I had no idea the temple opposite this clinic is one.'

Rafi snorts. 'There's nothing there,' he says, turning to go.

'What do you mean, there's nothing there? It's full of women.'

'A bunch of crones. Rural migrant workers, with nowhere to go.'

'But some of them are young, and really beautiful. You must have seen them?'

'There were problems. Fights and such. Place closed down years ago.' At which point, Rafi turns smartly on his heels and walks away.

The duty sergeant in front of her lowers his eyes and explains that, what with the recent bombings, Chief Superintendent Passang Kasturirangan is not actually able to keep his appointment with her today.

'But I made my appointment *after* the bombings. Why did you give me a slot when he wasn't free?' The duty officer tries to interrupt. 'Yes, I can imagine the bomb blast has put police forces nationwide on high alert, but you're empty.' She gestures around the waiting room. And it occurs to her that this isn't just someone being awkward for the sake of it, but that somehow being female and in need of help inflames a certain type of Indian male's sense of superiority.

She straightens her spine. 'Still, I am here now in person and I have risked sunstroke to get here. So, I suggest you take me to him now. I am not leaving until I see him.'

After a desultory search for a bomb in her bag, she is led not into the room she visited once before, just next to the front desk, but through a different door. It leads to a long dank corridor of low cells. In the dim light, Sara gradually makes out women huddled together on the dirt floor, maybe ten to a cell, some with babies at their breast or toddlers in their arms. One or two are muttering to themselves and scratching their arms. Everyone looks dazed, as though resigned to their fate, or drugged, their cheerful saris incongruous in this ghastly, dirty setting.

Something brushes at her bare legs. Sara looks down to find a hand stretched out.

'Please help us,' says the woman's voice, in an urgent whisper.

Sara crouches down. 'What's happened? Why are you all here?'

The woman struggles with her broken English. 'Bad things. We do bad things. But men make us.'

'What do you mean?'

But the lowering of the woman's eyes in shame tells Sara what she has guessed already. These women are prostitutes and they and their children are now being punished for it.

'Men hold our legs down, so we can't stop it happening.'

The duty sergeant has reached the end of the corridor and has only now realised that Sara is not following like an obedient spaniel. He barks at her to come.

Sara ignores him, and leans closer to the women, their hands reaching out like plants in search of the sun. The stench of urine makes her eyes water. Her heart is heavy. Maybe their stories are like those recorded in Shakeel's scrapbook, women trapped in a system which treats them like animals— no, worse. They may be out of their brothel, but they have just swapped one prison for another.

Passang is in a courtyard, at a table covered with maps.

'What are all those women doing in your cells? What on earth have they been charged with—' She stops herself. Firstly, this is not why she has come and secondly, she needs to keep the likes of Passang Kasturirangan sweet if she is to retain his help in finding out about Mike. Not, she concedes, that he has demonstrated much in the way of answers so far. 'Forgive me, I'm just shocked by what I've just seen—' She gestures back at the cells.

'And that is understandable, Memsahib Young,' says Passang fluently. 'The plight of women in India today is most hard. Most hard. Women must be kept pure.'

'But what are you going to do with them? There are children in there. They've got no light, no space to run around in. There isn't even a bathroom. I realise you're helping them, by rescuing them from such an awful life,' no harm, she feels, in a bit of flattery, 'but you can't keep them here indefinitely, surely?' And it occurs to her that the women and kids would be out of here immediately, if only they could do the impossible and stump up the cash to bribe their way out.

'Quite right. We be busy tracing their families and then they can return home. All will be well. All will be well. And you? Have you found your Missing Person yet, your husband?'

'No, which is why I'm here. Have you had any leads?'

Passang's eyes briefly cloud over. However, with a smile he orders one of his juniors in Hindi to get something and when the man returns he is holding a piece of A4. Sara's heart quickens.

'We blew up your husband's photo and sent it electronically, along with all the personal details you gave us, to every bureau in India,' Passang says proudly.

He turns the paper to show her. She remembers the photo she gave him, the one of Mike and her at a regimental dinner. This, its pixels dilated, looks nothing like him. In fact, the image doesn't even look human.

And she sees how it is, what a decent man Passang probably is and how the system often defeats him.

'OK. Because look, I was wondering, what with the recent bombing at the High Court and everything, what if my husband was working on the inside, trying to help improve India's bomb-disposal skills, or give advice about—'

Passang's epaulettes seem to bristle.

'Not that you don't—'

99

'It is you Westerners who need advice from us. Terror attacks have been a persistent issue for India since Independence. I cannot elaborate, but we be having much experience, much intelligence on the ground, much technological skills.' He pauses. 'I have to tell you I think it is highly unlikely that your husband, whether overtly or covertly, was helping us with something India has been dealing with, by and large, on the whole, successfully, for over fifty years.'

She wants to remind him that the Delhi police hasn't even got around to installing the much-vaunted CCTV cameras in a highly sensitive place in the capital which was first bombed two months ago. But although she can't explain why, something in what he says rings true. Mike wasn't here for his bomb-disposing skills. Mike was a good man, a man of vision, the kind of man who could imagine apricots as offering a safer future for Afghanistan. A man trading in hope.

❧

Back home, Sara takes Shakeel's scrapbook from where she has hidden it inside her wardrobe and sits on the bed to read more.

One page shows photographs of Indu's cigarette burns which have become badly infected. Shakeel has made a note of the topical cream he received from a compliant local pharmacy, the amount he paid in bribes to get the cream, and the dosage, presumably all for future reference.

Another page is Shakeel's hand-written account of being accosted by a pimp while walking through the narrow lanes of the red light district in broad daylight. It reads like therapy, as though Shakeel was, by putting pen to paper, trying to get the event out of his system. In the beating, he received a badly

100

bruised kidney and cuts to his face. He proudly reports how he told his clinical consultant that he sustained the injuries through a particularly rough game of football. The Shakeel she knows is not at all the sporty type, so she doubts Shakeel's boss was entirely taken in by the story.

On the next page Shakeel writes about Deepti. Deepti has a twin sister who has run away from the brothel, and this has led to Deepti being severely beaten. Apparently some men pay extra to have sex with twins, so the pimps are furious at losing out on this money-spinner. Deepti is terrified the traffickers will return to her village to kidnap her seven-year-old sister in revenge, and bring her to work in Mumbai. Shakeel would love to help get a message to them, but sadly Deepti is so green she can give him no information whatsoever about her village, not even its name.

Sara pads downstairs and shares supper with Rafi. She longs to talk to him again about the temple-brothel opposite their clinic, but the topic got such a ridiculous reaction last time she decides to leave it for tonight. And she isn't sure Shakeel would want his scrapbook discussed with anyone else, so instead she tells Rafi about going to see Passang for news on Mike but how she ended up discovering prostitutes and their children locked up, ten to a cell. 'It was horrendous. They just seemed dazed, resigned to their fate.'

Rafi shakes his head. "The greatest obstacle to India's progress is the very thing that underpins our life here. Our faiths. Or rather rebirth. *Moksha*. The release of the soul from the cycle of death and rebirth. If you are suffering physically, then it is thought that on some level this is your fault, bad Karma for your past. The same goes for mental illness. Mental illness is just something you are meant to endure. Until the next life.'

'So faith teaches people in India to endure? But that's absurd.'

Rafi nods. 'Absolutely. The ball and chain of rebirth.'

'So how do we fight that? How do we say, your religion is killing your people, making them suffer unnecessarily, stopping them seeking help?'

'Exactly. Or, we could say, your religion is keeping people apart, people from different castes who could happily coexist together. How do we lose the unhelpful bits of faith, and keep the rest intact?'

The evening news has started on the television. Delhi is getting back to normal after yesterday's terrorism outrage, which means that today's routine headline is of a village woman who died after being set on fire for giving birth to a girl.

'Oh my God, that's horrific.'

Rafi shrugs as if to say, what do you expect in India. 'It is called a dowry killing. The woman has broken her marriage contract by failing to provide a son.'

'But the family don't get away with it, surely?'

Shoving a post-supper fistful of fried potato into his mouth, Rafi gestures at the television, where the newsreader is revealing that the in-laws have now disappeared, presumed protected by village elders.

Sara tugs vigorously at her necklace. 'Everywhere I look, Indian society neglects and abuses its women. No wonder so many of them are trafficked. It's like no one cares. And even if they do care, the legal system lets them down.'

'Like I always say, the old India is hanging on for dear life.'

'I can't believe you can be so resigned about it all.' And before she knows what she is doing, Sara has stormed off up to the roof terrace.

She and Rafi often go up there after supper, but tonight she leans on the terrace balcony alone. The evening air is close, pushed up from the south of the Bay of Bengal. The weeks before the monsoon are always filled with anticipation, the precise date of it arriving always the subject of intense meteorological and media speculation. The flowers on the trees tremble and people get skittish.

A few minutes later, she hears dried leaves crackle as Rafi steps on to the roof terrace. Tonight, he is sporting new red Ferrari trainers. Rafi is not one to be seen in a dhoti anytime soon.

'Sorry about just now. It's not you I'm getting at.'

Rafi waggles his head sympathetically.

'The thing is, you and I, we have an incredible life here. We eat in amazing hotels with your lovely, well-educated friends, and then we drive home past beggars and lepers, while one block away off the highway, children are being used as sex toys.'

Rafi is silent for a while.

'How can you stand it?' She is, she knows, spoiling for a fight.

Eventually, Rafi half turns to her. 'There's an old story, I don't know if it's true, but it certainly contains a truth. Mother Teresa was once asked how she coped with all the upsetting things she saw around her in Kolkata every day. And she said, *I focus on what's in front of me.* She wasn't ignoring the rest of the shit, she was just acknowledging her limitations. It's all we can do,' he sighs. 'It is all we can do.'

And then Rafi steers the talk to Alok and Rupa, who have got engaged, with the wedding imminent. The recent terrorist attack wasn't exactly the trigger, but it has made the couple think. It has made everyone think; we don't know what the future holds. Seize the day. *And Alok and I thought, why wait and all?*

'Do you think you will get married again?' Rafi adds.

Sara takes a deep breath, holds it, lets it out slowly. 'I don't know. I fear there's a part of me which hasn't quite yet laid Mike to rest. Do you have a girlfriend?' she adds. It would be a shame if those red Ferrari shoes went to waste.

'No,' he says simply, staring ahead. There is a beat and Sara accepts that there will be no more on this subject, or at least not tonight. And then he turns to her and puts a kindly hand on hers. 'I'm just happy to be your Chota-bhai.'

'What's that?'

'Oh, you know. It's one of India's quaint old terms of endearment. Every declension of family relationship has its own special name.'

'Yeah, but how does it translate into English?'

'It means I'm very fond of you. In an uncomplicated way.'

'You're wriggling around something!' she laughs.

'It means I'm the Little Brother to your Elder Sister.'

'That's cute. So what would I be, then?'

'Didi. Sara-Didi.'

She repeats it.

'With a soft d, like *the*.'

'Sara-Didi.' Her heart glows.

The moon is small, but bright. The first dogs of the night are warming up. And under the trees in the lane she can make out a chap unloading the boot of a blue car.

'Fancy a quick stroll? Come with me?' she adds, taking a gamble.

Rafi declines the chance to take any exercise and they say goodnight on the landing.

In the lane she walks briskly away from the house and heads straight for the car. Inside, she is still annoyed at India, where women are patronised and abused and destroyed, and also worshipped and thought to be in need of protection to keep them pure. A country where some states still ban on-screen kisses, where the shameful behaviour of men is ignored and where mixed-class, inter-caste relationships are utterly, completely and stupidly taboo.

'Hello,' she says, softly.

Hemant turns, and for a fraction of a second his expression clouds. Ruined plans must be the bane of the life of a personal driver on permanent call.

'No, it's all right, I don't need you to drive me anywhere.'

Relief bathes Hemant's face and he resumes removing metal boxes with leads and knobs to take them, where? Where does he live? She is like a patient who can't imagine a therapist existing outside the therapy room.

He lifts something heavy to his shoulders, and she is aware of the worked-out muscles, the grey T-shirt lifted up from a flat stomach. He makes for a small building further under the trees. She has never noticed it before, since it sits completely hidden from the house.

She follows him. 'I just wanted to say thank you. For driving so carefully when I was hung-over this morning.'

He sets the load down in front of the building—it is the size of a lock-up garage—and unlocks the door. As it half opens, she catches a glimpse of a tidy room with a bed, neatly made. Hemant's home.

She follows him back to the car. 'Can I carry something? Is there more?'

He grins. 'You want to help?'

'Don't knock it,' she says, holding up her right arm, flexing her puny muscle.

They empty the boot in two more trips, although her presence, they both know it, is superfluous. Finally, they deposit the last items at the entrance to the lock-up.

She must say goodbye now. That is the right thing to do. The muggy air is confused with static, an electric charge sent ahead by an encroaching weather pattern.

'This is gorgeous,' she says, reaching for one of the long-necked instruments Hemant has propped against the wall. She crouches down to stroke its intricate carvings and feels happy. 'What is it?'

105

'It is one of my sitars.' He reaches forward and strums his thumb across a few strings. A haunting, nasal sound, quintessentially Indian, reaches into her gut and catches hold of her breath. Then he picks it up and twangs—she must learn the technical term—a dozen or so notes. Eventually she recognises the melody.

'The Beatles?'

Hemant tilts his head from side to side. '"Norwegian Wood." Can you play?'

Sara gazes longingly at the complicated ladder of keys. 'Not even the triangle!'

Hemant reaches into one of the bags and brings out a flyer, similar to the one currently nesting in her handbag in her bedroom. 'Take this.' She almost doesn't take it—thanks, but I've got one for your gig already—but then she studies it more closely. Music lessons, and a sketch of a sitar surrounded by notes of music.

'I teach on Wednesday afternoons. Come along. No one is born knowing how to play.' And he turns her flyer over, finds a biro and scribbles some words in Hindi, on the back. 'For the tuk-tuk driver,' he adds.

She walks away, clutching the flyer tightly. As she crosses the lane she glances up, sensing movement from the roof terrace, as though someone has just stepped away from the balcony, to be swallowed up by the darkness.

On the landing, Sara passes Rafi on his way to the kitchen for a glass of water. As she's about to switch on her bedroom light, Rafi says something; so softly she almost doesn't catch it.

'He's my driver,' he says, not even breaking step as he continues downstairs, his voice strangely calm for someone issuing a warning.

14

The hours between two and five. When sensible people are asleep. Sara creeps to the top of the house and steps onto the roof terrace. Dried neem leaves prickle her bare feet. It's like walking on nails. *He's my driver.*

The night is close, the patchy mauve cloudiness of the pre-dawn sky stretched out like torn silk. Insects flurry in a plume above the pot plants. *He's my driver.* As if anything would come of it.

Leaning into the wall, she can recall the precise pitch of Hemant's singing, the way the air around him seemed to vibrate and brighten. Hemant's creativity excites her, the way he strums with such masculine ease. Her need for Hemant's touch rolls inside like a wave making for the shore. But she can't. Not here, not in India. *He's my driver.*

Back in her room, she turns once more to Shakeel's scrapbook. Some of the girls—Sara still can't quite believe she is reading about children—prefer working in the temple to working in brothels. Shakeel has scrawled an interview with Indu: *at the brothel, I spent seven months living in an attic. There was no air. I couldn't stand up. There were six of us there. At the temple, I am able to stand upright.*

On another page, a girl called Pragya also speaks of why she likes the temple, *because I can hear seagulls from my room. When a man comes, I speak to the seagulls in my head. They keep me safe.*

Sara blinks and turns the page.

Here is a map, drawn in biro, where Shakeel has drawn the temple in relation to the clinic where he is training.

The temple is round the corner from sites Sara assumes are Mumbai landmarks, the Gate of India and the T.M.P Hotel, which both face the Arabian Sea. Hence the sound of seagulls. Yet it is also—coincidently—near to an area Shakeel identifies as *Kamathipura red light district*. At the bottom of the map Shakeel has written, *A B + D = HIV+*

Sara closes the scrapbook, barely one quarter of the way through. She rolls over on to her back. And it occurs to her how much it must pain Shakeel to pass this information on, a man so proud of his country. She thinks back to the squillion-pound pizzas and the swish cars on the roads. And she thinks about the dazed women and children in Passang's cells and about Akanksha and Deepti and Indu. And about Pragya, whispering to the seagulls to distract herself from being raped.

She leaps off the bed and carries on thinking about the women while she gets ready for work.

⚜

At the clinic, Sara has a quick catch-up with the Art Therapist, a woman who comes once a fortnight to release patients' suppressed emotion through arts and crafts. Apparently Pritti has used up the clinic's entire supply of black paint. But at least Pritti is again leaving her room! Sara thanks the therapist for this helpful information and makes a highlighted comment in Pritti's file.

Sara's next session with Pritti has a suspiciously easy swing to it. The bruises are still visible—they have turned green and yellow—and Sara mentions them only in passing—'I see they've changed colour a bit'—but focuses mainly on being empathic, regaining some of the trust lost.

'So, how are you feeling today, Pritti?'

Pritti vents a stream of consciousness about the imminent monsoon. She is keeping me out, thinks Sara, with a wall of words. Sara's heart goes out to her. What Pritti is really saying is, I don't know how to handle these enormous emotions within me, so don't make me do it. Or if I must, thinks Sara, I must do it cautiously. Still, it is progress that the emotions are coming out at all.

Again Pritti's talk meanders—'I like elephants, when I was little I used to dance in the rain'—and she appears to be taking herself back further in time with her memories, her anecdotes, until quite late in the session she is plumb into childhood, describing a dish her mother would make for her when she was poorly. A sort of milk pudding sprinkled with rosewater.

'It sounds delicious.' Very soothing, very feminine. 'And after your mother left,' Sara adds tentatively, 'what was your favourite thing to eat? When you got ill?'

Pritti starts breathing heavily through her nose, before swallowing hard several times and then standing up abruptly. Her eyes are panicky. 'I don't feel very—' and she rushes to the wastepaper bin and retches.

Sara stands up, passes Pritti a handful of tissues and takes the bin outside. She empties the contents—pale, watery—down the toilet, sluices it out a couple of times, shakes it in the absence of paper towels, and takes it back into the room.

Pritti looks shocked. 'You came back.'

'Yes,' says Sara, placing the bin where it was. Any closer and Pritti might assume she is expected to vomit again. 'How are you feeling?'

Pritti peers over into the bin. 'Where is it?'

'I cleaned it out. It's not a problem.'

Pritti slumps, or perhaps relaxes. 'You will leave soon, won't you?'

Sara breathes in. 'I don't know yet. I have to make sense of something first. But I promise you with all my heart, it isn't about you.'

She can barely finish the sentence. It is the thing she hates most about her work. Saying goodbye to her patients.

'They must be linked,' Sara says to Rafi and Shakeel when they meet later, to review various cases. 'The bruises and the vomiting and the mantra. Pritti is tiptoeing around something but I can't work out what it is. She won't let me in.'

She doesn't need to ask Rafi his opinion, his face says it all. He smiles kindly. 'It is not our job to find all the answers.'

Sara sighs. 'I know. We need to tolerate the unknowns our patients cannot tolerate. To show them it can be done.'

That afternoon, in between patients, Sara eases Shakeel's scrapbook from her bag and sneaks some more reading. She reads cuttings from newspapers, of police raids on brothels, and articles in the *Mumbai Mirror* about government crackdowns on Devadasi: *the number of children trafficked in India for the sex trade is thought to be seven hundred and fifty thousand.* Sara looks for the date of the piece: 2004. God knows what the figure would be now.

She carries on reading, almost in disbelief. In one cutting, a police chief is quoted: *there are no underage girls working in Mumbai.* Shakeel has ringed this heavily in red biro, with multiple question marks in the margin.

She sits back and thinks about Mike. She is sure he would have been as horrified as she is by the things that happen to women here in India. And she has a memory from just before she left for India, of Trevor being called as an expert witness in a trial of men who had groomed women in London. She is aware that women and children are abused and trafficked all over the world, but it is the scale of things here, and the way that desperate families often collude with it all, that deeply shocks her.

≈

Even up until the moment she leaves the clinic, Sara is not convinced she is going to go. And yet here she is, locking her office door, tripping down the lane, the music lesson flyer burning an impatient hole in her bag. Rafi has flown to Mumbai to check on the clinic down there so he won't be expecting her home for supper anytime soon. Yet even so, she was convinced she wasn't going to go.

A tuk-tuk driver outside the metro reads the instructions, with no hint of understanding them. She glances at the alien script from Hemant's hand, the writing precise and beautiful, like notes of music. And it occurs to her that the driver might not be able to read. What a farce. But eventually he nods at her to climb in the back and off they scuttle down the highway, to who knows where, the three-wheeler vibrating alarmingly in the back-draft of gilded lorries.

The class is held in a room in a block painted the popular if impractical Delhi favourite of egg-yolk. Candles glow in copper dishes on the floor. There is another woman present, eyes twinkling behind wire glasses and rolls of fat flopping over her sari skirt. Sara asks her whether this is her first lesson, but the woman speaks no English.

Hemant shows no surprise to find Sara here. In fact he carries three swan-like sitars by the neck which suggests he knew she would come, which slightly riles her. He invites them to sit cross-legged on mats on the floor, close their eyes and breathe deeply to settle themselves. Sara's knee creaks as she lowers herself and she waits for a giggle to burst forth at the ghastly new age-iness of it all, but the posture is surprisingly comfortable and she ceases to be self-conscious. Then he tells them to open their eyes and hands them each an instrument. The sitar is much heavier than Sara expects— her wrist bends alarmingly—but Hemant shows her how to balance it between her feet and knees to offset its weight. They are plainer than the ones Hemant had in the boot of the Merc, but their sheeny teak is deliciously tactile. Taking it in turns, he sits behind each woman and places their right hands in the correct position at the base of the swollen gourd, explaining how this will anchor their technique. His breath over her shoulder is warm and spicy, the grip of his hands on hers confident and knowledgeable. She listens carefully—he is explaining about plectrums and frets and string pegs—and tries to remember to breathe. His body is warm, cupped closely around hers as he demonstrates the finger positions. The thick strings pierce her skin, like tiny snake bites.

At the end of the lesson, Hemant picks up his own sitar and treats them to a raga. In its nasal notes she hears the tale of a stream, or more likely a wandering soul, searching for meaning, meandering yet with purpose. It is shatteringly beautiful.

And when the two women clap and call for one more tune, he lifts his guitar, the scarlet beast, off its bracket. Sara recalls the weight of it in her hand. At one point he appears to bend the music, one note with one upward slide of the finger, the tightest, smoothest vibrato on the string. She gazes at his hands, mesmerized by how much he can do with just his fingertips.

At the end of the lesson Hemant exchanges a few words with the lady in the sari. Whatever it is he is saying delights her hugely. Another satisfied customer.

In the street he hails a black and yellow cab for Sara, and gives directions.

'You did very well,' he says to Sara, as the driver revs up.

'Hardly,' she laughs. 'Cats fighting in a bag, more like.'

He laughs. 'That lady. She has been coming for a year,' he smiles. 'And after one lesson, already you are ahead of her.'

'Don't be daft,' she laughs, and the driver noisily sets off; in her hand a CD of Hemant playing songs he's written.

On the way home, she thinks about what he has said. The woman is probably rubbish on purpose, probably adores having Hemant enclose her in a weekly chaste embrace. Hastily Sara wipes away a tear. Still, thank goodness Rafi is down in Mumbai. Now she won't have to make up a story as to how she has spent the evening, and why she is so late home.

15

Later that week, Sara stares out of the window at the temple. The women in their red and white necklaces sweep and chat. Rafi is clearly completely wrong in saying the place has closed down.

In that moment, her eye is caught by movement at the left. Someone leaving the clinic. Sara would recognise that stoop anywhere. She races out of the clinic.

'Pritti,' she says brightly, loudly. With authority.

Pritti turns.

Sara takes hold of her arm and gently pulls. 'What are you doing out? Where is your one-to-one nurse?' She tugs at Pritti but the patient stands firm, as though her black plaits have rooted her to the spot. 'Come on. You know you're not allowed out on your own.'

'I wanted to find you,' mutters Pritti, or something like that.

'Next time you want to find me, your nurse can bring you. She'll know where I am.'

But Pritti doesn't seem to be listening. She is looking up and down the lane.

Eventually, Sara is able to coax Pritti back inside. That hopeless one-to-one obs nurse is in serious trouble. 'So tell me,' she says, trying to sound casual, 'how did you get out?'

But Sara knows there won't be a coherent answer. *Illusions, delusions, and confusions.*

In between patients, she reads more from Shakeel's scrapbook. She also starts making notes, of questions to ask Shakeel, and possibly Kate, should the topic of sex prove tricky to ask an embarrassed man. At one point he writes about girls who complain of having to endure the two-finger test. Sara jots this down. On a different page he records how sex is such a taboo subject in India that it makes education about HIV/ AIDS difficult: *the men I interview believe HIV/AIDS could be prevented if only the prostitutes would wash their hands.* Sara makes a note to speak to Dr Mathur about running health and sex education classes for local communities.

She finds photos of the girls, tatty ones, creased and torn, and very posed. Young girls with unsmiling eyes looking out to the camera, seemingly resigned to their fate. They remind her of the expressionless pictures she sees in the arranged marriage classifieds in the *Sunday Times*, and of the helpless faces of the women on G.B. Road or in Passang's cells. As she reads through Shakeel's captions she understands that these girls constitute some of the thousands of India's Missing Persons. The families have distributed these photos, in case their loved ones can be traced. And she is aware of how empty it has felt, to have had absolutely no response to her own poster campaign about Mike.

She turns the page. The fuzzy photo from a newspaper is of a young girl, maybe nine or ten, behind the grille of a padlocked gate. The child has short, matted hair, a grubby dress and wide, terrified eyes. The caption for the photo is, *Before the Raid.*

'Your file is extraordinary,' she murmurs to Shakeel in the canteen over lunch.

Shakeel tenses, despite the ready smile.

'Your file was about Mumbai. So, is it the same here in Delhi?'

Shakeel leans across the table. 'Yes. G.B. Road is the big red light district here.'

'I ended up on G.B. Road once. Horrendous place.'

'You went to G.B. Road?' Shakeel looks appalled.

She pulls a face. 'It was by accident. A friend and I got caught up in a demo and the traffic police detour took us right there. I couldn't believe what I was seeing. Our taxi-wallah got pretty spooked too.'

'It is the mafia. They control everyone. That is what makes it so hard to work with the prostitutes on things like HIV. The gangs beat up the girls who refuse to have unprotected sex. Some women are even killed by pimps or clients, and then their families are targeted for compensation by the very people who murdered their child!'

'Rafi is in Mumbai now. Is our clinic down there doing work with prostitutes?'

'We work with a few women, yes. But temples are tricky to deal with. It is like the one in the lane opposite. To suggest that temple women might need medical treatment—'

'So you've tried working with the women at the temple opposite?' She wonders whether Shakeel knows the beautiful woman and her small son.

'I did try when I first came here, but the bosses are very skilled at flying below the radar. They keep a very close eye on their women, keep them mainly out of sight.'

'What I don't understand is how India can be so uptight about sex and relationships, so socially conservative, while prostitution seems so blatant.'

'Women are voiceless. They marry young, they rarely divorce. Above all, women are expected to be pure and monogamous, but not the men. Ultimately, women can't stop their husbands straying sexually.'

Sara recalls some of the notes she made. 'And what's the two-finger test?'

Shakeel's face tightens. Sara holds his gaze, sees the shame in his expression but wills herself to ignore it. She is determined to know everything about this sordid industry.

When he finally speaks, she can barely hear him. 'The police conduct routine examinations of women they take in on raids, or who come to them complaining of having been raped.' He takes a swig from his beaker of water. 'If a woman's muscles down there allow the fingers to be inserted, she is considered to be "habituated to intercourse".'

Sara pushes her uneaten tiffin away, her stomach churning with an image of the women in Passang's cells and the junior sergeant on duty. 'Which means what?'

'It is taken as proof that the woman can't have been raped.'

Sara realises that this is the point when she stops being shocked by the demeaning lives women have in India. She can believe anything, now, and is just hugely saddened. She wonders what on earth she can do to help, and suddenly she has an image of Mike possibly thinking the same thing, and a light bulb goes on in her head. She can picture Mike, unable to father children, drawn to rescue others. Her spine tingles.

She is about to quiz Shakeel some more, when they are joined by Dana. They make space on their table for her tiffin.

'So,' says Shakeel quickly, 'who is planning to see the new Shah Rukh Khan film?'

⊗

Sara is pacing her room, the idea she had about Mike rumbling away in her stomach. She glances occasionally at the column of ivory silk hanging on the back of the door. She is desperate to speak to Kate about this idea, but Kate is not picking up her messages. Presumably this reception tonight at the Ambassador's residence is taking up all her time. Until then, Sara too must focus on work.

Pritti arrives, brought by her new, conscientious one-to-one obs nurse who then takes a seat in the corridor. Pritti is smiling, although the smile is unintelligible.

Sara smiles back. 'Sit down Pritti.' She pulls her own chair round from behind the desk. 'How do you feel after being outside in the lane?'

'Good.' Pritti looks away. Sara can see the rise and fall of her chest.

Sara leans forward in her chair. 'It's OK, Pritti. I understand that you wanted to get away from here. Can you remember what made you want to get away?' If it's someone at the clinic responsible for scaring her, they need to know so they can act quickly.

There is mumbling and Sara has to ask Pritti to repeat herself. 'Sad.'

'You felt sad. What were you sad about? Can you remember?'

Pritti looks up. 'I was happy, too.'

'Happy to be out of the clinic?'

And then Pritti starts giggling, clucking, and rocking on the chair. Her stare is defiant. Stop me rocking, it seems to say. I dare you.

'You're enjoying yourself? Having fun?'

The rocking intensifies. Pritti wriggles around on the chair, excited. Sara watches as Pritti's giggling increases, her voice panting, her eyes shining. Suddenly Sara understands what is happening. Pritti is masturbating on the chair.

Sara flushes hot with embarrassment, to be the voyeur. The wriggling is wilder now, the plastic chair scraping across the lino, the moans getting louder. Then Pritti closes her eyes for the last few seconds and comes with a shriek. She sits panting.

Sara waits until Pritti's breathing has calmed down and she has opened her eyes. 'You look as though you were enjoying yourself,' she says, with as much tenderness as she can muster. Above all, she doesn't want Pritti to feel judged.

It is as though Sara's voice has broken a spell. Pritti's face instantly twists into a grimace and she launches herself at

Sara. Sara yelps, tries to get off her chair, but Pritti is on top of her, grabbing her blouse, her nails clawing the skin on Sara's chest. She tries to grab Pritti's wrists, begging the woman to stop, while insanely conscious of trying to sound professionally soothing.

The door bursts open and the one-to-one obs nurse flies in, seizing Pritti by the shoulders. The nurse is a large woman, mother of six boys. Pritti stands not a chance against such experienced biceps.

Sara sinks to the floor, her heart hammering. But above all her brain is frantically trying to make sense of it all. The masturbation, the orgasm, the abrupt switches in mood. Why today? And why show Sara?

She uprights her chair, drags it to the other side of the table, grabs a pen and tries to write. Her hands are shaking. She has been shown something deeply significant, and she can't process it. At the edge of her consciousness, Trevor— urgently flapping one of his zany ties—is semaphoring something and she can't work out what it is.

16

At six o'clock, Hemant collects her and they drive into the heart of Lutyens' Delhi.

'Thank you for my lesson yesterday.'

Hemant smiles into the rear-view mirror.

She touches the opal at her neck. 'When you play, I feel the music on my skin.'

Hemant half turns round. 'Really? That is incredible.'

Sara wishes he didn't have to concentrate on the road. And she wonders what possible uproar there could be if, one time, she were to sit next to him at the front seat. 'Why incredible?'

'That is why I love playing string instruments. Sitars or my electric guitar, it is so physical. Sometimes, when I am writing music, I play without my shirt on, to feel the new chord sequences as they move across my body.'

She shivers. 'Do you write a lot of music?'

He holds her gaze for a beat and then looks back at the road. 'Only when I am inspired.'

When the traffic snarls up, she stops talking, respecting Hemant's increased concentration. Yet in the silence her brain is in overdrive, combing her memories of him, his fingers pressing hers to the sitar strings, his warm teasing of her Hindi, his chasing after her with the beaded purse that time she left it on the car seat. A smile flutters across her lips.

Two sentries in khaki watch them pull up with polite indifference. Pea lights twinkle in the bushes. Flashing her stiff invitation, she dashes through the doors of an enormous whitewashed villa and sprints past framed photos of

120

ambassadors standing with Thatcher or Indira to enter the packed back garden. Taking up position on the steps to the lawn to wait for her plan to unfold, she pretends to check her mobile. It is not long before she hears the expected restrained commotion behind her.

'Madam. I have a man outside. Says he has your bag, which you left in your car.'

'Oh, of course!' she says, slapping her hand to her head for added verisimilitude. 'Silly me. Tell him to bring it to me, thank you.'

The white-gloved flunkie trots off and, before long, returns escorting a familiar face.

Hemant hands her the beaded case, as once before. 'You really must learn to take your belongings with you when you leave the car,' he murmurs.

'Must I?' she says, scanning the garden. 'Take a glass,' she adds, as yet another tray hovers into view, 'you're my partner tonight.' Her heart begins to beat fast at her own audacity, challenging him, or society, or convention to defy her, rub her nose in their differences. But instead he takes a glass—a non-alcoholic lychee cordial, she notes—and takes his place by her side. She loves that he seems not at all fazed by the lavish environment.

'See that man by the palm tree?' he says.

She peers over.

'He wants to get into politics. However, the girl with him is not his secretary, but his mistress. That could complicate things.'

Trays of canapés glide by. The lamb koftas are moist, the samosas light and buttery on the lips.

'And that man by the fountain?' Hemant never points, he nods in the appropriate direction. 'He is a well-known fillim heart-throb. But in fact he is gay. The studios cover it up in case his box office popularity crashes.'

121

'How do you know all this?' she smiles.

'I am a driver. I watch. I listen.'

She is intrigued. 'What do you mean, you listen?'

'I pay attention to the differences between what people say and what they wish they could be saying.'

So your job is much like mine, she thinks. Accompanying people on journeys, paying quiet attention, keeping confidences.

'Sara!' cries Kate, bounding over. 'Great to see you. And Rafi—?'

'Sadly in Mumbai. This is my friend Hemant. He's—he's a musician.'

'Brilliant. I've got just the person I want you two to meet later. Radhi Chandramouli. Makes documentaries for *National Geographic*. Making a little fillim for us at the embassy. Needs someone good to do the background music.'

'Kate, do you have a minute,' Sara says, with a slight nod to Hemant who takes his cue to go for a stroll. Kate agrees, but her hostess' eyes continue to dart around the party.

'Look, I've had an idea. I'm appalled at what happens to women in India, the dowry killings, the two-finger tests, the sex trafficking. What if Mike was similarly appalled? What if he was helping rescue women?'

Just then, dinner is announced and all Kate's hostessing senses snap to attention, but not before she has whispered to Sara that the idea sounds very plausible, very plausible indeed and that they must speak tomorrow.

Sara's mind is whirring but Hemant is now by her side. Dinner is in another part of the garden and together they walk through a corridor of hedges. At the table, the chat bounces off the frozen apple mojitos and the tandoori sea bass and the cardamom kulfi, about the Slutwalk and the bomb blast and the general decline of Indian civilisation.

'It is dreadful,' says a bald man in a kurta. 'In India today there is too much of everything. Cars, inflation, casual sex—'

'India is out of control,' agrees his wife. 'Have you seen the bags of Lay's crisps? No wonder our kids are obese. We are emigrating to Singapore,' she adds proudly.

'So why don't you stay and make it better?' asks Hemant gently.

'Because the government has lost its grip,' cries the bald man. 'We need strong *boundaries*. Without them, we are undone. You know,' he adds, turning to Sara, 'we need a return to a proper hierarchy. The caste system made our nation strong. People knew where they stood. It is vital to our nation's survival.'

'Caste keeps us too fragmented,' chips in Hemant. 'We remain unknown to each other.'

'I agree with—' a trim historian from Nehru University glances at Hemant's place card, 'with Rafi here. Caste keeps us consumed by our hatred of the *other*. And that is how jihad starts—' He turns to Sara. 'Whereas you two,' he looks back at Hemant now, 'can be a beacon of light with your, if you don't mind me saying, your delightful multicultural relationship.'

She wants to laugh hysterically. 'We're not in a relationship.'

'Oh but we are, Sara,' says Hemant smiling. 'I am your driver, remember?'

And the table roars with laughter at the joke, the man driving the woman—whatever next!—when everybody knows that in a marriage it is always the other way round.

'I heard a joke like that once,' says the historian. 'British Encyclopaedia for sale. Just married; wife knows everything!'

And as the bald man chokes on his brandy and is slapped vigorously on the back by his wife—her expression hinting at the tiresome frequency of the task—Sara finds she has to stare down at the beads on her purse, to stop herself grinning stupidly.

With pillows propped behind her and Hemant's CD playing softly in the background, she turns the now familiar stiff pages and reminds herself of Akanksha and Deepti and Indu and Pragya, and the map of the part of Mumbai near their brothel. In one of Shakeel's interviews with Deepti, she tells him that *over half the girls in my village disappeared. No one ever goes back, so no one knows the lies we were told.* By 2008, the clippings are speaking of figures of over a million women and children trafficked into and around India. Shakeel interviews a patient who claims to come from Bangladesh: *my parents sold me to pay for my elder sister's wedding. We were told I would be a dancer in Delhi. Can you help me run away?*

At some point, in or around 2006, Shakeel obviously starts to download pieces from the internet. Whereas the pages at the beginning of the scrapbook are mainly Shakeel's interviews and drafts for a clinical research paper, with photos and quotes of the girls, now these are augmented with years of overseas commentary. The *Bangkok Post* points out the growing international dimension to sex trafficking: *girls from Nepal are at a premium, but in reality no village in Asia is safe from this dreadful trade.* The *Independent on Sunday* links *monies made from sex-trafficking in the subcontinent to funding terrorist activities in Britain.* The *China Morning Post* runs a four page spread on the connections in Mumbai between drugs lords and the brothel mafia, together with an interview with a self-confessed sex baron who claims sex with virgins cures AIDS.

In August 2007, Indu becomes seriously ill. On 3 August, Shakeel writes down how she is brought to his clinic by one of the madams: *11.04pm, H brings Indu. Indu symps = temp 103.7 headaches, wheezing, dehydr + <u>cough</u>. Chest exam. Abnormal. H refuses to pay for x-ray. 11.38pm, leaves clinic.*

On another scrap of paper, as if what he writes cannot be committed to clinical record, he writes, *Indu suffering acute AIDS-related pneumonia, brothel madam refused both x-ray + admission.* The next clipping is one single cutting, six lines short, from the *Mumbai Mirror*, dated 6 August. Shakeel has placed it on a page of its own, in the centre. Drawn a thick line round it in black: *Police in Kamathipura district last night report finding naked woman dumped in ditch with throat slit. Unidentified. Hospital tests reveal pneumonia. Anyone with information to come forward.*

In the scant lamplight, Sara reads until her eyes hurt, gripped by the horror of it all. She turns the page.

The clipping is very ordinary. She almost doesn't see it, tucked into the centre fold. It is an interview printed from the website of the *Croydon Guardian*, with a woman called Leela: *I was in the brothel for a long time. I don't know how long. I was ten when I went to the market to sell milk. A man I didn't know said I could earn a lot of money for my family working at his hotel in the big city of Mumbai. In the train he drugged me by putting something in my tea and when I woke up I was in a brothel room in a Devadasi temple with thirteen other girls. I started crying and wanted to go home. A girl called Jai slapped me and said if they heard me crying they would slash our faces with razors.*

Some awful fascination makes Sara read on. *A white man started coming to the temple but he only talked. He never did sex things, he only talked. We had to keep this a secret, because the madam wanted us to earn money. He came many, many, many, times. He said he was a soldier and had a plan to help us run away but we had to keep this secret too. He said the people who ran our brothel were bad people and that the money they made from us did bad things all over the world, but that we mustn't tell anyone. He had a plan to pretend to buy us and then take us to another part of the city to be safe. I was one of the girls he saw.*

125

One day the madam came to tell us that some of us were going to start a new life in Dubai. I was very surprised because the man had not said this. He came with a local lady and they took us in a minibus to the other end of the city to Sanjivani Home. I am very happy here. I feel safe. But I haven't seen this man again. I want to say thank you. His name was Andrew. He had funny sticky up hair and he brought apricots for us. He said he came from London. If he is reading this, thank you Andrew.

Something squeezes at Sara's heart.

17

Five thirty am but for Sara, time has derailed. The stamping of her boarding pass and luggage tag at security seems to last the entire day, while the wait in the departure lounge flies by in seconds. Normally at this hour she would be fast asleep, but today her mind is hyper-alert, falling down the rabbit hole. As the steward checks that her seat belt is secure she sends Rafi a text: *Urgent. Please text address of Mumbai clinic.*

If Delhi is hot, sultry, languid, Mumbai is like coming round after ECT. Disorientating. Sara isn't sure her lungs can cope with this much humidity, this much moisture, but her pulse is quick. Sprinting through Arrivals she shows a taxi driver the text reply she picked up surreptitiously before the seat belt signs were switched off.

The traffic jam to the tip of Mumbai is complicated by short if torrential monsoon downpours, turning the streets into choppy rivers ankle deep; it takes her twice as long to travel from the airport to Rafi's clinic as it did to fly here from Delhi. Her mind is so immersed in the cutting in her bag she almost doesn't notice the city with its brooding sky, its battered red double-deckers, its rustling palm trees.

At the clinic reception desk she explains her connection to Rafi and is told that he is off-site this morning at a nearby slum cluster. Sara doesn't trust herself, even with careful directions, to find him. Instead, she texts him, asking him to call her as soon as he can, and goes in search of bottled water and breakfast.

Just two blocks away she discovers Mumbai's waterfront and an enormous stone archway, with two little archways either side. Crowds are taking photos in between showers.

Seagulls cry out and she immediately thinks of Pragya, trying to use their calls to blank out what men were doing to her body. Near the water's edge she finds a sign describing how the Gate of India was built for the visit of King George V, and immediately she can picture Shakeel's biro map. Turning round she sees an ornate, almost Venetian building, in coffee and cream, which must be Shakeel's T.M.P. Hotel. Which means the red light district can't be far away.

Her phone rings. 'Rafi.'

'Sara-Didi. How are—?'

'Are you at your clinic?'

'Walking there now.'

She spins away from the archway. 'Wait for me there.'

'What? Where are you?'

'I'm in Mumbai. I'll explain when I see you.'

In his humid office she pulls out the folded article swiped from Shakeel's scrapbook. Last night she felt a twinge of remorse at violating his scrupulous record, but she got over it remarkably quickly.

'I've found Mike.'

'What? Where?' He takes the article. Eventually he looks up at her. On his face she reads empathy yet caution. 'I don't think I understand.'

'Neither do I, really.'

Rafi looks back at the article, skimming it. 'What I mean is, I know this woman, this Leela, says he was a soldier, but how do you know it is your Mike?'

She wants to say that it is the apricots, and the sticky up hair, known as a cow-lick. But it is not just those things. 'It's his name.'

'But it says here his name is Andrew. Not Mike.'

She bites her lip. 'That was his middle name. And he was passionate about apricots. Obsessed. They were a symbol to him of hope.'

Rafi puts his laptop at Sara's disposal while he sees a patient. Beyond his office, the sky darkens and the deluge begins again—people run for cover, shrieking joyfully—but Sara shuts her ears to it all.

Firstly she sends an email to Kate, telling her about the article and asking again whether the British army ever gets involved with rescuing girls in the sex trade. Then she emails Pradeep to see whether he or his chambers have any links to NGOs in Mumbai who might know about the Sanjivani Home Leela mentions. Pradeep replies efficiently with several names and by contacting two of them she eventually decides it could be the Sanjivani Community Care Home she is after. Pictures on its website suggest work with women, but the entire site is in Hindi, apart from the letters HIV/AIDS.

'Please can you translate?' she asks Rafi on his return.

Rafi leans towards the screen. 'Our stated aim is to rescue children trafficked into the sex trade.' He pauses, reading. 'Looks like they are a self help group, residential, committed to ending the abuse and exploitation, blah blah, we take in girls of all ages, donations welcome, close to the National Park. OK, that is interesting, they are right on the edge of town, in the north of the city. Presumably they have better security up there, so the traffickers won't bother so much to get the girls back.'

'Right, I've got to go there. Will you come with me?' The Hindi script makes her fear she will find it hard to make herself understood.

'Absolutely. When are you thinking of going?'

'Now.'

'Now?'

'Well, when you're done here today.'

'Today?'

'I'm *close*, Rafi, can't you see? This could be my one link to Mike. I'm going, whether you come or not, but I could really use your support.'

'But the weather.' A handy crack of thunder reinforces his case.

'I'm from *England*. We have rain there too. It's what we're famous for.'

'But the roads. It is a torrent out there at the moment.'

'So we'll take the metro.'

Rafi pauses. 'It isn't built yet.'

Sara runs her thumb and middle finger under her eyes, her soul swooning. 'I'm going to get a taxi.'

Outside, Sara stands shivering in the porch with other Mumbaikers sheltering from the latest downpour. It quite shocks her, this abrupt change in meteorology, with its glowering skies and cardigan temperatures and smell of mud. She pulls her pashmina tight. Ahead, people go soberly, steadily about their business, water sloshing around their ankles, as if there is no alternative. As though to wait for a monsoon to end would be a sign of madness.

Someone is pushing the clinic door into her back. She half turns, and finds Rafi.

'You will need a story. I doubt they will let you in unannounced. Security and all that. I shall call them on the way. Say we are from the clinic.' And then he launches into the flood, picking up his feet, until he disappears behind a small clump of palm trees. Minutes tick by and then a taxi putters into view, water pluming out either side like extravagant fenders. Inside, Rafi's trousers are soaked to the knees. He catches her glancing guiltily at his sodden clothes. 'Don't worry. Everyone in India keeps spare clothes at work for when the monsoon breaks.'

The journey takes over three hours, a grinding torture of vehicular slow motion. Sara snoozes for most of it, her early start and maybe the emotion of everything catching up with her. She doesn't so much dream as fret with her eyes closed, a patchwork of missed turnings and failed meetings keeping her in a constant state of semi-conscious frustration.

Yet when Rafi gently nudges her awake, it is as though they have entered a magical kingdom, a dappled corridor of trees and shrubs and sunlight shining on the opals of wet leaves. She wipes the condensation from her window with her sleeve and peers out. She spies small huts surrounded by thatched screens, some of which are draped with shirts and kurtas drying in the sun. Naked babies pat the puddles and young girls plait hair. A hand-painted sign sits on top of a corrugated roof. Sanjivani. Sara feels palpitations at her throat.

A square woman with a plait down to her buttocks steps out of a pale blue bungalow and stands on the veranda. In her eagerness to speak to this woman, Sara thrusts into the driver's hands an exorbitant wedge of rupees.

They perform namaste and the woman says, 'Welcome to Sanjivani.' Sara is so momentarily thrown by the pronunciation, San-JEEV-ni, that it takes her a few seconds to realise she is being spoken to in English.

'Hello, hello,' Sara says. And now she doesn't know what to say. Urgent questions swamp her mind. Did you know Mike? Did he work here? Do you know how he died? And a question she didn't even know she wants to ask: is my husband alive?

The woman introduces herself as Nidhi and invites them in. A guard with a rifle stands to one side. He looks docile, as many Indian security guards do, but Sara wouldn't like to chance it.

Inside the bungalow, the walls of the entrance hall are covered with coloured pencil drawings, of girls crying in rooms with bars on the windows and then of girls gathering flowers or having their hair brushed. In the next room, dominated by a wooden desk, hundreds of photos of girls line the walls.

Tea spiced with cloves is served, in honour of the cooler weather. Sara watches as Nidhi pours. The kind of woman

131

able to set a china cup down on its saucer without making a sound.

'So, how can I help you?'

Sara smiles back, aware that in the question lies its opposite, how might you be able to help us. Sara doesn't mind this. She wants the woman to have only the best interests of the Home at heart. 'I gather you work to rescue girls from Mumbai's red light district.' And she brings out Shakeel's clipping from the *Croydon Guardian*.

The expression on Nidhi's face changes. 'I thought you said you were from a clinic. Are you journalists?' Nidhi glares at Rafi, who is startled by the apparent accusation, and says something placatory in Hindi. Still Sara finds she does not mind. These girls need someone fighting on their behalf. And maybe Mike was a part of it.

'We don't talk about our procedures.' She turns back to Sara. 'We work to change girls' lives, providing health, friendship and education.' And from her desk she brings out a scrapbook, similar to Shakeel's, although not so bulging. Flicking through the pages she settles on one photo and spins the book so that Sara and Rafi can see. She taps the photo. 'Amrita. She has just completed School Certificate. Amrita.'

'Yes,' says Sara. 'Forgive me, but I think my husband was here. His name's Mike,' and she hands over the cutting.

Nidhi's eyes light up. 'Leela,' she says, tapping this photo too.

Sara leans across the desk and points at the lines where it mentions the sticky up hair and the apricots. 'I think this refers to my husband. He came to India and I can't find him and I think he was here.'

Nidhi looks shocked, pushing the article away. 'I can assure you, nothing like that happens *here*. We protect all our rescued girls. It is the cornerstone of what we do.' She rises in her seat, looking in the direction of the guard on the veranda. '*Nothing* matters as much as keeping them safe and away from men who want to abuse them.'

'He didn't abuse them, he helped them,' cries Sara, looking desperately at Rafi, at which point she realises she has no concrete evidence for this, either way. Maybe Mike flipped out in Afghanistan and came to India to rape under-age prostitutes and died of a heart attack, *in flagrante*. Why wouldn't you want to cover that up, as the MOD?

She feels sick. She doesn't know what to think, so she gets up and moves to the wall to calm down. Behind her she is aware of Rafi talking in Hindi. The only words she picks up are Sara-Didi and Mike. She glances at the woman, hoping for an expression of sympathy, but Nidhi's face is utterly unreadable.

Sara turns to the gallery of photos, stapled on to notice-boards covered with felt. Blurred and often creased, they are like the ones in Shakeel's scrapbook, girls alone, staring warily at the camera. Some of the photos here have hand-written labels above them, saying *returned*. There are also a few where Nidhi has her arm around a girl, and several more where the same woman is photographed with different girls, as though she might be a member of staff. Sara feels a flickering in her chest.

Moving quickly she scans each photo, willing a familiar face to leap out and finding, at the same time, that she has completely forgotten—how is this possible?—what that face looks like. It is as though the memory has been obliterated. Quickly she looks back at the line of photos just reviewed. Oh Christ, maybe she missed him. The faster she moves, the more jumbled the features become, the cotton kurtas and the nose studs and the plaits.

And then, 'Oh.'

At the cry, like that of a freed animal, Rafi is out of his chair and behind her. Her eyes are locked on the graceful

133

curve of Mike's cow-lick, as though to glance away for even a second would make him disappear again. But there he is, mid-stride, head and shoulders taller than five young women, in an unfamiliar pale cotton shirt, his sleeves rolled up to his elbow, laughing. He isn't looking at the camera, perhaps didn't know the shot was being taken, but it is him, his blonde hair so bright it is a halo framing his face. He is *this* close to her. She touches his chest, as though to feel it beating. And she is crying and laughing, shaking as though she has found him alive and breathing at last. It is all too blissful and confusing.

'It's him,' she says to Rafi, without taking her eyes off the picture.

And Rafi cups her shoulder, nodding in relieved agreement, unsure as to whether this *is* Mike or some sad delusion, but infected nonetheless by Sara's delight.

'It's him,' she says, to anyone, to her restless soul, to Tom who made it to the other side of grief, to herself.

Nidhi, standing on tiptoe, peers at the photo with reading glasses. 'Ah. *Andrew.*'

'You knew him?' Sara asks, unable to turn from the photo for more than a second.

Nidhi removes her glasses. 'Your husband?'

Sara confirms this. And Nidhi reaches for Sara's hands, clasps them in her own, brings them to her lips and kisses them.

'Where is he?' Nidhi beams. 'Where is Andrew?' And she looks to the door, as if this whole meeting has been part of some elaborate set-up and he is about to walk in.

'He died.' It isn't Nidhi's fault, but the tremulous bubble of Sara's reunion with Mike has now popped and she is plunged back into the real world. This time her tears are of pure pain. This time Rafi's touch on Sara's shoulder is of genuine solidarity.

'My dear girl, I am so sorry. And yet I don't understand.'

'The man you call Andrew died in India, or so Sara-Didi has been told. The article about Leela is the first clue she has had. We thought you might know something.'

'Anything,' adds Sara.

Nidhi thinks back. 'But this was some time ago, yes? We haven't seen Andrew for, I don't know, over a year?'

Sara nods. 'Did he come here a lot?'

'Oh yes. Many times. We are so grateful. So many women saved. So many women we have sent back to their villages, to their families. And for the girls whose families will not take them back, because they believe that working as prostitutes brings shame on the family, we find them work or study.'

'And then, what, he stopped coming?'

'Overnight. It was so sad. I had a message from him, there was to be a party at Dandy's. That was the type of message he always used to leave for us. *Get ready for a party*. So we knew to expect him in his minibus, with some girls. That was the plan. So this time he was coming from Dandy's, a brothel in Kamathipura. But on the appointed day, he never showed. And neither did the girls. I found out very quickly they were still in the brothel, so something must have gone badly wrong at the last minute. I thought at first it might have been the chaos of the terrorist outrage, which occurred around that time. Dreadful time. Mumbai was locked down for days. But even if that was the reason, there would have been other rescues, other deliveries. But after that, we never saw your husband again.'

'Did you not try to get in touch?'

Nidhi glances at her shoes. 'We never had any way of contacting him. He only ever contacted us. He said it was safer that way.'

'Well, was he ill? Did he ever say anything to you?'

Nidhi shakes her head slowly. 'We never spoke about anything other than the girls and what he had found out about

135

them while putting their rescue together.' Sara understands something else. That Mike never told Nidhi he was married.

Nidhi guides Sara back to the desk and pours more tea. 'Do you know how many girls he brought here over the years? Seventy-one. *Seventy-one!*'

'And how did you meet him?'

Nidhi chuckles. 'He came here one morning out of the blue. Just like you! Said he was a businessman. Said he had money to buy girls out of the sex trade and were we interested. He liked that we are out of the main city. We thought he was a god!'

Sara is about to explain that Mike wasn't a businessman but knows that for Nidhi, this is irrelevant. Sanjivani isn't about Black Ops or Special Forces or 'Trigger' and 'Pondy'. Its focus is the girls, girls needing refuge, girls deserving a new life. And Mike facilitated this. She still doesn't know how he died, but he died doing this. This is possibly the closest to the truth she is likely to get. She thinks her heart is about to burst.

Nidhi says, 'I must go now, but please,' she moves to the wall, 'take this.' And standing on tiptoe she unpicks the staples with her nails and hands Sara the photo. 'And stay, look around.' Thunder rumbles in the distance. 'Or come back tomorrow.'

Sara looks at Rafi.

'Well, there won't be many planes out of Mumbai tonight,' he says, gesturing at the weather beyond the window. 'We can ring for a room at my hotel from the taxi.'

Outside, their taxi is starting up. Their driver must have thought Sara's wedge of cash meant Wait and Return.

Sara thanks Nidhi, who leans in for an un-Indian hug. If Mike was going to die anywhere, Sara is pleased to think that one of the last people to see him alive might have been this lady. When she gets back to Delhi tomorrow she will go to the temple, for this glimpse of closure. The scent of cloves lingers on her skin long after they have driven away.

After much negotiation, which includes emphasising his status as a much valued, repeat guest, Rafi manages to book Sara a room at the hotel where he is staying, round the corner from the clinic. But Sara is beyond caring where she sleeps. At last she can visualise Mike, and what he was doing in the end. Rescuing girls. She reaches into her bag and touches the photo. The holes from the staples are like Braille. It is not the truth, but it is a truth, a truth she now knows.

She wants to feel content, but something gnaws away. He died for this, working to save girls. Yet was it worth dying for? Her heart judders.

And how could she have had no inkling? How is it possible he never wanted to share with her this incredible tale, that he had begun to save lives in a different way? How could he not have whispered it to her, when home on leave? She looks down and realises she has been holding the photo so tightly it is scrunched up. She attempts to smooth it out on her knee.

Eventually they reach the tip of Mumbai, and their taxi pulls up in front of the ornate building on Shakeel's map, the Taj Mahal Palace Hotel.

'Terrorists landed by boat right there,' says Rafi, gesturing at the Gate of India.

'Then what happened? Nidhi implied the attacks went on for days.'

'There were eleven separate attacks across the city. Bombs, machine guns, hostage-taking. They knew exactly what they were doing,' he adds.

They wait as their hand luggage trickles through the hotel's security scanner.

'What do you mean?'

'This is the most iconic hotel in Mumbai. Every visitor to the city tries to stay here, what with its views of the Gate and its luxury. By choosing this place, the terrorists were striking at India's leaders, investors and tourists, as well as the city's social elite.'

The low-lit lobby is packed with Japanese tourists, but soon Sara is sinking back on to her bed, spreading her limbs on the cool counterpane, reliving the conversation with Nidhi. Although she is still angry at him for keeping secrets, the fact that Mike died doing something so noble feels like some sort of resolution, and for that she is immensely relieved. And it occurs to her to send an email to Tom. *The other side: I got there in the end.*

Her phone rings. 'Kate!'

'I've just got your email and BBM. I can't believe it. And you saw a photo?' And for one very strange moment both women are laughing through the tears. 'So where are you now?'

Sara glances at the notepad beside the phone. 'The Taj Mahal Palace Hotel.'

There is a beat before Kate says, 'That's brave.'

'I know. Rafi told me the whole story. It's been fully refurbished apparently, but even so. I keep expecting to find bullet holes and blood on the carpet. What a dreadful episode.'

'Ghastly day. Everyone knows someone who died.'

Sara starts doodling on the notepad. 'It's like that conversation we had last night at your reception.' She can hardly believe it was last night, it feels like a month ago, so much has happened. 'So does it make sense to you, that Mike was in the army, but posing as someone else, in order to rescue girls?'

There is another beat. 'I'm looking into it right now. Just don't tell anyone, OK?'

Sara feels the sting of a reprimand. 'Well, it's a bit late for that. Rafi was with me the whole time. He heard everything.'

Kate clicks her tongue. 'Well, let's speak tomorrow. And sleep tight—if you can sleep at all with all the excitement!'

After a sushi supper in the hotel, Rafi retires to make calls. Pining perhaps for her Majestic days, Sara takes a stroll round the hotel's polished shopping arcade. She browses the well-stocked bookshop, buys a souvenir T-shirt to sleep in and some deodorant to supplement the copious teeth-cleaning amenities in her bathroom.

Back in the main lobby, although it seems morbid to do so, she visits the monument to those who died in the terrorist attacks. In one corner stands a glass sculpture, at the bottom of which reads the inscription: *For now and forever you will always inspire us.*

She reads a brief description about the night of 26 November 2008, and learns about the hundreds killed and wounded, about how Westerners with foreign passports were singled out, about the other co-ordinated attacks around the city on a synagogue and a café, the three-day battle with the gunmen, and the programme to rebuild the hotel. The closeness in dates to Mike's death gives her a surge of feeling, a connection to the sheet of glass engraved with the names of the dead, to the small waterfall next to it, and to the memorial book now opened casually at the page signed by Hillary Clinton. There were people mourning at the same time Sara was, people wading through similar tar.

On a table in front of the memorial lies another book, an oblong book. Leather bound with thick cream paper. A Visitors' Book.

But evidently not the current Visitors' Book. This is the very one in use back at the time of the attacks, a relic of the horror.

She flicks back through the pages, 26 November, then the day before. One entry in Japanese characters, a *Muchas Gracias* in the comments column.

And there on 24 November, a hand she recognises, two words grabbing at her windpipe. Andrew Young. And underneath, sharing the same box—the same room, in other words—in an unfamiliar hand but definitely in the same pen, another name. Mira Mittal. A wave of hotness floods her system and she feels herself swaying. Her eyes rapidly scan the glass, darting in every direction until she finds the two names again, her husband's name forever above an unknown woman. *For now and forever you will always inspire us.* Her heart implodes.

⚬

'Did you know?' she seethes. She wants to scream, but in the background she hears Tom's wife Danda trying to soothe a crying baby. Pride stops her sinking to its infantile level.

'Know what?' says Tom. Either he is stalling for time or there is a delay on the line.

'About Mike's girlfriend. Is that what you wanted me to find out? Is that why you told me about India?'

'Sara. Shhh. What are you saying?'

'Mike died in the Mumbai terrorist attack in the Taj Mahal Palace Hotel, where he was staying with a woman. Did. You. Know?'

'No. I mean, that's impossible.'

'I've seen his writing with my own eyes. I am staying in the same hotel—' The weirdness of this freaks her, and she yelps as though in physical pain. 'It makes perfect sense. His whole wretched life here was about secrets.' She is shouting now, doesn't give a toss that jet-lagged guests in the next bedroom can hear her.

She hears Danda demanding the phone, but it is Tom's voice which remains on the line. 'Sara, listen. I can't believe he was having an affair. He adored you—'

Does he really think she believes him, clutching at straws again?

'I only wanted to help. You've been so stuck.'

'Grieving a man who had a secret life, a secret woman.'

'No. Not Mike. Not Mike.' As though he really has no idea. As though he really needs his best mate to remain the hero.

She drops the phone. Briefly it occurs to her to ring Pradeep, instruct him on her behalf to see the paperwork, the hospital records. But after all she has seen of Indian bureaucracy, what would be the point? She is drowning, her lungs sore, fighting for air. Every few seconds she has a soothing image of Mike, of his smile, his generosity of spirit, his stable presence in her life, which is then immediately forced aside by the sickening discovery that this version is flawed. Which version can she trust?

She flees her room. Outside the hotel, she crosses the street in a daze, jaywalking through the gridlock of limos and taxis blasting their horns. In front of her stands the Gate of India, staging post to royalty and terrorists alike. Swatting at midges, she stares at its solidity. She waits for the tears to flow again but, for now, something more neutral has taken hold. Gradually her breathing normalises and she doesn't feel quite so suffocated. Yet she is now certain of nothing.

Mike must have walked round this structure too, heard the gulls, smelled the fried snacks. She doesn't want to think about it, but she can't help herself, Mike and Mira, Andrew and Mira. Maybe they strolled here hand in hand. Maybe he convinced himself that rescuing women justified lying to his wife, in which case he was lying to himself. All the humidity in Mumbai, and she is actually shivering. What fresh hell is this, seemingly back from the dead only to drive a new blade through her heart. So many women saved, and her destroyed.

Child hawkers crowd her, touting postcards of the arch, and lurid coloured sweets. Eventually Sara gives in to their pester power and bends to look at the knick-knacks spread out on plastic sheets. Some of the bracelets appear to be made from irregular seeds, drilled and threaded with black twine, and then painted various colours. She picks up a red one, tests it against her skin for no reason at all. She is hardly going to buy souvenirs here. And then she sees a white one. Red and white. The colour of the necklaces worn by the Devadasi.

'*Yeh kit ne kah hai?*' She holds up two fingers. The girl names her price.

Reaching into her bag she sees the Sanjivani photo. Looking away, she fumbles for some loose notes and hands them over. The girl on the plastic sheet insists on tying the bracelets on, her dark fingers strong and wiry, fluttering at Sara's skin like a tiny bird. It is hard to imagine such a fluttering touch bringing the comfort it does.

With the crowds out relishing a rare dry evening, she joins the surge round the Gate to the waterfront. At her feet, she hears the gentle slap of seawater against the stone of the harbour wall, but ahead is only darkness. The future feels dreadfully heavy.

In the beginning she thought she came to India to find out where Mike died, the actual inch of ground, as though this would be healing, like someone nudging the needle of her stuck record. Months ago she grieved for Mike but also for the end of her marriage. Now she is grieving for the loss of the man she thought she knew, and a marriage that feels increasingly like an illusion.

142

What she wanted to believe was that knowing where Mike died or how he died would change everything. And it has been easier, lately, to let him go, knowing he died in a country which has nourished her, which she has grown to love. But what she sees now is that there is no one concrete moment of loss, no one defining moment of closure. Instead there are a million moments, of joy as well as pain, but that the single truth is that Mike is dead. When Tom was telling her about talking to his stroke-felled father, she wanted to ask, how do you get there, how did you pass over to the other side of loss? And now she knows. You get there by not fighting it, by accepting it, by accepting the only truth that counts. By creating your own closure.

She opens her bag. Her heart jolts, to see the blonde cow-lick again. Photos of him around the house in London have long ceased to have impact, out of familiarity. Photos of Mike hitting a six, of them sipping honeymoon cocktails, or signing the register. Photos which once meant so much, evidence of happiness and pleasure, a validation—hopefully—that she was once loved.

But this photo, this is a permanent reminder of a man she never knew existed, a man who looks exactly like her husband but with crucial chromosomes altered, a kind, loving man who danced with grannies at weddings, a man inspired by the apricot growers of Afghanistan, yet a man capable of secrecy and lies and therefore marital disrespect.

She brings out the photo. So flimsy, and yet so disturbing. How much would she give now to have never come to India, to have never read Shakeel's scrapbook, or taken that flight to Mumbai. She looks about her. Couples, families, even two Japanese businessmen, hold out their phones and wait for smiles. Memories of the good times, moments to be captured for posterity.

She feels on the very edge of things. Holding the shiny paper she tears her photo in half, into four, eight, sixteen, and holds the pieces over the low harbour wall. And in a gesture to the past and all that has happened, but also as a sign that this is a line finally crossed, she drops the pieces one by one on to the black water.

18

Rafi looks up from his dosa and sambal. 'Don't you want breakfast?' he gestures at the chair opposite. 'Don't you want to go back to Sanjivani this morning? I could go with you. My flight to Delhi isn't until this afternoon.'

'I think I've got a mild dose of dysentery, so I'm flying straight back to Delhi.' My patients, she adds, deeply conscious that she has rather abandoned Pritti and the others for what has turned out to be this horrible wild goose chase over Mike.

She tries to avoid Rafi's gaze. Surely he can see the facial evidence of her sleepless night. But—and if there is one thing Sara will always remember, it is this kindness of Rafi's tact today—he simply rises, clasps her shoulders and says, 'Sara-Didi. There is always sunshine tomorrow, and we all get our share.'

Sara can feel her eyes welling up.

'Although probably only in India,' he grins. 'Not sure it always holds true for somewhere like England!'

On landing at Delhi, Sara phones the clinic to say what time—traffic permitting—she will be in, and then listens to a voicemail from Kate. She braces herself and twiddles her necklace. She swings from picturing Mike singing Afghan ballads, outlining his dream of investing in an apricot farm or running a hand through his cow-lick, to recalling with a violent lurch to her stomach his increasing withdrawal from her and the two names carved on the memorial. In one way his infidelity seems absurd, and in another it makes perfect sense.

'Hello,' she says cautiously, on Kate's pickup.

'Hello lovely, how are you feeling? I bet you didn't sleep a wink!'

Sara mumbles that yes, it was rather an odd night.

'Listen, email me everything you found out in Mumbai. Any information at all.'

Sara is trying very hard to blank out the bits of information she won't be passing on.

'You never know what might be useful and what not, so best to chuck it all in.'

Efficient commands fall from Kate's lips, but Sara isn't really listening. The last thing she needs is Kate worrying away at the topic.

So she politely ends the call and spends the rest of the journey to the clinic drafting a simple prayer to utter at the temple, suitable for an ending. Then she retrieves her e-ticket to London from an email on her phone and saves the relevant phone number in order to contact the airline when they open later today. She will close her work with Pritti, say a fond farewell to Kate and Rafi and Hemant, and leave India. And as though this has already happened, she finds herself gazing wistfully at the Delhi street scenes—the litter, the cow-shit, the traffic jams—as though memorizing it all for the very last time.

❧

As soon as Sara steps from the taxi it is clear that any healing trip to the temple will have to wait. Dana is waiting for her in the lane, bobbing on the balls of her feet.

'Pritti has gone missing.'

'What?' Sara dashes in to the clinic, Dana following hot on her heels. 'Where was her obs nurse?' Sara demands of the ward staff. They stare at their painted toenails. On a toilet break, apparently. 'Did you tell Pritti I was coming back today?'

Apparently so.

'So, Pritti waits several days, while the clinic is two senior staff short, and then absconds the day her therapist returns? Anyone would think it was for maximum impact.' Sara smacks the wall with a Manila folder. If only, in more senses than one, she hadn't gone to Mumbai.

For the rest of the morning, she tries to put thoughts of Mike's secret life aside and instead listens to meagre police reports of what has been done to try to find Pritti, the loudhailers used, the places searched. She also throws herself into soothing the patients left disturbed by the woman's disappearance, all of whom seem delighted for a change to talk about someone other than themselves.

'So Deepak, how are you feeling today?'

Deepak's alcohol detox has not been going well. His bloodshot eyes still droop halfway down his face. His theory is that Pritti has been kidnapped by her own family, to pay off a debt.

Sara tries to retain a degree of therapeutic neutrality, and fails. 'What do you mean, pay off a debt?'

Deepak shrugs, as if this kind of thing happens in his world all the time. 'Someone in the village owes money. They can't pay. They give their virgin daughter—' (she notices the relish with which he says this), 'to the man calling in the debt, and the debt is cancelled. Of course, if you find Pritti and bring her back here, then the debt transfers to you. They will come after you for the money. And if you don't pay—' he mimes slitting a throat.

'So Manu, how are you feeling today?'

Manu lost her parents in a stampede at a temple in Jodhpur, so she went to live with her brothers. One of them raped her and when the other brothers—or rather, their wives—found out she was pregnant yet unmarried, they threw Manu out. Last month she was picked up, hiding in a goods yard. She had lost the baby. Manu and Pritti are known to be quite close, a relationship Sara has long been nervous about, given that Manu has lately been found inhaling detergent stolen from the clinic's cleaner.

Manu's theory, presumably based on her own experience, is that Pritti is pregnant. Sara racks her brains as to whether she has noticed any changes in Pritti physically, but then her pulse skips a beat to recall the session when Pritti vomited.

'And where might she go, if she was pregnant?'

Manu isn't sure, but probably Las Vegas. Or the moon.

'Kanan, how are you feeling?'

Kanan is typically measured and reflective. The clinic has been talking to her recently about having skin grafts for the acid burns on her arm. She has even been in discussions with Dr Mathur and the Art Therapist about setting up a stall on the highway and selling some of the pottery the patients make in Arts and Crafts. Despite her modest background, Kanan is showing a head for business and an inspiring streak of get-up-and-go. Sara suspects Kanan is the sanest person in the clinic, including the staff.

'How do you feel, about Pritti gone?'

'I'm scared for her. India is brutal to its women. But she was constantly looking for ways to escape.'

Sara knows this to be true. She remembers the time she caught Pritti leaving the clinic unattended, and the time she became violent and had to be restrained. 'What was that about, do you think?' she adds, swallowing the guilt for blurring the therapeutic boundaries.

'Miss Sara,' smiles Kanan. 'You know that as well as I do. All Pritti wants is to find her mother.'

❧

Sara leaves the inpatient ward, the security grille clanging shut behind her, and tries to work out where Pritti would go to find her mother; and how, on no money. Yet blundering into her brain is Mike's handwriting and the grenades of those two words, Mira Mittal. How long had they known each other, and what did she look like? Was she able to give Mike the deep closeness Sara feared? Sara tugs so hard at the opal at her neck she almost breaks the chain.

Two flights of steps back down, and the sweat slides down the inside of her thighs. The stairwell is Blu-Tacked with stained notices urging patients to continue taking their medication. At the bottom of the stairs she reaches into her bag for a bottle of water. Empty. She steps into the scorching sun and crosses the courtyard. Sara unlocks her office door and shoves it so hard it bangs into the wall.

After lunch she tries to flesh out her notes about Pritti. She doodles on the page, and for several moments at a time is able to forget about yesterday's discoveries. Something tickles the synapses of her brain but it won't come. She stares at the wall opposite, where a dent the shape of a door handle stares back at her with contempt. Pritti and Mike, fighting it out for space in her head. How hard are the police trying to find Pritti? And did Mike love Mira? And in that moment she understands that she has been wounded by what seems like a lifetime of tall tales, by the ground constantly shifting beneath her; like her mother's stories about her absent father, stories which have never hung together, which rarely made sense. Lies, basically.

149

She gets up, her heart racing. What if Pritti believes she is being lied to? And what if the person she thought had lied to her most recently was Sara, Sara the mother figure, who suddenly one day ups sticks and disappears?

Sara crosses to the window and starts talking to herself, trying to put a jigsaw puzzle together in her head. 'What if Pritti's recent disturbances—the vomiting, the attack, the attempt to abscond—are in fact signs of a woman getting in touch with her feelings, groping her way towards health?'

The blue Mercedes pulls up between the clinic and the temple. The airport run is evidently complete. The back door opens and Rafi emerges, his face that of a prisoner back once more outside his old jail. Hemant is already at the boot, removing matching designer briefcase and holdalls. The sight of Hemant in chivalrous mode weakens her.

Sara is about to turn from the window when beyond the car she notices movement, a watching woman, half-hidden behind one of the pillars at the entrance to the temple. Her punished frame, the line of her neck, the intensity of her leaning. If she was any closer Sara would be able to see the wisps of honey hair unravelling. Hemant and the luggage are now following Rafi into the clinic and the woman turns around, tucking stray tendrils back into a loose bun. Sara's stomach falls away.

⚜

Early evening and Pritti has still not been found. Staff on their day off have been summoned back in, and the police have arrived to take statements from staff and patients. Rafi is unconvinced this will help matters and Sara, remembering the general air of good-natured incompetence at Passang's station is inclined to agree. Still, a woman with no money has evaporated. The one oddity is the family. Sara keeps waiting for

Pritti's uncle to arrive, demanding action. Keep us informed, they say flatly, on the phone. But no one bothers to come in person. It is as though they are glad to be shot of her.

Towards the end of the day, Rafi appears at her door. 'So what is your gut feeling about Pritti?'

'Obviously, I'm terrified something awful has happened to her.'

'Counter-transference,' says Rafi. 'You are feeling what she is feeling.'

Sara nods. 'I know. But what is Pritti afraid of? And in the transference, I've become her mother, the mother who disappeared, who waltzed off without a word. It was while I was away that Pritti absconded.'

Sara locks her office and they leave the clinic. Rafi says, 'Why don't we grab something to eat on the way home, to celebrate you finding Mike yesterday. There is a new Brazilian at the Sheraton. Or Barkha says the Lebanese at Hauz Khas is good. I can get Hemant to drop us anywhere you want.'

She still can't bring herself to tell Rafi about what she found at the hotel after he'd gone to bed. Or not yet. 'Do you mind if I make my own way home?'

Rafi agrees—*absolutely*—that it has been a long day. That maybe another restaurant supper is the last thing he needs.

They part, leaving Sara alone in front of the temple. Twelve hours ago, before the revelation of Pritti's escape she had intended to say a prayer, to say goodbye to Mike for good. But that would mean remembering. And right now, she doesn't want to remember.

Briskly she sets off down the lane towards the metro on the highway. Behind her she hears the clunk of a door closing and the streamlined sounds of a Mercedes pulling effortlessly away. At the cluster of tuk-tuk drivers, she turns to wave at it, but the dull blur of streetlights makes it hard to see whether either Rafi or Hemant has seen her.

She isn't sure where she wants to go. To one of the shopping malls maybe—the biggest in Asia!—or to a movie. Mike is in her head on a loop, the twin notions of him as someone who lied to his wife and someone who rescued women fighting for space, for clarity, for supremacy. And now crowding into her head are the women not rescued, Akanksha and Deepti and Indu, and the women in Passang's cell and the girl in pink polyester sucking her thumb. Women in desperate need of rescue.

'G.B. Road,' Sara says, sliding the opal from side to side.

The driver coughs. You can tell he wants to challenge the request, as though it is somehow a commentary on his own predilections. Or maybe he just fears for her safety. He mutters something to his fellow drivers, who look similarly disgusted. She pulls out a wad of rupees. 'G.B. Road,' she barks, before her courage runs out.

G.B. Road at night, she discovers, is a more manic version of itself at dawn. There are more girls plastered in make-up, more madams sweeping, and more men cruising. She doesn't see actual assignations, but she does see girls escort men into buildings or down seedy passageways.

She taps the driver on the shoulder; she will get out here. Up close, the area reeks of sex and sweat and rotting food. At a mom-and-pop convenience store she buys half a litre of whisky, unscrews the cap and takes a swig. Then she walks up and down the road lined with waiting women. Some have the glazed focus of a drug-fuelled stupor. Outside one property stand two girls, plastered in make-up, welts on their arms, playing pat-a-cake. Sara turns away, awash with sadness.

The pimps and brothel owners stand in doorways, whispering to each other, staring at her, a white woman. One bold lad falls into step with her and asks, *You want Nepali girl?* Another asks if she is a journalist. Maybe she should pretend to be. But if she was, would the girls talk to her?

And if they talked, what would lie in store for them? And she remembers Shakeel's scrapbook with the newspaper cutting referring to the prostitute, presumably Indu, found in a ditch with her throat slit. A woman who maybe had once been seen talking to Shakeel.

She takes another swig of alcohol, and her sinuses sting. She looks at her watch. She has been here nearly two hours and she still isn't sure exactly why she has come.

Three girls sing along to tinny radio music.

'Hello,' Sara says, holding tight to the neck of the whisky bottle.

'Hello,' they repeat, all high voices and painted smiles. When they catch Sara looking at the bruises on their legs, they tug their skirts lower.

'What's your name?'

'Nita.'

'And yours?'

'Mita.'

She looks at a third girl.

'Gita.'

She doesn't believe that for a minute. 'And how old are—?'

'Nineteen,' the girls say quickly.

A madam comes lolling over. 'Welcome, lady. You want something?'

'I was just asking how old these girls—'

'Nineteen.'

Sara glares at the woman. 'Right. And how old are you?'

'Twenty. Twenty…five.'

"Twenty-five? Right." And the rest.

The madam lays a fat hand on one of the girls' shoulders.

'And are you well?' Sara asks Nita or Mita or Gita.

'Very well madam.'

Sara crouches down. 'Do you get sick? Are you worried about getting a disease?'

The fat hand is pulling at the girl. 'Nothing to say.'

'And where are you from?'

'Nothing to say.'

'What? They're nineteen and they aren't allowed to speak to me themselves?'

The madam yells out something. A man strides out of the sub-continental gloaming. His teeth are stained with red paan. In broken English he asks, 'What be your business?'

Sara stands up. 'I'm interested in the health of these girls.' She is conscious of a small crowd gathering, of lots of chatter in Hindi.

'Very healthy. Very healthy girls,' says the man, standing in her face.

Another man steps forward. The madam shrilly gives her version of events. The paan chewer pushes Sara roughly away.

'Don't touch me,' she says, more sharply than she means to. Everyone is watching her closely, and for a moment Sara sees herself through their eyes, a white lady asking awkward questions, possibly losing them income or getting them thrown in prison. Someone spits at her. The blood red betel juice lands on her foot.

The ageing madam has reached hysteria pitch. Other men, possibly clients, start to jostle Sara. Sara puts up her hands and walks off, fresh whisky on her lips.

As she walks, keeping to the well-lit parts of the street, she imagines, from the increased presence of madams and pimps on the pavement, that word has got around. She picks up speed, hoping to outrun the gossip. The whisky is warming her blood.

Someone grabs fiercely for her hand. Sara tries to break free. 'You doctor?'

Sara looks down. 'Sorry, no.' Then she sees the urgency in the girl's eyes, registers the ill-fitting sari. 'I mean, yes. Sort of. Are you OK?'

154

'Yes. But my sister, no. Very sick. Help us.'

'Sick?'

'In bed. Very thin. No eat. Help us please.'

'Help you escape?'

'No, help her get better again. Earn money again.'

'It's better you try to leave.'

'It is better to get money than have wet man play with his thing in you for free.'

Sara's heart aches. 'What's your name, little one?'

'Swarti.'

'And how old are you, Swarti?'

A madam waddles over, calling for Swarti. In front of her tiny body, where the madam cannot see, the girl splays her fingers, all ten of them. The madam draws her income source away from the foreigner, cuffing the child sharply around the head.

Sara's eyes rim with tears and she walks away, hating herself. Ten years old. If she could, she would grab the girl—the *child*—and take her home right now. And she has a vision of Mike picking this girl up easily, in a fireman's lift. That noble side to him she wants desperately to hold on to.

Standing in a dim doorway, she types notes into her mobile phone while the events are fresh in her mind. When finished, she sets off, glancing back at where she last saw Swarti. Through an open doorway she glimpses the child bent double under blows from the madam's hands. Sara steps off the pavement, yelling at the madam to stop.

The people who surround Sara, who hit her, who cause her to choke, are here one minute, gone the next, walloping her, shoving her, pitching her forward into smelly rubbish at the kerb. It takes Sara several seconds to realise what is happening, that she hasn't just been accidently bumped into, but is being slapped, kneed in the kidneys, kicked in the shin, smacked on the shoulder, and pushed to the ground.

Something cracks her around the head. She shields her head with her arms and is hit sharply on the elbow. She cries out, a taste of blood in her mouth. Suddenly this stretch of busy road is utterly empty. At her ankles, the bottle of whiskey lies smashed on the road, the shards of glass like scattered diamonds at her feet.

She stumbles, aware of a soreness at her neck, like whiplash. And she is weeping now, not for herself but for Mike, in case he too was ever beaten up for trying to rescue children. Mike, wonderful Mike, how can she ever apologise enough?

And all of a sudden Hemant is there, pulling her upright. Together they hobble to the car. The familiar scent of his ironed clothes makes her want to cry. Wincing, she slumps into the back seat.

'Are you badly hurt? Shall I take you to hospital?'

She doesn't feel too damaged—it was a warning, nothing more—but she is dizzy, bruised and definitely drunk. She can barely get the sentence out. 'How did you find me?'

Hemant shrugs, but he is out of breath, as though he has been chasing something.

An idea pops into her head. 'You came here to meet a girl!' she slurs.

His face darkens. 'I went back to the tuk-tuk drivers at the metro. They told me where you had gone.'

Her addled brain is struggling to keep up. 'Why?'

'You shouldn't come to places like this. It is not safe.'

'Yeah, well imagine what it's like for the girls working here, every day. I'm all right, I've got you to rescue me. Who do they have?'

He presses his foot on the accelerator. He is not the petulant type—he has the perfect temperament for negotiating Delhi's vehicular chaos—yet tonight, something simmers, so much so that Ganesh, the bronze elephant statue below his dashboard, seems to be alive, pulsing with energy. 'They don't care, about you or the girls. All they care about is making money. Next time, they will throw acid in your face.'

She is weeping again, knowing he speaks the truth. 'I hate it here. India. I hate it, the way women suffer.'

Hemant passes back a gilt box of tissues. 'Life in India is hard. People have no money or they have no home or they have no independence. But we are alive. That is worth celebrating, yes?'

She blows her nose. 'I suppose so.'

'Forgive me, I did not mean to be so outspoken, but—'

'No, you're right. Go on.'

'My father is a tuk-tuk driver, my mother keeps house. I have three older brothers, who are in Dubai. Construction. My parents want me to move there, my mother worries I will end up like my father. And there was a time when I think I would have gone. But now my mother spends all day looking after one of my cousins. My cousin is not well, I think you call it cerebral palsy. She was thrown out by her own family so my parents took her in. Much of the money Rafi gives me, I give to my parents to pay the hospital bills.'

'I'm sorry, I had no idea—'

Hemant waves her comment away. 'I am just saying, everyone has their own hardships. Now you. Tell me about your life.'

So she tells him about her mother's death in the hospice and about Mike being in the army, and about his death and the funeral and the medals. And about Tom's visit. 'He told me Mike didn't die in Afghanistan, but in India.'

His eyes lock on hers in the rear-view mirror. 'So that is why you came to Delhi?'

Sara nods.

His hands tighten on the steering wheel, his knuckles turning pale. 'But it must be like a wound opening up again.'

157

If only he knew. If only she could bring herself to tell him about Mumbai. 'I don't know what to do.'

'I guess that depends on what you want.'

She doesn't understand.

'We all want truth. In India, we demand truth from our government. Who attacks women, who plants bombs. But what if there is not one truth, but many? You already have one truth. Your mother is dead. And your husband is dead.'

When Hemant puts it like that, factually—decently—for some surreal reason it doesn't sound nearly so dreadful, nearly so insurmountable.

'Grief reminds us to go out into the world and serve the living,' he adds, his fingers instinctively stroking the bronze statuette of Ganesh beneath his dashboard.

'So our philosophies overlap,' she says, quietly.

Hemant looks at her curiously.

'In my therapy world, the past is always with us but this can also inspire us to live more fully. And that's how you live?' she adds, just to make sure.

'I live in the present moment. I live for the joys in the present moment. Like now,' he adds quietly, for once not quite catching her eye.

At the house, he helps her out, proffers his arm. She tries to drape hers around his shoulders but misses. Instead he cups her elbow and walks her to the house, slowly. At the door she leans forward and tries to kiss him, or thinks she might have done. He rings the doorbell, hands her over to Rafi, points out all the cuts which need washing with antiseptic, and then bids them both goodnight with a deep, employee's namaste.

19

In the morning, Sara avoids Hemant's gaze in the rear-view mirror. Her mind is all over the place. She wants to apologise profusely for the dreadful state she was in last night, and to thank him for his tender care, but she cringes to think of the kiss, if indeed she did kiss him. It is an enormous relief to find him still employed, to see that Rafi hasn't fired him for *her* lapse of judgement, but all the same, she wishes he wasn't currently driving her.

She slinks down in her seat. Thank God she's decided to leave Delhi and all its complications, although she hasn't yet got round to contacting the airline. Even so, she has an image of arriving at Heathrow Customs surrounded by girls from G.B. Road. Anything to declare? A dozen prostitutes.

She taps her phone. In the night, when a raging thirst and a bruised hip forced her to get up for a glass of water, she scoured Shakeel's scrapbook, for any information about raids or rescues. And it occurs to her that Kate is one of the few people she knows who is likely to be able to wangle senior level, reliable contacts with the local police. And so she weighs up the pros and cons of phoning Kate. Kate who, she suspects, will want to quiz her again about heroic Mike.

She can sense Hemant trying to catch her eye in the rear-view mirror.

'How are you feeling this morning?'

She flinches as, in his focus on her, he inadvertently drives over a pothole. 'A bit sore. But as you said last night, I'm alive! That's what matters.'

He smiles. 'What you did last night. Going to G.B. Road. I think you were very brave.'

'Mad, more like!' And in that moment she is reminded of Trevor's warning, of the India Psychosis, where a traveller becomes so consumed by their quest they lose touch with reality. 'I think,' she says, half to herself, half to Hemant, 'that all my life, I've been trying to protect myself from being hurt.'

Hemant looks at her quizzically.

'Staying slightly detached. It's been the perfect way to live if you're a therapist. But maybe not if you're a wife.' And she smiles, at how Hemant's car has started to become her couch.

She calls up Kate's details on her phone and her fingers scurry across the keyboard. She suggests a quick chai at the Hyatt and gets Hemant to make a detour.

'Hello lovely.' Kate swishes in, in a lemon sari. Her arrival sends waiters into frenzied activity. 'I'm dying to hear all about Mumbai. Did you send me that email? I don't think I've seen it.'

'No, sorry. One of my patients has gone missing. And last night I got into a bit of a fight.'

'Good grief. A fight?'

Sara tells Kate about going back to G.B. Road, about the girls she saw there and about getting beaten up.

'You went alone?'

Sara nods.

'You're mad. Why? You saw what it was like when we accidentally ended up there together.'

Sara stirs her sugarless tea. 'I don't know really.'

'Sara. I'm serious. The people who run the sex trade, this is a war for them. This is dangerous stuff. You rescue a girl and you're taking away their profits.'

'That's hardly the point, surely?'

160

'No. What I mean is, they play dirty. If they need to kill, they will.'

Sara blinks. 'Do you think Mike was murdered? By the rape trade mafia?'

Kate purses her lips. 'No,' she says slowly. 'I think the irony is, he got bitten in the arse by a terrorist operation no one saw coming. No one in London, anyway.'

The mundane nature of this chills Sara. 'What, you mean right place, wrong time?'

Kate sips her iced tea and waits for Sara to absorb this sad news. Eventually she says, more brightly, 'So, tell me about Mumbai.'

With a jolt, Sara sees again Mike and Mira's names cosying up together in the Visitors' Book, and wonders whether the city's name will always trigger this Pavlovian reaction. Pushing this ugly image away, she tells Kate in great detail about the trip, the monsoon, the slow traffic, the Home, the guard on the veranda, and the drawings in the lobby. She talks about Nidhi's description of the code phrase about getting ready for a party, and about the photo gallery of girls rescued, and how Mike had rescued over seventy. And she describes showing Nidhi the article from the *Croydon Guardian*, which talked about 'Andrew's' gifts of apricots for the girls, and how Nidhi had recognised Leela's photo.

'Don't suppose you still have this cutting?' says Kate, casually. 'Did Nidhi mention any other names? Mike's contacts? People he might have gone to Sanjivani with?'

'No, there was no one else.'

'And in terms of security, you only ever saw one guard, on the veranda?'

Sara nods.

'And just to be clear, Mike only got in touch with her, not the other way round?'

161

'With the code phrase, yes.' She can imagine Kate mentally scribbling. Why?

But in an instant she can see why. Kate is using her, just as she once used Kate, to unpick Mike. Mike, who was working undercover. Mike who must have had masses of information. Brothels, mafia bosses, trafficking routes, dates. Maybe the information was all in his head, or maybe on a memory stick. Either way, it must have been lost when the Taj Mahal Palace was attacked. And now Kate, warm and friendly Kate. Can she still be trusted? Or does she need to be distracted?

Sara catches her breath. 'Nidhi thought I was saying Mike came to have sex with the girls, so she got really offended,' Sara wipes away a tear, 'which at the time I thought was a ridiculous thing to think about Mike. But then we went to the Taj and it turns out I didn't know him at all.' She grips her glass of tea. 'Mike was having an affair.'

'What? No!'

'He was sharing a room with her in the Taj.'

'What do you mean? Who? How do you know?'

'They wrote their names in the same box in the Visitors' Book.'

'But the things you've told me about him, you sounded so good together.'

Sara keeps silent.

'And it couldn't have been a friend visiting him? A relative?'

How is it possible that after discovering so many secrets, Sara cannot interpret this any other way, cannot stop blaming herself, that she let her husband drift away. Sara shakes her head. 'It was an Indian name. Mira Mittal.'

Kate gasps in sympathy and reaches out, clasping Sara's hands tightly across the table. Sara can feel the woman's lively pulse. 'And now it makes sense of everything, his remoteness, the lies.'

'Sara. In my line of work, I suspect in yours too, the truth is rarely simple.'

'I know what you mean. Truly I do. I'm always telling my patients how we often make sense of the world by imagining things and then, I don't know, in our mind these things become true without them necessarily *being* true…'

And then until the bill comes, she is capable only of focusing on Kate's firm stroking of her hands.

An hour later, with the bitter taste of chai still in her mouth, Sara's tuk-tuk pulls up at the clinic. She looks over at the temple. Like a patient bunking off therapy, she knows that the one thing she is resisting is the one thing she should do. For an ending of sorts with Mike, for gratitude at surviving last night's assault on G.B. Road, but above all to pray for Pritti's safe return, she must buy marigolds this evening and drape them over one of the temple's altars.

What with giving further statements to the police, having her office finger printed, and having to soothe agitated patients, the day flies by so that by the time she eventually leaves the clinic, night has fallen and the temple opposite is brightly lit. And although many of the lights stutter before popping for good, she interprets a welcome even if none is intended. Wrapping one of Mr Pants-U-Like's fabrics around her waist she approaches the cart selling marigold garlands. The pungent flowers feel fragile in her hands.

Tonight the temple seems busier than usual, full of gaudy saris, glinting nose-chains, and necklaces of red and white beads. Sara fingers the coloured bracelets at her own wrist and steps into the courtyard. It echoes to the sound of anklets and bangles and women gossiping. Sara wanders around, aiming for elegance while gripping marigolds in one hand and trying to stop her cotton sheath unravelling with the other.

This far back in the compound, the walls are lined with identical wooden doors, as though someone was once sold a dodgy job lot. Leading to more penis shrines, no doubt. She tries a handle, but it remains firmly locked.

A loud noise, part bugle, part scream, makes her jump and turn. From the direction of the lane comes raucous, tuneless music. Space is being made in the crowd for a procession. In the middle, walks a young girl of maybe nine or ten, weighed down with jewellery and looking glum. The older women push her roughly.

In the centre of the courtyard they stop, as thankfully does the music. Everyone turns to face the girl, and an old woman drapes fabric over the girl's head. There is chanting and the muttering of what could be prayers, with all the solemnity, all the ritual of a ceremony. And she remembers Shakeel, describing women being married to the deity.

Looking at the small girl in the centre of things, Sara's stomach turns over. The young girl—no more than a child— hasn't stopped staring at her embroidered slippers. Sara looks around the courtyard to see whether anyone else is as shocked as she is, and suddenly sees her, those plaits and that familiar submissive stoop emerging from one of the locked narrow doors.

'Pritti,' she yells, above the chants, the fresh wailing. Sara tries to run to her, hobbled by her impromptu skirt. She stumbles. 'Pritti. Wait.' Yanking off the fabric, she flings it to the floor. She hurries to where Pritti is being ushered by an elderly woman with matted dreadlocks through a different door. Sara reaches it as it clicks shut. She calls Pritti's name and bangs on the door, but the old woman whacks her on the arm.

'Ow,' she cries, dropping the marigolds. 'Give me back my patient.'

164

The woman ambles off.

'Pritti? It's Sara. Are you OK? Talk to me.' Pritti's passive-aggression is well-documented in the notes, but this smells different. 'I'm worried about you,' she shouts. 'Really worried.' She presses an ear against the door, but there is now only silence.

The woman with dreadlocks and the martial arts tendencies returns, smoking a fat roll-up the colour of bamboo.

'Excuse me,' Sara barks. The woman might not understand polite Received Pronunciation but people always turn round at sudden noises. 'Excuse me. I need to get my friend out of that room. There's been a mistake.' Those fabulous miming skills again.

The old woman takes a long drag on her bong and wanders off again.

The night staff. She must get them to help her.

Sara fights her way through the crowds in the courtyard and lane and reaches the clinic door.

Locked. An extra precaution since Pritti's disappearance.

She smacks her hand against it. And she doesn't even have a main key, has never needed one. She rings the ward on her mobile, but the night staff speak no English. Sara rings Rafi but his phone is turned off.

Pushing her way back into the compound, one or two of the narrow doors are now open. She peers inside one, a small, airless, windowless room, empty but for a mat on the floor. Like a cell. The fetid stink of sweat makes her heave. It is now twenty minutes since she last saw Pritti. Could a person suffocate in that time?

She scans the crowd, trying to find someone to help her. And then she remembers, and rummages in her bag for a business card.

Pradeep takes twenty minutes to reach the clinic. She meets him at the front of the temple.

'Sara. This is an odd place for you to be. How did you know the ceremony was happening? They keep these things very quiet nowadays.'

Sara beckons Pradeep to follow her into the temple. 'I didn't. As I said on the phone, one of my patients is here. She ran away from the clinic, I came here to pray for her safe return, and I've just seen her here by chance.' Sara is now banging on every door, yelling Pritti's name above the crowd. She tugs on each door in turn, but they are all locked. 'And now I need to get her back from the old bat over there.'

In Hindi Pradeep appeals to the woman sucking on her cigar and Sara suggests Pradeep throws in a few choice allusions to AIDS, hoping to render Pritti repulsive to her madam.

A sum of money is mentioned. Contagious or not, clearly Pritti can be bought or sold like any other commodity. At an ATM on the highway Sara and Pradeep each withdraw the maximum daily rate of rupees. Not quite the donation to the temple she had envisaged earlier this evening.

When Sara and Pradeep return and hand over the money, the old witch leads them to a door. Just as they reach it, Sara hears a female scream from inside.

'Pritti, it's OK. We're getting you out,' she yells, thumping the door.

The old woman unlocks the door and barks into the room. A man hurries out, tying his loin cloth. He limps away, one leg polio thin. Then Pritti emerges, crying, muttering her mantra. *Illusions, delusions, and confusions.* She looks at Sara but nothing registers. Christ almighty, she must be drugged.

'Pritti, I've come to take you—' she almost says home. 'To keep you safe.' This close, the room stinks of semen and something metallic like blood.

Pritti recites her mantra, her eyes to the floor. Like the girl from the ceremony. If I don't look, none of this is happening.

'I'm here to look after you.' Sara holds out her hand.

The madam speaks to Pritti who mumbles. Sara looks at Pradeep. 'I know it breaks all therapeutic boundaries, but tell her she can sleep over at mine tonight. I'll get Rafi on side later.'

Pradeep presents his case, but the madam interrupts. There is a short exchange and then Pradeep says, 'Your patient doesn't want to leave. I'm sorry.'

'What? Pritti.' She is pleading. 'Pritti. I know it's hard, but what we're doing at the clinic, it's really helping you. I really believe that.'

Pritti's mantra is louder now and she is rocking on her feet.

Sara knows there is usually no way past this barrier of words, but she can't help trying one more time, grabbing for the girl's shoulder. But the madam slaps her hand away. Limply she watches as the madam chaperones Pritti to where a new client waits. Somewhere in the dirt Sara's marigold petals lie crushed underfoot.

Pradeep offers to give Sara a lift home.

On the way, she quizzes him, 'Is there any way we can legally get my patient out of the temple?'

'Yes, but it could take months even for a judge to read our deposition. By which time Pritti could have been moved on, or—'

'Thanks, but I don't even want to think about *or*.'

'Of course you could always try and persuade the police to organise a raid.'

'Something tells me organising a raid isn't as easy as you've just made it sound.'

'Secrecy and trust are vital, since some of the senior police often tip off the brothels in advance, so there are no girls on site when the raid takes place. Or there might be a shoot-out. Or the police might allow the girls to "escape" only to round them up again and sell them back to the pimps.'

'Ah. That explains it. I went to the main police station recently and found dozens of women and children locked up in squalid cells. They were definitely prostitutes, but I couldn't work out what they were doing there, locked up.'

'They will be sold on at some point.'

'But it's like the whole country is in collusion to see women as objects, which makes trafficking them so easy.'

Pradeep tilts his head.

'It's tricky in India, but many men in all levels of society believe they are doing a good thing, atoning for a woman's lost honour. And when so many families refuse to take back relatives who have ended up in prostitution, for the shame it brings, often on the whole community, then sometimes the only option is to move the women on to a different brothel.'

Pradeep isn't sure how to get to Rafi's enclave, so when they get close, she must concentrate—there is a crafty double back near the golf course involved—since someone else usually takes care of directions, in the posh car. Like the one up ahead. A sleek limousine eases out of the enclave's entrance and glides towards them. It is the correct shade of blue.

She checks her watch. Nearly midnight. Where is Hemant going at this hour? And she has a vision of Rafi, slumped across some bar, jeered by waitresses, needing rescue. Soon, Hemant's face will pass within inches of hers. There he is, gliding towards her, looking ahead.

But as the car passes it is the silhouette of a woman sitting in the back, sweeping her long hair up into a bun, bangles sliding down her wrist, which sears itself on to Sara's retina.

A chill sweeps through her. In her mind she sees with painful clarity the curve of Hemant's neck as he plays guitar, the side of his thumb where the skin is gnarled, the way he tries out chords on the steering wheel when they are stationary in traffic. Composing songs. Songs she now realises she had once hoped might be for her.

20

In the house, Rafi is still up, sipping cola and chomping crisps. Urgently she explains about finding Pritti, and about Pritti's refusal to leave the temple.

'You shouldn't have gone there,' is all Rafi says. His mouth contorts into an enormous yawn. Orange potato mulch clings to his incisors.

'I don't see why not. It's a temple, it's not private property. People wander in and out all the time. And if I hadn't gone, I wouldn't have found Pritti. The main thing is, we've got to get her out. Half the women there have been trafficked or abused, maybe both.' She takes a fat pinch of crisps. She hasn't eaten all evening. Her body swoons at all the salt, the additives, the E-numbers.

'It is not a temple.'

'OK. *Brothel*, then," she snaps, seizing more crisps. And she has a sudden flash of the woman with the bangles, the unravelling hair, the little boy. Of course, the woman is a prostitute too. Which means, Hemant—. She shakes her head. 'Tomorrow?'

'Tomorrow what?'

'Tomorrow, will you come with me to the temple and get Pritti back?'

He opens his mouth. He is about to remind her that it is not a temple. 'You don't understand,' he sighs. 'We can't just go in and take one of their girls.' He has the grace, she thinks, to sounds regretful.

'She's not one of *their* girls, she's one of *our* patients.'

'Sara-Didi, we have talked about this before. India is still ambivalent about mental health. And besides, Pritti's family won't go on paying for her treatment forever.'

'They said that?'

'You know as well as I do, someone with Pritti's history is going to need lifelong care.'

'And you think she's going to get it in a place like that? She's *ill*.'

He heads up the stairs. 'Look. Pritti has no education, no resources. And the girls there, they can make so much more for their families this way. Paying medical bills, paying for schooling, for weddings, for food.'

Sara stops on the landing between their two floors. 'You're saying you'd sooner one of our patients got pimped out than that we try to get her back and continue treatment? You know Pritti. Mentally, she's a child. This will terrify her. She will never get well.'

'Did she look scared to you?'

'No, in fact she looked doped out. They've probably drugged her, to make her do what they make her do.' She doesn't even want to think about it.

'Look, you don't know much about places like that—'

'No thanks to you. When I asked you about it, you kept fobbing me off. Told me the place had had to be closed down. Utter rubbish.'

Rafi looks weary all of a sudden. As though women calling attention to his deficiencies happens with alarming frequency. 'The set-up there,' he can't, or won't say brothel, 'it makes some women feel empowered. Village women, they have no hope. They travel to the big cities and *still* there's no hope. These places provide hope. It might not be much, but for some, the work gives them an income, status, security.'

His voice sounds flat, as though he has tried to convince people—maybe even himself—many, many times before.

'But it's a *brothel*,' she seethes. 'We have a Duty of Care to our patient. And leaving her in a place like that, to get raped,

171

possibly AIDS, is *not* a responsible course of action. It makes us complicit.'

'You can't come here and be a role model. Your country and mine, we tried that before, remember?' And he starts wearily up the next flight of stairs. He half turns, as though it pains him to say this. 'In the long run, we have to be left to make our own mistakes. That's what I think, anyway. Goodnight Sara-Didi.'

She tries to slam her bedroom door shut but it catches stubbornly on the pile of an expensive rug. She flops on her bed and kicks off her shoes. Stares at the ceiling. Rafi. Mild, funny Rafi. All the fight drained out of him.

She cleans her teeth. Perhaps over breakfast, she will ask Rafi again. She swabs cleanser and toner around her face. Outside, a floorboard creaks. There is a tap at the door, a dormouse scratch of a sound, someone considerate of the late hour. She pictures Rafi's face on the other side, tired but persuaded. What a relief.

But Rafi mustn't think her a pushover. Pritti's safety is the absolute priority. She slips off the bed.

'So what's the plan,' she says, opening the door.

'Sara?' whispers Hemant, glancing nervously up towards Rafi's floor.

She tightens her grip on the door jamb, although it costs her dearly—her heart hammering—to be this unyielding. Dark circles have appeared under his eyes. Well, serves him right for driving his prostitute home at this hour.

'I—I wanted to know how you are. After, you know…'

'I'm fine. Thank you.' For Hemant to be here, on the landing, with Rafi's floor immediately above, speaks of desperation. She is on the verge of closing the door, but can't quite make it happen. 'I'm sorry, I owe you an apology. More than one, actually.'

Hemant looks puzzled.

'Firstly I want to apologise. You were right. I should never have gone alone to G.B. Road.'

Hemant shifts uncomfortably on his feet.

'No, hear me out. I did a stupid thing, going there alone and getting drunk. And you saved me.' She can feel herself colouring at what she needs to say next. 'And I think I might have tried to kiss you afterwards, so I'm also sorry about that—' she wishes she hadn't put it like that, with its implication of complete regret. 'What I've been meaning to say is, I wasn't really myself that day.'

'I understand.'

'No, you're very kind, but you don't understand because you don't know. I think I got madly drunk because I'd found out something about Mike—'

'Yes, you remember? You told me in the car. That he died not in Afghanistan, but in India.'

She waves her hands. 'No. What I didn't tell you was that in Mumbai, I found out that he, uh—' she catches her breath, 'was having an affair.'

Hemant smashes his hand—oh God, his precious hand—against the door jamb. She recoils. If Mike were alive, Hemant would, it seems, now kill him.

There is a creak, of Rafi moving around upstairs.

'You should go,' she whispers.

'I came to tell you, Rafi's friends Rupa and Alok have asked me to play at their wedding.' He has come steeped in happiness, with good news, news he wants to share, in spite of the immense risks. 'But Mike…' But his face is anything but joyful. 'You will be there?'

She has certainly been invited. Rupa and Barkha are taking her shopping for outfits for all the many parties. Purple chiffon has been mentioned, plus a ton of jewellery. 'I'm not sure—' she swallows. Hemant's eyes are on her. She hopes to God him whacking the door with his hand hasn't destroyed his second career, his true calling. 'I'm probably going back to London.' Like it's nothing to do with her. Her fingers tighten on the door handle. 'Who is that woman?' she says quietly, lobbing in her grenade.

'What woman?'

Don't give me *what woman*. 'The woman with the bun and the bangles and the little boy with the torn T-shirt.' Given this deeply personal description, Hemant doesn't have a clue which woman she is talking about. 'You know *exactly* who I mean,' she hisses. His expression unnerves her. She cannot read it.

'I'm not sure—'

'I saw her in your car earlier tonight. She is a Devadasi.'

'Her name is Ammu.'

The simplicity of this sentence winds her. And when Hemant fails to add anything else, she asks, 'Is she your girlfriend?'

Hemant stares at her and for one pure moment his expression, his micro-gesture, is of horror, disgust. It seems he is about to deny it. Don't be ridiculous. It's you I've grown to like. And then she watches the light in his eyes go out and he says simply, 'Yes.'

21

That night she dreams of Mike and Hemant. The shape of them, walking away from her, hand in hand, into a ball of fire. She wakes in a sweat, her legs tangled up in the sheet.

In the car the following morning she is relieved to find that Hemant's hand appears undamaged. She avoids his gaze, but is grateful he hadn't lied about having a girlfriend, hadn't humiliated her further by imagining her gullible.

At the clinic, she can't bear to look at the temple but makes straight for Shakeel's office and knocks on the door. The Devadasi, Mike, G.B. Road, she barely knows where to begin. 'I've found Pritti. She's in the temple opposite, and I need your help getting her out.'

'The temple?'

'Yes. There was a ceremony and I saw her there. You know what that means.'

Shakeel blinks.

'You compiled the scrapbook. Pritti's been kidnapped, or she wandered in there by mistake, I don't know. But she is now being pimped out as a Devadasi.'

Shakeel sinks into his chair. 'You went to a ceremony at the temple?'

'Believe me, that's nothing. I went to G.B. Road the other night and got beaten up by pimps and madams.'

Shakeel runs a shaky hand through his maroon hair.

'Look. I've read all your cases, from years back. Akanksha and Deepti and Indu and Pragya. But it's happening *now*. In our lane. And here's the thing. In your scrapbook I found an article about Mike. Turns out that before he died, he was rescuing trafficked women in Mumbai. I see it now, it was my fault. I lost him. I am *not* losing Pritti. But I need you to come with me,' she says, standing up.

'You found Mike?'

She ignores what she decides are his stalling tactics. 'Look I can't speak Hindi, the brothel owner has money of mine, and she's a witch.' She rubs her forearm.

'It is not that easy. These places are run by violent gangs—'

'I get that. So, we'll only take Pritti, I promise. One girl. What is it you guys say in India? *Doing the needful?* Help me do the needful.'

Her use of the Hinglish phrase clinches it. He even pulls on his authoritative white coat and stethoscope, for which she wants to kiss him.

Yet when they explore inside the temple, they find it completely deserted. No women idly sweeping, no mothers shepherding kids and, inside the penis shrine, no flickering lamps. Towards the back of the courtyard, doors even hang off their hinges. Overnight, someone has destroyed all evidence of the brothel and its nefarious activities.

They are back out in the lane, looking around. 'Ask him if he knows anything,' she says, nodding towards Mr Pants-U-Like. They jog over and Shakeel questions Mr Pants-U-Like who, with expansive gestures to his own building and the temple, is clearly loving having a new audience beyond friends, family and customers for the whole story.

Shakeel turns to Sara. 'Apparently this good man and his good lady wife were woken up in their flat above the shop around two in the morning.'

'Did they see anything?'

'They looked out the window, but because it faces the road they couldn't see what was going on. But he says it sounded like trucks or minibuses being filled with women and children. Then, after they had driven off, hours of crashing and banging.'

'Ask him, does he know where the women were taken?'

Mr Pants-U-Like looks apologetic.

Sara paces in a circle. 'I should have gone to the police last night.' It is Pritti she is most worried for but, in spite of herself, she wants Hemant's woman to be safe too. Or maybe it is just her son. And it occurs to her, who on earth is going to tell Hemant that his girlfriend is missing?

In Shakeel's office, Sara is adamant, 'We need to go to the police. There's a senior policeman I know. Or my friend Kate may have even higher level contacts.'

Shakeel's mouth twitches. 'We must be careful. Many in the police force regard prostitution as acceptable. The same men who grant us clinical licences to trade without bother in this area—' He shrugs. Sara gets the drift. 'It is a hornet's nest,' he adds, flatly. This development, she sees, has unnerved him. Having kept detailed notes for years, he knows how hard it is to fight the system. It has worn him down. And now Sara won't let the topic drop.

Out in the desiccated courtyard, she pulls out her phone and rings Kate.

'Thank God you've rung,' says Kate breathlessly. 'How are you feeling?'

'That's normally the therapist's line! But listen, I know you're busy, so I'll be quick. Does your embassy have good contacts with Delhi's Chief of Police?'

'Sure we do. But I was about to call you anyway. I really need to talk to you. It's pretty urgent. Can you meet me for a drink this evening? My treat. Or rather, our government's! I'll have a dig around and bring you the contact details then. You're sure you can meet?'

Sara says yes, and they zone in on the Oberoi as a venue before hanging up.

She is just unlocking her office door when her mobile rings. It says unknown number. Maybe Kate is ringing back on a secure embassy line. She answers it.

'Sara,' says the man's voice.

Sara feels a chill wash over her and instinctively moves to stand in the lozenge of sunlight on the floor by the window. 'What do you want?' She will not give him an inch, after what he withheld from her. She hears him take a breath, as though choosing to let her hostility go.

'I have some more information.'

Sara marvels to hear herself actually laugh. 'What? Where they met? How long he'd been fucking her? Tom, do you think I even care now?'

'Sara.' His voice is stern, reining in her pretence at indifference. 'Are you listening?'

'No Tom, are you listening to *me*? Because frankly I don't have the energy to repeat myself. Whatever you have to tell me, I don't want to hear it. It won't change anything and it won't do me any good. Do you hear me? I'm ending this call now.'

Yet her thumb hovers over the red button.

'Sara. Please listen to me. It might help you, to hear what I've got to say.'

'You mean it will help you, assuage your guilt.'

There is a beat, the sound of someone consciously maintaining self-control. 'The reason I didn't tell you wasn't because I thought it was for the best because, as it happens, I don't. The reason I didn't tell you was because Mike asked me not to. Begged me.'

'And what was so awful he wanted me kept in the dark?'

'Mike was put on sick leave.'

She doesn't think she has ever stood more still. 'What do you mean?'

'Before he went to India.'

'Why?' She pictures missing limbs, him screaming in agony. She cannot swallow.

'He had some sort of breakdown.'

'What?' That can't be right. And yet something stirs. 'What do you mean, a breakdown?'

'In the field. Look, as you probably know, as his ammunition technician it was my job, ahead of the Long Walk to each device, to get him into his bomb suit. But it got to the point we couldn't get the damn thing on, he was shaking and sweating so much. He was a wreck. No longer trusted himself. Kept saying he wasn't good enough any more.'

A ringing sound starts up in her ear, to think of her husband sliding secretly into her world, a psychiatric world of personality changes and stress disorders and low self-esteem. She rests her head against the window. 'Why didn't he tell me?' But she can guess. Her husband, devastated by infertility, feeling less of a man.

'Sara,' he says gently, 'don't be so hard on yourself. He wasn't your patient.'

'So what happened?' she asks, numbly. 'What did they give him? Drugs? Counselling?' She could almost be back in Trevor's consulting room, taking the case history of any random patient.

'They sent him to India. A desk job. Paper pushing. I promise you, this truly is all I know.'

Sara pulls away from the wall and stares into the lane. She is stunned to see it is still the morning. 'And you didn't think to tell me—'

'He made me promise. Said he wanted to protect you. And of course, when he died, the army were only too happy to have an excuse not to reveal they'd had a nutter in their ranks—sorry, I didn't—'

'I know.' She takes tight hold of the windowsill, to steady herself, and closes her eyes. Rafi is right. Some things can never be known. Patients can talk for years and yet never quite bring themselves to reveal the kernel of their pain, instead hugging it close, where they know they left it. The containment of toxicity. She wants to howl and smash her hand though the window. People claim they want to keep things to themselves to protect other people, when in fact deep down they hope to protect themselves. She leans her head against the cool pane of glass. She is overcome with sadness, for the vulnerable man she couldn't reach and the marriage she didn't know how to save.

❦

Mid-morning she emerges from her office wearing sunglasses. In the courtyard, she sees Rafi coming towards her. Dark circles draw attention to his bloodshot eyes.

'How's it going?' he says, with the air of hoping to discover that someone else is having a dreadful time too. A part of her hopes he has been up all night regretting his obstinacy over rescuing Pritti.

'I was heading to the canteen,' she says. 'Join me?'

Watching him stirring three sugars into his coffee, she sees that his hands are shaking. 'The temple has been closed down.'

'I saw that.'

'So now we've no idea where Pritti is.'

He looks up. 'Pritti?'

'My patient? The clinic's patient? I told you last night she was there?'

Rafi nods. 'Sorry. Bad morning.' He downs his coffee like his beers. He is silent for a while. 'When I went to England I had this idea that when I came back, things would be different.'

She is drawn to the sight of Rafi's hands hugging his cup. She touches his wrist.

'But now I know that's not true. People don't change.' He looks up at her and pulls a face. 'Isn't that an awful thing for a psychiatrist to say?'

'We all have stubborn cases—'

'I'm not talking about patients,' he snaps. 'I'm talking about Baba-ji. I have to be the perfect son. Yet he is so backward, so reactionary. He would disown me if I said the wrong thing, prayed to the wrong god, dated the wrong girl—'

Sara notices the ugly sludge at the bottom of his cup. 'I know—'

'What do you know?' says Rafi's voice is harsh. 'You have never had to crawl out from under your father's shadow.' He laughs once, humourlessly. 'Although we in India have been doing that for decades, learning how to crawl out of the shadows of you British.'

Sara doesn't know what to say, although a part of her is just dying to snap back, at least you've *got* a father.

'You don't really know Baba-ji. He has been good to you. You are grateful. But what you see is not what you get. You see what he wants you to see. Noble doctor, helping the poor. I'll say this for him, he is very good at PR. But it is all a fiction, don't you see? Everything is for show. He is always acting.'

Sara stands up abruptly. In her head, all she can hear is Tom words, *he wanted to protect you*. 'Well, aren't we all,' says Sara, screwing up her napkin and flinging it on the table. 'Aren't we bloody all?'

Pleading the need for fresh air, she returns to the courtyard. A lizard zigzags across Sara's path. There was a lizard here when she first arrived in Delhi, sunning itself in the dried-out bird bath. That was three months ago. How much has changed. And then again, how little. The bird bath is still dried up, turns out she didn't really know Mike at all, and now her favourite patient has gone missing.

From her bag she pulls out a bottle of mineral water and tips the entire contents into the bird bath.

⚜

The bar overlooking the golf course is all fake mahogany and platoons of whisky bottles. Kate orders a pink gin and Sara a lime soda, which are brought with a flourish and a dish of spiced cashews.

They clink glasses and Kate knocks back most of her drink. Then she embarks on a long story about meeting an Indian MP who demanded a full briefing on the current plots of various British soap operas, convinced that his meeting the next day with the visiting British Foreign Secretary would require such detailed knowledge. Sara does her best to see why this tale—a one-liner at best—is taking so long, before it dawns on her that Kate is, for once, gabbling with nerves.

Kate raises her empty glass at a passing waiter and signals for another pink gin.

Sara also notices that the blue eyeliner, usually so immaculate, is smudged. 'Is everything o—'

'So, you wanted to know whether we have any leads with senior police?' Kate begins digging around in her handbag. 'What's it for?'

'Remember the patient I told you about, the one who went missing? I found her last night in the Devadasi temple opposite the clinic. But overnight the whole place has been closed down. Presumably all the prostitutes have been moved on.'

Kate has found her piece of paper. She grips it tightly, like a gambler clutching their last chip. The ridges of her knuckles are tinged white. 'How weird. Where to?'

182

'No idea. But someone must know something. The local police have been hopeless, so I need someone higher up. To help me organise a raid, or something. That's why I'd love your contacts.' She nods at the paper in Kate's fingers. 'Who do you know?'

Kate thanks the waiter for her second pink gin and drinks deeply. 'He's the new District Commissioner. Haven't got his name yet, but here's the main number.' She drinks again. 'Seriously, I hope you pull it off. Someone needs to. Trafficking of women is getting completely out of hand in India. And of course the money from sex trafficking in India often funds organised crime around the world.' Her glass is now empty.

And Sara has an image of Kate's discreet, industrious enquiries, of hushed yet urgent conversations in sweltering corridors, of communications with MI5 and MI6, their obstructions confirming more than they deny. Mike working not just to rescue vulnerable women, but covertly to disrupt organised crime in Britain. She isn't sure how she feels about this latest revelation, a residual flicker of wifely pride, definitely, and yet a sadness that this only confirms how remote the two of them had become.

'Another drink?' asks a waiter, smoothly. Kate readily agrees.

Sara is determined not to follow Kate's slide into inebriation. Instead, she focuses on the call she will make to the senior policeman, to rescue girls like those in Shakeel's scrapbook, betrayed pawns in a global chess game, young enough to be sucking thumbs, but rubbing their nipples and glancing coyly. 'When I see the street women, I just want to scoop them all up and take them back home, care for them. Repair the damage.'

'And I should imagine that's how Mike felt— No, hear me out,' Kate adds, putting up her hand as Sara tries to interrupt.

'I don't know exactly what was going on in Mumbai, who was running who, who the handlers were. I don't know what leads Mike had, who he was tracking, how deeply he had penetrated the traffickers, nor what links he left behind. As you can imagine, all that intel disappeared the night Mike died. But I do know this much. Mira Mittal wasn't interested in men.'

Sara jerks backwards, a loud hum in her head. 'Not interested in men?' Not an affair then. Sara's tries to reach for her glass, but her fingers are trembling. She is acutely conscious of her own body, her knee bumping against the low table, the citrus sting in her mouth.

Kate accepts the latest gin and takes a swig. 'I didn't tell you before, because I wasn't sure I was cleared to.'

'Cleared to?'

Kate avoids Sara's stare. 'And in any case, Mittal is not such an uncommon name. I had to check a few things.'

'So?'

Despite finally putting down her glass, Kate waits a long time before speaking, wiping her palms on her sari. 'I knew a Mira Mittal. She was a friend. A good friend. In the service. What we would call Special Forces, so secret operations. Died in the terrorist attacks, although I never knew the full circumstances. No one ever does.' She tries to smile and fails. 'After you mentioned her, I did some digging around. Funny how much you can uncover once you have just one piece of information. Seems she was working on trafficking.'

'Mike was apparently plucked from a desk job, although I never got the bottom of how he came to be doing that, I'm afraid. His role was to play the businessman, offering vast sums of non-existent money to the traffickers to ship the girls out to the Middle East. Mira's job was to pretend to be his colleague, arranging the paperwork, when really it was her job to befriend the girls, make them trust her, trust the process.' Kate takes another swig. 'Apparently they made a great team. Some reports speak of over a hundred and thirty girls rescued. I hope this makes it easier for you.'

And now Sara is fuming, not just at Kate for messing with her mind, but also at Mira Mittal, a woman she has never met, for having worked *so well* with Mike, for making such *a great team*. 'And you didn't think to mention this to me yesterday?'

'It was a hunch I had, that's all.'

'Believe me, I would have considered all hunches.'

'I know, but I had to be sure. I had to think things through.'

'What things? Think what through?'

'I don't know. Lots of things. I didn't even know if it was my, you know, the same Mira Mittal. If you're working out in the field, as Mira was, your activities won't be common knowledge, even in the Embassy, let alone to people closer—'

'You could have rung me. Texted me. I've been going out of my mind.'

'I know. I'm sorry, Sara. Really. It was never my intention to hurt you. Never.'

And in truth, the dark pressure on Sara's heart has now dissolved. Her husband was heroic and selfless and she had been wrong to fear getting close—afraid to feel connected to a man—yet so right to adore him; which shames her afresh, after learning of his breakdown, that she could ever possibly have doubted him. And she is reminded again of the psychosis Trevor once mentioned, a search for meaning so pure, so focused, that the quester loses their grip on reality.

And she wonders too what turmoil Kate has been through this past twenty-four hours, to psych herself up to reveal secrets and truths and yet at the same time to hold back with such obviously feeble excuses. And she thinks again about Mike keeping his breakdown from her, and about how hard it can be to heave your heart into your mouth, to let someone else in on your innermost secrets. Because this is what she sees clearly now. Kate's delay, the obstacle, lies not in what Kate has said, but in what she has not said. *My Mira Mittal.* Kate, capable Kate, pissed as a newt, nervous as hell, slaving away for the good of the service, apparently married to no one but her job.

Sara leans across the dish of cashews, takes Kate's clammy hands in her own and says simply, 'I'm truly sorry your friend died.'

22

The new Police Commissioner for the Chandni district is, say his juniors, very busy, but happy to see Sara. Waiting in the swept if dingy reception of a marginally grander police station than Passang's, she practises her cover story, to avoid getting the clinic involved for now: she is a journalist called Claire writing about women's issues. She was here covering Delhi's Slutwalk, and now she just wants to talk to someone important, someone in the know, someone who clearly has women's best interests at heart.

Passang Kasturirangan stands up as she is shown in by a junior officer. Both she and he blink on discovering themselves face to face with each other.

'Sara,' he says, with a half-smile, checking a notepad. 'I was told I was meeting someone called Claire.'

Sara blushes. And then she notices the block of wood on the desk, decorated with Passang's name in brass letters. 'Congratulations on your promotion.'

'It is nothing,' says Passang, proudly, and he invites her to sit. In front of her on his new desk squat two fat tomes: *Preventions of Immoral Traffic and Law* and *Criminal Minor Acts, Volume 4*. Yet another small flag of India flutters in the token breeze of a tiny fan. 'I am delighted to see you again. And so may I be asking, what is the purpose of your visit this time?'

'One of my patients has gone missing.'

'My word! So you have another Missing Person to report?'

Sara smiles thinly. 'There's a temple on the lane off Vikas Marg. Do you know it?'

Passang is delighted to announce that yes he does.

'It was closed down last night, and all the women working there have been moved on. Do you know anything about that?'

Passang regrets that he does not.

'But you knew the temple was really a brothel?' Passang is non-committal, so Sara presses on. 'Some women there had been kidnapped and now they've disappeared.'

'Since 2007, there be no kidnapped girls working in this district.'

Sara pretends to read from her notebook. 'Well, one girl at the temple was originally taken from my psychiatric clinic, and girls from Nepal are being pimped on G.B. Road. G.B. Road is in your district as well, isn't it? Trafficked girls. And girls under eighteen.'

'No trafficked girls and no underage girls. Not in my district.'

'Well, I've been there and I've seen them. And their madams prevented them from speaking to me.'

Passang extracts a file from a precarious pile. Waving it, he announces that all district prostitutes are over eighteen, are not exploited, and don't face violence. 'You see, that is why we must legalise prostitution in India. Prostitution is important.'

'Important?'

'Very much so. You see, if there is no prostitution, then civilisation will collapse.'

'Collapse?' Sara cannot quite believe she is hearing this.

'Male persons have needs and if the needs are not met then they will commit rapes, or some other immodesty against the ladies.'

'So you're saying society needs brothels to prevent rape?'

'Exactly so.'

'Which you think makes them a good thing?'

'Exactly so.'

'But if the women are kidnapped or trafficked, then that makes them sex slaves, being held and being made to perform sexual acts against their will. So, I would have thought, if any man has sex with such a woman, this is also rape?'

Passang smiles as though she has just agreed with him.

'So, if you knew that a girl had been kidnapped or trafficked and was now being forced to work as a sex slave, you would help rescue her?'

'Most definitely. But as I say, that is not happening in my district. All the girls working in the industry are there voluntarily. So there be no need for any raiding.'

Sara has an image of ten-year-old Swarti in her head. She isn't quite sure how she manages to stop herself from standing up and punching Passang in the face.

❧

Once the clinical day is over, with the apricot wash of evening settling over the city, Sara and Rafi climb into the Mercedes.

'So what did the Chief of Police have to say?'

Sara is relieved to see that for once, Rafi is not glued to his phone. Instead his BlackBerry rests inert on his knee. In fact, he seems disturbed by its inactivity. 'Turns out I'd met the man before, when I tried to get help finding Mike. A man now promoted above the level of his own incompetence. And not only that, he believes brothels stop society collapsing.'

Rafi passes his hands over his eyes. 'I knew it. We can't rely on the police. We have got to find the women ourselves.'

She would love to know what has happened these past couple of days to bring about Rafi's marvellous change of heart. Whatever the reason, she is delighted he is finally on board to find Pritti. 'Maybe we could try the other temples in Delhi.'

'Do you have any idea how many there are? Tens of thousands.'

'OK, but there must be rumours, surely?' She is thinking of the night she went to G.B. Road, when word got round so quickly that she was asking questions. 'What we need is info on the ground. Has anyone heard about a new batch of girls arriving, that sort of thing. Maybe I could go to some of the red light districts, ask around.'

'You'd stick out like a sore thumb, and get beaten up again. More importantly, the pimps would move them on in no time.' Rafi drops his head.

The enormity of Rafi's grief surprises her. That he should care for Pritti so much.

'OK,' she says, 'so what we need is someone who won't be noticed, who can bond with young girls and ask questions without arousing suspicion.'

'My sister,' says Hemant, hoarsely.

Sara and Rafi glance up. Sara has never heard Hemant address Rafi in the car before, certainly never in English. Bless Hemant, and his habit of eavesdropping. In the tawny light she sees his eyes on her in the rear-view mirror, a look at once desperate and hopeful. And she has a vision of brave Varsha, waving a placard on the Slutwalk.

'What do you mean, your sister?' asks Rafi.

'At college, she works with women's groups, improving women's health and empowerment, that sort of thing. She could ask on the ground.'

'Yes,' says Sara eagerly. 'I could go around asking medical questions to distract the madams, while Varsha could speak to the young girls themselves to find out if they know anything.' She is thinking of Swarti again, as much as of Pritti. 'If they think I'm a medical doctor, I think they would talk to me more freely about their lives and their environment. It would be a great cover.' She is so thrilled to finally have a

plan that for a moment she can ignore the slight rumple to
her equilibrium, that someone has obviously told Hemant
about Ammu, and that Hemant is obviously doing this to
get his girlfriend back. Although on some level she admires
his consummate professionalism, his ability at work to hide
personal distress.

'You would do that?' says Rafi, as if he means to add,
for me. There is something about the way he didn't snap at
Hemant, the way he doesn't appear perturbed that Sara knew
Hemant's sister's name, that makes him seem on the back
foot. This business with the temple has subdued him.

'Please can you speak to Varsha for us?' she asks into the
rear-view mirror.

Hemant tilts his head. For his bosses? Anything.

23

At lunchtime the next day, Hemant collects Varsha from college and brings her to the clinic. Sara witnesses the protective look in Hemant's eyes as he takes leave of his sister.

Sara shows Varsha into Rafi's office—Rafi sits chain-eating crisps—and introduces her to Shakeel. Varsha lowers her eyes and tugs her ghoonghat over them before this unfamiliar man and they namaste each other shyly.

'So how is this going to work?' says Rafi.

'While I'm distracting brothel madams with questions about their health,' says Sara, 'Varsha will speak to the girls in Hindi and try to find out if there have been any new arrivals in the area.'

'In which case you must take clipboards,' says Shakeel. 'The brothels will be expecting health professionals to use clipboards for their surveys. And pens. Everyone you talk to will want free pens.'

Rafi goes to a metal cupboard, pulls out boxes of pens bearing the clinic logo and leaves them on the desk with a self-conscious flourish.

'And I can go "desi", so I'm less conspicuous,' says Sara.

Everyone nods their approval.

'So, when shall we do this?' asks Sara.

'We must move quickly,' says Shakeel. 'It is amazing how rumours get out.'

Varsha agrees. 'Your girls could be moved on again at any time.'

'Tonight?' says Sara.

'Sadly we are speaking at my father's conference on Hindu Psychosis,' Rafi says, gesturing at himself and Shakeel.

Sara doubts Pritti can survive much longer in the world of rape and violence and degradation. She looks at Varsha. 'Hemant could drive us tonight, keep his phone on in case anything happens? What do you think?' In her head she can hear Passang saying to her, *Speed is of the very essence.*

Varsha tilts her head now. 'Tonight, then.'

＊

Sara and Varsha systematically walk the murky streets of the red light districts in the Old City. Light is leaking out of the day. Sara's nose detects cooking fat, leather, urine. They walk past crumbling shops, and betel-stained doorways, through lanes the rust colour of rogan josh. Men on their haunches, chewing paan, watch them go by, while women and girls primp and jiggle.

Sara finds the experience even more disturbing than the first time, partly because she is stone cold sober and partly because sharing it with young Varsha brings home the horror of it. If circumstances had been different—if Hemant and Varsha's parents hadn't been so protective, or so stable, or if life had simply taken a different turn—Varsha could easily have ended up on the streets, being raped for small change.

They set to work. Sara bonds with brothel madams about backache and inflated rents and hopeless men, while Varsha flits like a moth, in and out of the crowds, whispering to the girls while their madams are being dazzled by the promise of free biros. Sara slaps at a mosquito at her neck and carries on to the next brothel, the next madam. Women line the street while men in groups amble by, window-shopping.

'The clients in this area are migrant workers, mostly,' murmurs Varsha, when they meet up in a disused doorway, as Sara hands her a few more pens.

193

'Presumably, if ordinary men didn't feel able to enjoy sexual freedom, the traffickers would have to find new ways to make money, and leave women alone?'

'Apart from the fact that some women end up in the sex trade precisely because they experience violence at home, from their husbands or fathers. It is all they know, about relationships with men.'

Sara and Varsha separate and Sara moves on to approach a new group of blousy brothel madams, her patter now fluent. *Good evening. How are you coping, looking after so many girls? Are you looking after yourself? Can I have two minutes of your time? And by the way, here is a lovely free pen.*

An hour later and Sara and Varsha meet up back at the Mercedes, tucked in a lane behind a derelict rice warehouse. Varsha has picked up news of a new consignment of women on G.B. Road.

'Temple girls?' says Hemant.

'Possibly. Apparently the man who sold them on has made six hundred thousand rupees.'

G.B. Road is even busier, even dingier than Sara remembers, but even so, at the risk of being recognised, she lowers her ghoonghat. Prostitutes stand with their arms folded, or twist girlishly on low stools. Their eyes reveal nothing. Sara recognises the defence mechanism of disassociation: physically these girls are ready to have sex; mentally they are somewhere else entirely.

She talks to around thirty brothel madams while nearby Varsha whispers to young girls, making them smile, fishing out their secrets. After a while, Sara realises she has also been trying to glimpse again the urgent face of ten-year-old Swarti. Yet every putrid shopfront she passes looks like all the others. Every few minutes she wants to double back, thinking that was the building Swarti sat in front of.

Suddenly, Varsha appears, bumping into her, apologising. A prearranged signal. With as much speed as they can muster without drawing attention to themselves, the two women melt away, gravitating to where Hemant waits in a back street in the Mercedes.

Varsha has so much to say, she is nervous her English is not good enough, so she asks Hemant to translate.

'There is a brothel two blocks from here, next to a big money changer. It's called Domino's. A new group of women and children arrived two nights ago, which has put many local noses out of joint. Apparently the man who bought them had to pay six hundred thousand rupees so they are working all night and all day, to make him his money back. The story is that they are weavers from a factory in Pune which was flooded out due to the rains.'

'So not our girls, then,' groans Sara.

'Wait,' says Hemant, his eyes shining at his sister's tale. 'Apparently none of the locals believe this story, partly because the women speak with Delhi accents and partly because all the new women are wearing red and white necklaces.'

'Which means they are Devadasi,' cries Sara.

Hemant nods. 'Which means there is every chance they are our girls.'

'Plus,' says Varsha, fishing a mobile phone out of her bag. 'I took these.'

Sara scrolls through the photos. They are grainy, having been taken covertly, and the women waiting on the streets look emaciated. Like husks of women. But two frames make Sara go cold. She would know that self-conscious stoop, those girlish plaits anywhere.

'So let's go there now. Get them out.' She will not—if she can help it—have Pritti stay one more night in this horrific meat market.

Varsha tugs her ghoonghat over her head. 'They will be under close supervision.'

Hemant agrees. 'We are only three of us and we have no weapons, no strength.'

Sara holds up her arm again, flexing her puny muscle as she did once before when offering to help Hemant carry equipment into his home. Hemant's amused expression says, Exactly.

She hesitates. Passang was pretty useless over Mike—but then so was she. At least this time round she would be giving him and his men a clearly defined task. 'OK. So I'll call the Commissioner for the Chandni district. When I tell him one of my patients is definitely being held there, he'll have no option but to authorise a raid.'

24

Two nights later—forty-eight wasted hours later, with Police Commissioner Passang Kasturirangan refusing to return Sara's calls, while girls like Pritti spread their legs on filthy mattresses—synchronised drumming is audible in the distance. Sara wriggles out of one of a long convoy of imported Porsche Cayennes, slumming it with all those not arriving by helicopter, and prays the luminous threads of her sari aren't unravelling.

The main wedding party is being held on the irrigated lawns of an estate on the outskirts of Delhi. Sara stops and looks about her, partly to disguise further checks that the pink chiffon is firmly in place and partly to rein in her anger at having to be here at all—pleasure at supporting Rupa and Alok on their special day excepted—when she could be out stalking Passang Kasturirangan and organising a raid to rescue Pritti. Security is extremely tight after Delhi's High Court terrorist attacks and everyone— judges, cricket stars, cousins writing for the *Washington Post* or trading oil in Dubai—is being searched. Were it not for Shakeel's scrapbook and its revelations about police duplicity over trafficking, she would be very tempted to sideline Kasturirangan and recruit some of these policemen personally for a raid on the brothel.

At the estate entrance, a greeter in a turban of purple silk holds fast to a thick chain at the end of which lies a panther. A ripe, almost glandular smell hits Sara as she walks past and she is reminded once more of seamy G.B. Road. She tightens her grip on Rafi's arm.

Beyond the estate, fields have been transformed into a maharaja's palace, with thousands of candles, and pavilions strung with pea lights in case the monsoon officially arrives in Delhi tonight; churning clouds suggest it might. Giant television screens will show a continuous live feed of the wedding ceremony. Not that Sara and Rafi will suffer the indignity of watching second hand. In her matching purse Sara carries their VVVIP tickets for the main betrothal marquee. They were delivered with a topaz bracelet for her and topaz cufflinks for Rafi. Cheapskates, joked Rafi, when he saw them.

The cocktail reception lasts hours, the auspicious timing of the marriage ceremony—nine twenty seven pm—having been ordained by an astrologer. She and Rafi stroll, while white-gloved waiters hand round platters of sushi and spoons of pomegranate sorbet, and play spot the politician or tycoon or fillim star. As the air hums with jasmine and money and sex—the frenzied drumming verges on the orgiastic—Sara fingers the under-blouse of her sari where it scratches her skin. In the background she has picked up the sounds of live music. Hemant is playing somewhere here.

Sara spots Pradeep. 'I'll join you in a minute,' says Rafi.

Pradeep smiles as she approaches. 'How are you enjoying the party?'

'It's like I've walked onto a film set. The lights, the colours, the smells.' She is trying to ignore the sitar she can hear over by the artificial lily pond. 'But listen, I've got an update for you about my patient—'

Pradeep takes her arm and steers her gently yet firmly away from his little group.

'She's being held in a brothel on G.B. Road.' She takes a breath. 'Can you help us organise a raid?'

'I can help with the legal side, for sure,' he whispers, 'but the police would have to conduct the raid itself.'

'I had a horrid feeling you might say that.'

'Don't get me wrong, the Delhi police are quite capable of bungling a brothel raid on their own, but without them taking part, nothing will ever stand up in court and, more importantly, you lay yourself open to being accused by the pimps of stealing or kidnap.'

'Well, I've tried the police but I think they might be stalling me.'

'And you're absolutely sure where your patient is?'

She nearly mentions Hemant's name. 'The sister of a friend of mine took photos.'

'That's good. Keep them, in case by some miracle it ever does go to court.' He pulls her further into a quieter part of the garden. 'Now listen, if you are going to do a raid, you have got to get it right first time. The girls are always in great danger at this point. If the gangs get trigger-happy they might just eliminate the evidence.'

'Get it right?'

'Get a layout of the brothel itself. I have some contacts who might be familiar with the brothel you have in mind, so they might be able to draw you a floor plan. They might also be able to give us the name of the man, the pimp in charge. It's always a man.' Sara bristles with pleasure at his use of 'us'. 'And above all, and this is really important, don't tell the police raiders which venue it is. That way they can't tip off the brothel owners ahead of time.'

'Layout, owner's name, and secrecy. Got it.'

Pradeep is studying her. 'I suspect you won't agree with my last bit of advice, but in my opinion you'd be mad to go on this raid, too.'

'But she's my patient. I have to be there.'

Just then, there come drifting across the lawns the sounds of a loving parent calling for hush. Rupa's father—all political waving to the crowd, and unaccustomed as I am—is standing on a far-off stage, tapping a microphone. His voice is hoarse from last night's traditional party for the men, carousing to folk songs (Rafi was also in attendance and had to be driven home by Hemant at four in the morning and later threw up while shaving). Quickly Pradeep and Sara dash towards the main marquee.

And then Sara hears it, the sitar, calling sweetly through the diminishing murmur of the guests, as Alok arrives resplendent on a white horse. Both Alok and the horse are smothered in tassels—both might be said to wear bashful expressions—but Sara can only hear the sitar. Nasal and thoughtful, its hum reverberates right though her. It sounds so near, he could be standing next to her. Its music burrows unbidden into her heart.

Hurriedly, she rummages in her bag for her camera and snaps away frantically. Alok and the horse process towards the main marquee, as though lured there by Hemant's playing. Those with the correct, gilt-edged authorisation press into the marquee and take their seats. Having been helped off his horse, Alok makes his way to an elaborate canopy on the stage, where a curtain separates him from Rupa. A group of male relatives gather behind her. Dressed in sumptuous red she could be a piece of jewellery, a small yet precious ruby on a pillow, and they her bodyguards.

As Sara sits down next to Rafi, she notices Hemant seated cross-legged beside the raised dais. He wears traditional dress including an enormous purple turban wrapped round his skull. She is conscious of the broad sweep of fabric across his shoulders. Surely, if women are defined by their hips or waist, then men are defined by their shoulders. She holds her breath, remembering the bulk of him at her back as his hands adjusted her fingers fumbling on the frets. Around her she is conscious of appreciative murmurs. Guests adore the effect created by his lone sitar, its pared-back sophistication.

And it occurs to her, with the pandit chanting—wailing, really, as though privy to her discomfort—that in another life, another India, she and Hemant might have had some kind of beautiful future together.

'Weddings always make me cry too,' says Rafi, handing her a tissue, along with some rice and petals to throw at the happy couple. In front of her, Alok's silk turban shines in the light as he leans down to kiss his new wife's tiny hand. Around her people stand to take photos of the garland exchanges, the prayers, the ghee offerings, the dabbing of the forehead with sandalwood, the final walk round the fire.

'So when's yours going to be?' she sniffs, just to see what he says.

A micro-gesture, impossible to read. He chuckles and throws himself into the chanting and ululating, encouraging her to do the same.

Cocktails and canapés flow abundantly, and the buffet supper doesn't disappoint. Later, a second marquee, as large as the first, houses the dance floor and cabaret. A singer in a sequinned catsuit leads the line-dancing gyrations to various Bollywood hits. She doesn't realise quite how tipsy she is. Three raspberry mojitos and nearly a bottle of champagne and the floor has become strangely uneven. When she falls for the third time against the thrilled—if wizened—chest of Rupa's uncle from Trivandrum, she suspects she might need some air.

Outside, after the sweaty fug of the marquee, the cool is a slap in the face. She pulls from her bag a purple pashmina—the table gift for all female guests—and wraps it round her shoulders. She would have liked to have had one dance with Hemant, to have felt before she leaves India the pressure of his arm at her back.

Angrily Sara pulls out her phone. When she manages to get reception in this enormous field in the middle of absolutely nowhere, she tries Passang's office again. Sadly, many regrets madam, but Commissioner Kasturirangan, he is not at the station tonight but away on important business. She leaves a message similar to the numerous others she has left in the last forty-eight hours.

She drifts, not knowing what she is looking for, not knowing that she is looking for anything, until she sees him. He is dragging an amp out of the back of the main marquee. The gentle smile on his face is of a job well done.

She strides over. 'Well done.' She swallows a hiccup. 'Everyone loved your playing.'

He turns towards her. His traditional brocade coat reaches in long panels to below the knee. He looks suddenly very regal, very serious. The smile has vanished. 'What did you think?'

'What does it matter what I think?' She doesn't mean to sound surly. Although some part of her obviously does.

Hemant visibly exhales. 'About the other night—' he starts.

'It's fine. I appreciate you telling me. Being honest.'

A voice in the dark barks out in Hindi and Hemant spins round. A party planner with an iPad and a Bluetooth earpiece signals for him to *buck up, do the needful*. Hemant turns back, bows his head, and resumes dragging the amp to a waiting lorry.

Sara watches him leave, but he doesn't look back. Maybe she can let the man go after all.

Back in the dance marquee, Sara looks around for Rafi with a view to going home. The politicians, cricketers and businessmen are looking very pleased with themselves, their families rubbing shoulders with all sorts of influential types: NDTV journalists, fashion designers. Senior policemen.

She marches straight up to him. Today he sports a burgundy Nehru suit but its shoulders are wide enough to bear an entire district's worth of imaginary epaulettes.

'I've been trying to get hold of you for two days.' With a tinkle of bangles at her wrist, she points a finger in the direction of Passang's Kasturirangan newly-promoted chest.

Passang Kasturirangan is evidently not as pleased to see her here, now, at this prestigious party, as he was a few days ago in the privacy of his office. In the intensity of his stare, the rigidity of his smile, she sees a state of panic. He wants her gone but he is also acutely aware of the influential people around him. This man, with his pleasant wife and teenage daughter, who believes the rape trade to be an essential part of a functioning society. 'If you make an appointment we can talk next week in my office.'

She decides to ignore the fact that she has repeatedly tried to make an appointment. If Mike and India have taught her anything it is to know when to abandon her well-honed therapeutic attitude of non-judgemental patience and to become a thorough bloody nuisance.

'Oh, it can't wait,' she says. 'You're the only man to help me.' And for a moment she feels imbued with something of the spirit of the women on G.B. Road, of women up and down the country, or around the world, desperate women forced to play a role. 'This man is a brilliant officer,' she adds to the small throng, making strenuous efforts to correct a slight list brought on by one too many mojitos.

He wants, she can tell, to contradict her, but in this audience, pride defeats him.

'When I met Commissioner Kasturirangan recently, I was struck by his concern for women. He also has some fascinating views on prostitution and sex trafficking.'

Passang's wife beams but Passang's face falls flat. One of the men in the group leans in. Sara has often seen him on TV, thinks he might be the Minister for Finance.

'So I thought, I must tell you immediately. Underage girls have been kidnapped for sex this past week and are being held in a brothel *in your district*.'

Prassang tries to say, *this is minor matter*, but the man who may or may not be the Minister of Finance tilts his head. 'Tell me more, young lady. This is exactly the kind of thing which gives India a shocking reputation around the world.' He says this wearily, suggesting that in his travels he has received such accusations first hand.

'I agree,' says Sara, warming to her theme. 'And the police are just the men to stamp it out, organise a raid, rescue women. Don't you think?' And with a sweep of the eyes, she includes all the men in this, men who miraculously have provided an audience of sufficient weight and social standing to make it hard for Passang to contradict her.

Although he does try. 'There could be problems with local mafia.'

'Yes, but you're the police! I couldn't possibly do it on my own.' They all laugh.

'And you know exactly where these women are?' chips in the Minister.

'Oh yes. And I have photographic evidence.'

'So how many are we talking?'

She thinks back to the women sweeping and chatting outside the temple. 'At least forty. And at least one of them is no older than Mr Kasturirangan's daughter here.'

Up until now, Passang's expression has been sending her covert messages of dismissal but at the mention of his own daughter she catches a flickering of real pain beneath the skin. Passang pulls his daughter closer.

The Minister's gaze has now been distracted by the arrival of one of Rupa's father's parliamentary colleagues, and the group shifts to watch a light-hearted political scrap begin.

Sara steps towards Passang and his family. Now that the buzz of confronting him has worn off, Sara recalls Shakeel's scrapbook, and Pradeep's advice. 'The raid must be kept a secret.'

'Quite so. Secrecy is paramount.'

'But how can you ensure it?'

'I'll deploy staff from a force outside my own.'

'And I shall only give you the name of the brothel at the very last minute.'

'Quite so.'

'How soon, then?'

Passang's eyes flick to his daughter. 'The sooner the better.' He gives her his card.

Long after they make a plan to speak tomorrow and finalise logistics, long after she has told Rafi, in the Porsche Cayenne home, what has been agreed, and long after she sees Rafi discreetly wipe away a tear, she can still feel the touch of Passang's wife's hennaed hand on her wrist, in a gesture of gratitude.

25

'Do not be fobbed off. I want you to be doing the needful, trying every door handle, every broom cupboard, every locked room.'

Passang is in his element. Less than twenty-four hours after the wedding, Sara and Rafi are huddled in the police station waiting room where eight uniformed officers also sit receiving Passang's instructions. Sara is relieved to find that the chosen officers look slim and fit, although she worries that their youth won't count for much against a pimp with a gun or a middle-aged madam in full war cry.

In her hand she holds a piece of paper. On it is sketched the floor plan of the brothel, sourced from one of Pradeep's contacts familiar with the brothels on the G.B. Road strip. It also has the name of the main pimp and a photocopy of his face.

Passang smacks his baton into his hand. 'Now, I don't need to tell you, but secrecy is absolute number one top priority. This is why no cell phones, no walkie-talkie. We will wait here until the evening trade is in full swing and then we will make our move. We want to catch these guys in action. From the minute we leave the van, we are on the raid, so—' Passang mimes zipping up his mouth. 'And I will not be giving you the venue's name, so keep your eyes peeled one hundred per cent on me.'

Then he introduces Sara, who introduces Rafi. She namastes the men. 'Thank you so much for agreeing to help rescue our friends.' Some of the men, she feels, receive her gratitude with thinly disguised smirks.

Passang starts distributing torches, and also crow-bars and hammers to knock down any stubborn partitions, together with photocopies of Varsha's photographs of the girls.

'Aren't they going to use more hard core weapons?' Sara asks Rafi out of the corner of her mouth. 'Hand guns or rifles perhaps?' And it occurs to her that no one has been given padded or protective clothing either, least of all her and Rafi. And she remembers the dreadful copy the police made of the photo of Mike, how it hadn't looked like him at all. Not for the first time she wonders whether it really was a good idea to get the police involved.

⚜

They all move from the police station to the parking lot outside. The policemen clamber into a battered, unmarked van to wait for further instructions. Sara sees one of them pull out a pack of cards, and his colleagues gather round, in high spirits. Rafi and Sara loiter in front of the clinic minibus, where Hemant sits at the wheel. Rafi chain-smokes, inhaling desperately, the smoke passing in front of his face giving it a ghostly countenance. Sara, despite the night-time mugginess, is hugging herself, shivering and wearing down tracks in the ground.

'I am very glad you are here with me,' Rafi says.

'Me too.' She looks back to check whether Passang has given the order yet to move, before resuming her pacing up and down. 'But what if we never find Pritti?'

'You are the only one she *would* go to. You are her Good Object. Before you came, no one could reach her. Remember what she was like when you first arrived? Pritti just sat on the floor, rocking, muttering. But something shifted when she started working with you. Something big. She stopped the rocking, and the mantras. She stopped picking at her clothes.

She began leaving her room, going to Art Therapy, engaging with people.'

'And look where that got us. She attacked me and absconded, which laid her open to kidnap. I made things worse, not better.'

Rafi shakes his head. 'You got her engaged with her own feelings. You got her talking. In months, none of us had managed that. Trust me. I feel like the fever's about to break.'

'I don't know.' Sara hops from one foot to the next. There is something she still hasn't quite understood about Pritti, perhaps one final piece of the jigsaw.

She turns round again to see if there are any signs of movement from Passang or his men. The policemen in the van are still playing cards, although a couple of them make no secret of staring at Sara and Rafi and muttering between themselves. 'I wish I knew how those guys are feeling about rescuing prostitutes.'

'Huh?'

'Do they see it as acting nobly, do you think? Or does it go against the macho spirit?' She digs deep into her pocket and touches the folded paper floor plan.

'Stop fidgeting, Sara-Didi,' snaps Rafi. He lights a new cigarette with the old one and grinds the butt beneath his shoe. 'I need to tell you something. Something I should have told you a long time ago. I kind of don't want to tell you, but I must.'

'I know. If Pritti comes, she comes. And if she doesn't, it's not my fault.'

'Sara. Please. Just shut up.'

She stops jumping up and down on the spot.

'When you arrived, I didn't know what to expect. I didn't even know if you would stay long. But you came highly recommended from Papa's old friend. And since then, I don't know. Shakeel is somehow looser, more relaxed. As though a large burden has shifted, or something. And the rest of the staff like you. The patients like you. And you know, I like you.' He takes a long drag. 'I like the way you came to find out about your husband. I like the way you have fought for Pritti.'

'But you've fought for Pritti too. You want to get her back just as much as I do.'

He takes another long drag. 'I want to get them all out, not just Pritti.'

'Of course—'

'All the women. Or rather, one in particular. My girlfriend.'

And in that beat, Sara realises that all this time she has been running just to play catch up. Rafi's edgy attachment to his phone, his strident disinterest in the temple, his disappearing act at the conference when the subject of Devadasi was raised. And the lithe woman gazing at the clinic. The woman with the little boy. 'Ammu?'

Rafi's face floods with relief. 'You know Ammu?'

She nods cautiously, remembering Hemant's confession.

Rafi seems on the verge of tears. 'I used to see her standing in front of the clinic, sweeping the steps, her long hair falling over her shoulder. She is so beautiful, so graceful, so self-contained. And so I would talk to her, buy her small things. And before I knew it, I had fallen in love.'

Sara can imagine what it must be like, the relief to feel you can now talk in public about someone you have loved in secret. She touches his arm.

Rafi takes a drag on his cigarette. 'So you're not appalled?'

'About you and Ammu? Far from it. But I'm just thinking, how could you stand it? With Ammu right across from the clinic, and, you know…?'

Rafi shudders. 'I know. I've been a coward,' he says, flicking ash on to the ground. 'My father is a scientist, but I love an Untouchable, which is unthinkable in my father's system. So, if it is unthinkable, it means it doesn't exist.'

209

'That doesn't sound remotely scientific.'

Rafi rolls his eyes. 'That's India for you. Chauvinistic superstition trumps science. So he sent me to England, to get her out of my system. But it only made me love her more. The thing is, he has threatened in the past to disinherit me. Kick me out of the clinic. So I have another confession to make, which is that I used you. I think part of the reason I invited you to move in is that I hoped that if my father ever caught a glimpse of a woman in the house, he would think she was a friend of yours.'

Her brain is trying to process all this while another thought strikes her, about whether Rafi knows that Hemant also regards Ammu as his girlfriend.

'For example, and this will make you laugh, Ammu didn't believe I'd gone down to Mumbai. Got Hemant to drive her most nights, to the enclave. Even slept over once. Got it into her head you were my girlfriend!' He chuckles uproariously at the very idea.

'But why didn't you tell me? I would have understood.'

'Habit, I guess. In India, as you know, we are very good at all kinds of repression. And before now, I've never known how to fight that. Never even really seen, despite all my clinical training, that I should. And then you arrived, fighting for the truth about your husband, and now fighting for Pritti. Whereas I have not stood up to my father, not stood up for Ammu—'

Suddenly behind them Passang claps his hands. It is time to move. Sara's stomach shimmies.

The raid has begun.

The officers climb into their van, while Passang heads with Sara and Rafi for the front of the clinic's minibus.

Sara looks over at Rafi. His eyes are filmy with moisture, the liquid shimmering there catching the light from the beams of the headlights.

He takes a last puff and stamps out the stub. 'Right, I guess it's time to grow up.'

❧

G.B. Road is as busy as ever. The main strip crawls with scooters and rickshaw-wallahs and pedestrians, the night-time haze thick with exhaust fumes and incense and fried food. The alleyways are crammed with painted women and men sizing them all up. Sara peers out the window into the gloaming, hoping for a glimpse of Pritti or Swarti or even the girl in pink polyester sucking her thumb, but no one looks even vaguely familiar.

Passang asks to see the map. Sara rummages in her pocket and hands it over. He unfolds it and studies it, the number of floors, the lines indicating staircases, the possible secret rooms. 'Buildings like these have many hiding places,' he says, tapping the paper with one of his many pens.

'They would be small spaces, even for very small people,' says Sara. She imagines Pritti, her stoop worsening.

Passang gives Hemant directions in Hindi and after a time crawling through the crowds, the minibus slows to a stop. Passang turns round. 'Do you want to stay here—?'

'No,' the colleagues say, in unison.

'Good,' he says, handing them each a torch. 'There may be less aggro if you're present. Just stay close to me.'

A chill ripples through Sara, at how none of them is wearing any protective clothing.

Passang indicates to Hemant to stop the minibus. Sara and Rafi follow him out and Passang grabs his baton from his seat. He points ahead with it so that his men, emerging from their own bus, can see him, and he waits for them to huddle around.

211

'The target is here,' he says, tapping his own head, 'so follow me. And,' he clears his throat, 'remember. They could be your sisters or daughters inside.'

As a pack they all head off down G.B. Road.

Locals stare, but not so much as to draw attention back to themselves. She wishes Passang and his men weren't so conspicuous in their crisp police uniforms, but decides that their very visibility might keep crowd hostility at bay.

They tread on.

'Hear that?' says Passang, glancing around. 'Whoo whoo. Warning calls.'

'Who's warning who?' she says, running to keep up with Passang's stride.

'The pimps see a uniform and they get twitchy.'

Sara is amazed he can hear anything at all above the loud radio music, the car horns and the chatter of people. But she can hear Pradeep in her head, saying how some of the gangs get trigger-happy. And is it her imagination, but doesn't the crowd now seem eager for confrontation?

Suddenly, Passang doubles back and ducks behind a clothes stall. Following him, their full posse enters a non-descript entrance, with loops of flowers above the lintel.

Rafi and Sara exchange excited glances. *This is it.*

Inside the building, the corridors are tight and airless. Cockroaches scuttle across the chipped tiles. Passang twitches curtains obscuring doorways and they peer into cramped rooms decorated with collages of pictures torn from magazines. At the same time, he gestures an instruction for some of his men to try the basement.

Over-made-up young women press themselves into the wall as the raiders pass. Sara tries to make eye-contact, but they stare back warily. A couple of women spit at the policemen, once they have passed, and one jiggles a crying toddler on her hip, but no one stops the progress of the police. It all seems too easy, and Sara wonders whether the pimps have had a tip-off after all, and are not on site tonight. Or maybe Pritti and the others have been moved on again?

Seconds later, older women burst from the shadows, hurling obscenities. Passang barges his way through them, his wooden club held high. The women snatch at him, and then at Rafi and Sara, drawing blood with their fake nails, but Rafi and Sara manage to wriggle free. Sara cannot think straight, for all the ear-splitting shrieks, and reaches for the wall to steady herself. It is slimily wet, from condensation and sweat.

Up the first flight of stairs, the light dims and they switch on their torches. On the first landing, Passang pulls back a curtain. Sara sees shelves of plastic washing baskets. As he pulls it back further, their collective torch beams find six narrow cubicles, maybe four foot by three. They are plastered with pictures of Shah Rukh Khan in various uninhibited dance poses. Crouched in each cubicle is a female of indeterminate age, wearing a thin dress and the traditional red and white beads. These girls look up at these strangers with blank expressions, ready to do what they're told.

Slowly, the girls unfold their skinny limbs and climb out. After one girl emerges, another does too, and then a third, then more. *Five* to a tiny cubicle. But no Pritti.

The girls are silent, scratching their skin, while back down the stairs behind them, all is shouting and scuffles.

'Rafi, tell them we're here to help them,' Sara urges, as each girl passes, 'tell them, don't be afraid.' He murmurs the phrase to each girl and Sara visualises each syllable, engraving them onto her heart: Daro mat. Daro mat.

'Wait. Count them,' says Rafi. He calls out to the policemen behind them, 'I'm saying, get your guys to watch them.'

Upward they go, with Passang and his men bashing the walls with his baton, checking for rickety partitions.

Out of nowhere, a man appears, holding a gun. Momentarily stunned at finding two white people in his corridor, the man stutters. Passang clubs him around the face and the man falls towards Sara, dropping the gun. Her legs shaking, Sara steps over the gun and the man. How many more men are in here, with lethal weapons?

Passang is calling out. Rapidly one of his men leaps up the stairs and handcuffs the bruised man, before pocketing the gun. Behind them, madams are screaming hysterically.

'What are they saying?' hisses Sara.

'Get out. Leave us alone. All our girls are twenty-one,' says Rafi, rolling his eyes.

At the top of the next dark flight of stairs, Passang's baton smashes through a fake wall. 'Next door building,' he says, climbing through.

The building is dark, the staircases narrower; Sara has never known claustrophobia like it. As they climb in the beam of their torches, they pass pinched rooms with single beds, where the girls are sent to have sex. These walls too are covered with escapist pictures from magazines: of skincare products and film stars and wide open spaces.

At the top of the stairs they reach a dead end. Above them in the low ceiling is a locked trapdoor leading up to the attic. Passang pushes at it with his hand, tugs at the padlock. Calls are yelled down for heftier implements.

Soon one of Passang's officers is squeezing through the raucous crowd of madams with a crow-bar and a hammer, which he hands to Rafi. Looking back, Sara sees another man being dragged away in handcuffs.

Using the crow-bar the officer smashes the padlock and then Passang and Rafi and the officer bash away at the trapdoor. As they do so, Sara can hear the cries of females on the other side. They sound terrified. Under her breath she polishes the precious syllables: daro mat, daro mat.

There is more shouting. The trapdoor swings open. Someone brings a crate. Standing on it, Passang and Rafi heave themselves up through the tight opening and into the attic, and then they pull Sara in too. The space is huge and thick with dust, and stinks from lack of air.

It is also empty, bare but for the wonky wooden struts supporting the corrugated roof. Sara's eyes meet Rafi's, acknowledging each other's disappointment. Once they were on the raid, it simply hasn't occurred to her that they wouldn't find their women.

She is about to lower herself back down to the landing when she hears Passang urging, gently, 'Come, come.' In the dim light she sees movement beyond his beckoning hand. And slowly, from the shadows, around a dozen barefoot females start crawling out from between the struts, shielding their eyes from the modest light of torches.

'Daro mat. Daro mat,' she says.

A line of unfamiliar women crawl by in thin dresses, sharply slapping down Passang's manly efforts to guide them through the hatch. Sara is amazed at how many have been secreted here. And then two more. Behind one trails a small boy and behind them, the filthy hair of another is—miraculously—still in plaits.

Sara sees the moment Ammu recognises Rafi and crawls eagerly towards him, her body still supple, bending herself towards his eager contours. He caresses what Sara has until now not registered before, Ammu's softly swelling belly—Hemant has obviously been cuckolded for months—and, with Passang's help, carefully eases his girlfriend and her little boy through the hatch.

Behind them, Pritti kneels, the only movement coming from her lips, reciting her mantra. Sara couldn't bear it, if Pritti was lost to her forever. And it's all her fault. If only she hadn't gone to Mumbai. Even now, she can't believe she

215

behaved so badly, so *unethically*. If only she hadn't abandoned her patient. Pritti, who has waited a lifetime for her mother to come back. Perhaps she, too, told herself she had behaved badly, to explain her mother's failure to return.

A shaft of coldness rips through Sara's body. Of course. Behaving badly. Finally she understands her patient, what information Pritti has been withholding in order to feel safe, what musty room from childhood has been boarded up where, with the self-centredness of a child, she has held herself totally to blame.

Behind her Sara can hear madams yelping and the sound of wooden clubs on bone.

Sara crawls forward, her legs shaking, her hands slipping in the dust. 'Pritti. It's me. Sara. Let's get out of here.'

Pritti doesn't move.

'Come on Pritti. You can do it.'

Behind her she can hear the voices of madams coming closer up the stairs and Rafi and Passang fending them off. Any minute now, she expects to hear gunshots. 'Pritti, we have to get out *now*.'

Pritti sways, her lips parted, but still makes no move.

Sara rapidly scans her mind for her recent interpretation of Pritti's disturbance, waiting her whole life for her mother to return. 'I've come back,' says Sara. 'I've come back for you.'

Pritti hesitates and looks up, her face a blend of sharp delight and disbelief. 'Sara.'

This is the very first time Pritti has used Sara's real name, made real contact.

Sara holds out her trembling hand. 'Come with me. Quickly.'

Downstairs, all is chaos. Madams scream and snatch at Sara's clothes and try to prevent her escorting Pritti, slapping at both women with their bony hands. Shielding Pritti with her arm, Sara drags her through the scuffling people, out of the brothel and into the street.

She casts wildly around for Rafi. After the success of tonight's little enterprise they could easily organise another raid on G.B. Road, maybe next time for Swarti and her sick sister. And she thinks back to the women in the cells at Passang's old police station. So many women. But they could do it.

Eventually, in the distance she sees the clinic minibus. As they approach she sees Hemant at the wheel and, in the seats behind, Ammu and her boy, along with one other prostitute. She wonders what has passed between Hemant and Ammu tonight. And it crosses her mind that maybe Rafi will fire Hemant. No point having a daily reminder of one's indiscretions.

'There you are,' cries Rafi, running up. 'My God, it's a farce.' He is out of breath.

Instinctively Sara grips hold of Pritti more tightly. 'What do you mean?'

He leans over, hands on knees, to catch his breath. 'They have let them escape.'

'What?'

He rights himself again. 'The police. The girls, they have let them go.'

'The girls we've just rescued?'

'Ran off into the crowd. The police did nothing to stop them,' he slaps his head.

Passang extricates himself from a screaming madam and joins them, beaming. 'You have your girls, I see.'

'But where are all the rest?' Sara says. 'We rescued about sixty women, but your men have let them escape.'

'We will find them,' he says plainly, as though he isn't even surprised to be put on the spot like this, as though such confusion, such madness is all part of the process. He gestures at his men, whose slack postures and diffident expressions give Sara no confidence at all.

And it occurs to her that maybe this was why they didn't meet much resistance. Such raids are really only for show. 'You'll round up all of them?'

'Hundred per cent.'

'Because you know they're likely to get picked up again by new pimps and forced to work as sex slaves in new brothels, don't you?'

'We will find them. Rest assured. We will find all of them.'

She feels Pritti's hand in hers. 'And once you've caught them, what will you do with them? Where will the women go?'

His silence cuts through her.

There is nowhere for girls like these to go.

26

Hemant drives them all in the minibus, back to Rafi's house. The full moon is high, washing the potholes and litter and bodies dozing on the pavements in its pure light.

Once back in the enclave, Sara and Rafi wake up the sleeping cooks and get them to make up beds for Pritti and Lapi, the other rescued girl, and a small cot in Rafi's room for Ammu's little boy; Ammu will sleep in the bed she already knows, where her second child was conceived.

Sara shows Pritti to the bathroom and hands her two towels. As she closes the door she glimpses Pritti smelling the new bar of soap. Gone is her patient's mantra and the anxious twitches, gone too is any sense that Pritti is locked in the past, seeing her mother in Sara, wishing her returned.

Instead, what has emerged is a young woman cautiously delighting in her new surroundings, feeling the clean tiles under her feet, gazing as though for the first time in the mirror. On emerging from the shower, she even asks Sara if she can borrow a pair of scissors. 'My mother used to cut my hair,' she adds, shyly.

'And no one has cut it for you since?'

Pritti juts out her lower lip. 'I said no. But now—'

Sara watches as the blades slice into the thick ropes of hair. Not a cure. She wouldn't be so presumptuous as to call it that. But a step in the right direction. Snip, snip, go the scissors.

There are so many things she wants to ask Pritti, she doesn't know where to begin. Who caused the bruises on her arms, how did she end up in the temple, what happened to her in the brothel, how did she block out what men did to her there? But guilt stops her. She took her eye off the ball and put her patient in danger, and no medical tribunal would see it any other way. And as she looks at Pritti stroking the shorn nape of her neck, fluffing out the new bob, she reflects on how there were two people in her life who went missing, but how miraculously one of them is found. Or on some level, maybe both of them were. And she understands that in life, what matters is progress, not perfection.

Sara sits on her bed and waits for Pritti to finish enjoying the bathroom.

'Am I really sleeping in this house tonight?' Pritti grins, as she enters the bedroom.

Sara nods.

Pritti sits down at the opposite end of the bed. 'Are you sleepy?'

Jangly with adrenaline Sara wants to keep busy. She can see herself leaving the house and walking the streets of Delhi all night.

Before Sara can answer, Pritti says, 'Can I speak?'

Sara is acutely conscious of her own body, of the blood pumping through her veins, the skin stretched and every sinew straining towards Pritti.

'When you went away. I didn't think I would see you again.'

Sara's shoes feel glued to the floor. 'Why was that?'

'Me.' Pritti bites her lip. 'I thought it was me,' she whispers.

'You thought you were to blame for me going away?'

Pritti tilts her head again.

'In what way?'

The old Pritti would have started rocking here, muttering her mantra, the old defence, but not tonight. Sara knows from the brightness of Pritti's eyes that she is no longer trying to block something out, but instead is actively reliving the past.

'You're remembering something,' Sara states calmly. 'Where are you?'

'I am in my playroom.'

'And where is your playroom?'

'It is on the first floor. I am leaning out of the window.'

'What can you see?'

'I am looking out at the garden. The old gardener sweeps the dry leaves off the lawn. His broom is going swish, swish. The sun is warm.'

Sara sees the micro-gesture alter Pritti's face.

'What can you see now?'

Pritti's breathing changes. 'My mother—'

'What about your mother?'

'My mother—' Pritti stops and swallows. 'My uncle—'

Instinctively, at this mention of her uncle or at this fresh memory of him, Pritti touches the place on her arms where the bruises are now but pale shadows of themselves.

Sara understands. 'Your uncle is hurting your mother?'

Pritti takes in a gulp of air. 'He drags her across the lawn.'

Sara watches as Pritti's eyes dart from side to side as she speaks, as she remembers, as her mind processes exactly what happened in the garden.

'And what happens then?'

'My uncle hits the gardener, shouts at him to go. Then he pulls my mother over to the guava trees. I want to stop watching but I can't. He throws my mother to the ground.' Pritti wipes her eyes. 'He kneels over her. Takes off his belt. I think he will kill her. My mother is screaming, hitting him, but he is too strong.' Pritti rubs at the bruises on her forearm. 'Now he lies on top of her.'

221

'And you're watching…'

'I want to run down the stairs and save my mother, but I think he will kill me.'

'You want to stay safe.'

Pritti nods. 'I run from the window, I pull my chair from the desk and sit down. I wriggle to make the nice feelings come.'

'You are keeping yourself safe.'

Pritti blinks away tears. 'But when I go down for tea, Mataji is crying in the kitchen.' Pritti is stroking her arm. 'My uncle says I make Mataji sad, and sends me to bed without supper. The next day, Mataji is gone.' Pritti looks at Sara. 'She never came back. She was cross I didn't protect her from my uncle and so she ran away from me. It is my fault.'

Around them the house is settling to sleep, but Sara is alert. Her voice is lower than usual, its syntax and cadences vibrating on an unplanned frequency. 'I think you believe that when people disappear, it's because they are angry with you, that you have been a bad person.'

'I am a bad person.'

'But sometimes people disappear for other reasons.'

Pritti tilts her head. 'At the temple, they made me do things I didn't want to do, and when men knelt over me, I wanted to get away.'

Sara watches as understanding flits across Pritti's face. She lets out a small cry.

Sara has always wanted to hate this unknown woman for abandoning Pritti, but in that moment she can picture a variety of scenarios featuring a desperate widow, victim of incestuous rape in India, perhaps banished by her own brother, or most likely murdered. Who knows what that desperate woman endured? Although Sara can hazard a guess.

'I am not a bad person,' Pritti says, and it is as though the weight of these spoken words has finally grounded her.

222

The tension in Sara's chest fades away. Processing the past has desensitised Pritti to the memory of her trauma. Now the healing can begin.

And in the dusty light, Pritti reaches for Sara's hand.

27

With Pritti now sleeping, Sara steps out into the lane in front of the house and breathes in. Delhi. After the recent rains, the enclave smells sweetly of jasmine and comfort and hope.

As she stoops to pass under the trees she glances at Hemant's lock-up. Hemant is off returning the minibus to the clinic and presumably bringing back the Mercedes. Apparently after Rupa and Alok's wedding, calls have been flooding in for that *genius with the sitar*. Hemant has had dozens of meetings with happy couples—or rather their proud, efficient, bankrolling parents—all over town. According to Rafi, there is even talk of Hemant appearing on *Music Maestro*, a reality TV show which helps Indians get their needs met, seize their own destinies, change lives. None of this old-fashioned karmic destiny nonsense.

Still, destiny is something Sara has been thinking about these past few hours. How she got to here, and where she is going. How she came to find Mike and instead has found herself.

It's time, she knows, that she emailed Dr Islam—Trevor— to tell him that she won't be coming back. 'I'm doing this to get you back,' he had said. Well, she *is* back, but probably not in the way he had meant. But of course it is! She sees that now. She smiles to herself, at how annoyingly right Trevor is about everything. He'd been showing her that to move on, you have to let go. He had let her go.

For an hour she walks in the dark around the enclave, seeing no one, although the odd dog barks, the odd owl hoots, the odd dark shape scampers into the nearest bush. She abandons herself to the mildly narcotic rhythm of walking. Gradually she is aware of her own body, the lilt of her hips, the easy swing of her arms, the rocking of her feet on the leaves on the ground with each step. This walk, this gentle bilateral stimulation settles her, and now her mind wanders freely.

She knows exactly how she wants her Refuge for Women to look.

It will be an unthreatening low-build, two storeys maximum. She will buy Dr Mathur's overgrown plot next to the clinic and link the two buildings by turning her office into the lobby. This way, like Sanjivani Home, its location on the lane will seem like the edge of the city. This way, the girls originally from villages might feel more at home. And all its inhabitants can benefit from the simple pleasure of being able to walk into the field beyond the temple, see a goat, buy a lime soda.

Her Refuge for Women will have a well-stocked art room and a large communal kitchen. There, the girls will be taught basic home-making or tea-serving or catering skills which in turn could lead to paid employment as a domestic servant. And maybe a hairdresser could come once a week to teach basic haircare techniques, both for good grooming and self-care, and the potential to learn a reputable trade.

Seeking out enlightened potential employers, Sara foresees, will be essential in combating both the stigma and trauma her girls have suffered. She will go and visit the concierge at the Majestic, for an introduction to the senior management team. With them she will discuss opportunities for job placements, as chambermaids or in the kitchens, to build up both the women's CVs and their self-esteem.

And she will buy fabric from Mr Pants-U-Like, for the curtains and to upholster the furniture. And for cheerful cushions, for all the therapy rooms. Perhaps Mr Pants-U-Like could even be persuaded to give dressmaking classes? And in the evenings there will be communal suppers and discussions. Maybe even play readings, or poetry. One for Barkha, she hopes.

Above all, there will be story-telling, a chance for the rescued women to write the script of their experiences, re-write the narrative of their future. Maybe the Refuge for Women could produce a magazine, filled with poems and tales and drawings, to be sold in the city, with the money distributed among the women.

Talking of money, she also plans to buy the women and children out from Passang's old cells. Money talks here in India, she knows that implicitly. And she will talk to Nidhi, maybe even fly down to Mumbai again, and grill her about running a refuge, about funding options and about whether single rooms or dormitories are better. And she sees a time looming when she will be able, while in Mumbai, to go to the Gate of India in front of the Taj Mahal Palace Hotel and throw marigolds into the water, for Mike. She will sell their old London home to buy the land next to the clinic. She hates the triteness of the phrase, *it's what he would have wanted*, but somehow she just knows that it is.

And music. The girls must have music. And now she knows she cannot put this moment off any longer. She re-traces her steps through the slumbering enclave, her body feeling strong and balanced.

The Mercedes is back, parked under the trees, its bonnet warm. Above her, it is as though someone has scooped up all the stars in the world and sprinkled them like luminous seeds over Delhi.

At Hemant's lock-up she knocks on the door and thinks back to that night a short while ago when it was Hemant risking the wrath of his employer to come and stand outside her bedroom. She hopes he is more forgiving, possesses greater self-composure than she showed that night.

226

His face, when he sees it is her, lights up. 'So you've come for another sitar lesson,' he teases in a whisper. He opens his door wider.

Her heart thudding, she steps for the first time into his neat room, his territory. A bedside lamp casts a golden glow on the walls. A breath of wind strokes her spine as the door closes behind her.

'I hear you might be trading in driving for life as a rock star,' she grins.

'Maybe. And what about you, now your patient is free. Will you return to London?'

She takes a step towards him. 'I'm going to set up a refuge for trafficked women.' She hesitates. In telling Hemant this fantasy, this first manoeuvre in her own personal war against the rape trade, she is affirming it to herself, making it more real.

'But that is truly wonderful. Where?'

'Here in Delhi. I'm going to buy the overgrown plot next to the clinic.' Just seeing the delight, the enthusiasm in his eyes, tells her it is going to happen. 'A place where women can get support and companionship and practical help to boost their confidence, raise their self-esteem, help them heal from their traumas. Empower them. I want to help women take control of their lives.'

'Hey, what about the guard who works at the clinic. You could ask him to give the girls advice on personal safety. Self-defence classes, that sort of thing.'

'Brilliant. And Varsha, I hope she might want to be part of things.'

'She would love that. And you could give English lessons.' He pauses. 'And I could give music lessons. That is, if you want me involved.'

Sara takes in a breath. 'Why did you tell me Ammu was your girlfriend?' She hates herself. If she didn't care, she wouldn't ask.

Yet in that fraction of a second, she witnesses a startling change come over him, another incongruous micro-gesture, the almost imperceptible spasm of emotion, as shame ripples through his entire body. And she is right back, that night on the landing, asking if Ammu was his girlfriend.

And then for one pure moment she realises that she *had*, that night, been shown Hemant's truth. His horror and disgust that she should ask such a thing. His expression betraying his true feelings, before he had to give in to the reality of life in India, a country where knowing one's place in relation to another person is more vital than breathing. As much as he longs for it to be otherwise, what matters even in the twenty-first century is that Rafi is his sahib, and Hemant's duty is to protect him.

'You lied for Rafi?'

He tilts his head. Would rather not call it a lie.

She feels the air solidify between them, binding them together or maybe keeping them apart.

'We in India must confront the old order,' he says. 'India must change. We must believe in our capacity to learn and grow and change. Otherwise life has no meaning. Life must have meaning. Otherwise, we are like music no one hears.'

And in her mind Sara sees Varsha who inspires her, tugging her ghoonghat over her face, Shakeel who guided her, patting the dashboard of his clapped out car, her patients who gave her a lifeline back to full engagement in the world, including Pritti, currently sleeping in Sara's bed. And she remembers Rafi, explaining about rebirth in India, a nation congenitally blighted to endure. When what is needed is rebirth *in* life, not after it.

She steps forward and kisses Hemant, properly, deeply, on the mouth. Hemant who has restrung her, with his capable hands. There will be times when she will struggle to breathe through this much reality. But maybe that was the point of

228

coming to India. To know that as long as you can breathe, you can survive.

He pulls her close, cradling her head. They kiss each other to say thank you, aware that the answer to *what for* is too complicated to be put into words. He pulls her closer, every part of them touching, creating their own private moksha, releasing each other's soul. Above all, she kisses him because deep down she knows that India hasn't changed enough for them to be together publicly, and he kisses her because he knows it too. These next few hours is all they have, a gift between friends.

For a long time they simply hold each other tight, enjoying the weight of the other, luxuriating in each other's smell. And then he lifts her, as though she weighs no more than one of his instruments, and lowers her gently on to the bed. He kneels above her, removing his shirt. His brown chest blooms before her, and there is a moment, a pause, as they gaze at each other, delighting in their contrasting pigments, each the reverse of the other, pale where he is dark, dark where he is lighter, when the silent agreement is made. To cross the line. Then he leans in, his hot soft mouth taking in hers, and his hands, those clever hands, with those magical fingers, rough at the tips from all that strumming, lifting up her sari, tracing her belly-button, finding her wetness. Once he is inside her, they are the same, outside of their past, outside of their lives, their differences eliminated.

※

Later, they lie on the mattress, she in the crook of his arm, his fingers stroking her hair. And her heart, still pumping. There are many kinds of heart rhythms: fear, guilt, panic. Tonight all is ecstasy. Tonight she has reclaimed her body. Tonight she feels whole again.

Something shifts inside her, a movement as subtle yet as precise as an oven reaching the correct temperature. Somewhere in Mumbai, traces of Mike lie unclaimed. In Delhi, a diplomat removes her blue eyeliner, a cleaner flicks dead marigold petals from behind an ECT machine, a woman in a police cell nurses a baby to sleep in her arms. All this is a part of Sara, of who she is, just as India is made up of slums and celebrities, ruins and skyscrapers, tolerances and prejudices. Just as life has death threaded invisibly through it.

Hemant checks his watch, and then sits up, reaching for his trousers. From inside one of the pockets he brings out the keys to the Mercedes and dangles them in front of her. 'Come on. One last thing. Let's go for a drive. Before anyone else is up.'

They dress hurriedly and creep out of the lock-up. Sara slides into the driving seat, feeling the stitched leather contours beneath her legs. Hemant takes the passenger seat alongside her. She clicks the seat belt into place and turns on the ignition, feels the yield of the pedal under her foot, the sheer awesome potential of the machine currently in her control.

She pulls away and takes the route out of the enclave, towards the city. The car obeys her seamlessly. She doesn't even need to ask Hemant for directions. They do say that once you can drive your way around a city, you have a right to call it home.

Up ahead, a camomile dawn melts through the early smog. Confidently she flicks a button on the steering wheel which activates the CD player. And as the morning ripens and the streets of the capital city yawn around them, the sounds of Hemant's songs fill the car. The air is alive with strings, drums, vocals. She doesn't yet understand the Hindi lyrics, but she has listened to them enough times to have committed them phonetically to memory. The cadences, the intervals, the hypnotic chord changes, are all known to her. It is as though she first heard them in the womb.

For one priceless hour, the Mercedes purrs around Delhi, the engine pitched in uncanny, immaculate harmony to the songs. And as they head east, towards the sunrise, the two of them sing together, at the tops of their voices.

ACKNOWLEDGEMENTS

Enormous thanks go to Shomit Mitter for guiding me elegantly on this incredible journey I've started, and also to Fiona Macnaughton-Jones.

To Dr Sunil Mittal and the staff at Delhi Psychiatry Centre, Rockwell Hospital and Sanjivani Clinic in New Delhi, and to my colleagues at the Priory Hospital, Roehampton.

To Sam Kiley, for taking the time to speak to me. And to Toby Parsons, for being so generous with his time, and also to Richard, for conversations we never had.

To Steve Rothwell, for being there at the beginning and single-handedly fighting off the kites.

To Chris, eagle-eyed David, Francisco, Graham, Laurel and Ronan, at the RFH Writers Group.

To others for their invaluable support and inspiration: Nikki Bedi, Christine Campbell, Kate Christie, John Costello, William Dalrymple, Grace Dugdale, Sophie Hopkins, Jackie Macdonald, Radhi Mathur, Vikram Mathur, Paul McWilliam, Mary Mike, Piers Northam, Anthony Quinn, Dr Alexandra Samways, Mike Samways, Sunny Singh, James Stanbridge, Hannah Tallett, Sasha Waddell, Martin Vander Weyer, Virginia Whetter and Sean Williams.

And to the gang at Quartet, especially Naim Attallah, Gavin James Bower and Grace Pilkington – forces of nature all, who know how to make things happen.

To Derek Costain for lighting the fire of my passion for India, and to Sir Robert and Lady Wade-Gery and the late Jeremy Seddon for fanning its flames.

And finally, mostly, to Guy, who lights the skies above me.